Jerry Bauer

About the Author

Colin McGinn was educated at Oxford University. He has written widely on philosophy and philosophers in such publications as *The New York Review of Books, London Review of Books, New Republic,* and *New York Times Book Review.* McGinn has written sixteen previous books, including *The Mysterious Flame; The Character of Mind; Ethics, Evil, and Fiction;* the novel *The Space Trap;* a memoir, *The Making of a Philosopher;* and, most recently, *The Power of Movies* and *Mindsight: Image, Dream, Meaning.* He has taught philosophy at University College of London, Oxford, and Rutgers University, and is currently distinguished professor of philosophy at the University of Miami.

Shakespeare's Philosophy

Discovering the Meaning
Behind the Plays

Colin McGinn

HARPER ⬤ PERENNIAL

NEW YORK • LONDON • TORONTO • SYDNEY

HARPER ● PERENNIAL

FIRST HARPER PERENNIAL EDITION PUBLISHED 2007.

Designed by Christine Weathersbee

The Library of Congress has catalogued the hardcover edition as follows:
McGinn, Colin.
  Shakespeare's philosophy : discovering the meaning behind the plays / Colin McGinn.—1st ed.
    p. cm.
Includes bibliographical references and index.
  ISBN-10: 0-06-085615-7
  ISBN-13: 978-0-06-085615-1
    1. Shakespeare, William, 1564–1616—Philosophy. 2. Philosophy in literature. I. Title.
PR3001.M38 2006
822.3'3—dc22   2005055008

ISBN: 978-0-06-085616-8 (pbk.)
ISBN-10: 0-06-085616-5 (pbk.)

07 08 09 10 11 ID/RRD 10 9 8 7 6 5 4 3 2 1

Contents

Preface

Like many another person, I first encountered Shakespeare at school, where I studied *Othello* and *Antony and Cleopatra* for A-level English. I was particularly struck by *Othello,* though I would have found it hard at the time to explain my reaction. It was, in truth, all rather above my head, but something about the emotional articulation appealed—and I always liked words. In subsequent years, during which I became an academic philosopher, I would attend a performance of this or that play, finding that my own advance in age and sophistication would deepen my response to the plays. But I never made a proper study of Shakespeare during these years, not supposing that I might have anything to contribute to understanding his work, and having quite enough difficult material on my plate anyway.

Then, while on sabbatical in 2004–5, I found myself with a block of time and my philosophical projects completed—so I decided to make a detailed study of Shakespeare. I had recently seen a production of *King Lear* at Lincoln Center, and some lines had struck me as having philosophical import; I wondered how much philosophy was embedded in the plays. I began to watch DVDs of the plays, read commentaries, and study the texts carefully. After a while, it seemed to me that a philosophical study of Shakespeare would be worthwhile. The result is the book now in your hands.

I am well aware that there is some presumption in my enterprise, since I am not professionally a Shakespeare scholar or any other kind of literary expert. But I am not attempting to do better what earlier scholars have labored to produce; I am approaching Shakespeare from a specifically philosophical perspective. The book, as its title suggests, is about the philosophical ideas embedded in Shakespeare's text—though of course there is no avoiding questions of character, history, and poetry. What I have attempted is a systematic treatment of the underlying philosophical themes of the plays, themes of some abstraction and generality. These themes include skepticism and the possibility of human knowledge; the nature of the self and personal identity; the understanding of causation; the existence and nature of evil; the formative power of language. I claim that these themes are woven deeply into Shakespeare's plots and poetry. I write, then, as a professional philosopher with an interest in Shakespeare, not a professional Shakespeare scholar with a passing interest in philosophy.

I am grateful to Jonathan Miller for some conversations on Shakespeare, to my agent, Susan Rabiner, for suggestions about the structure of the book, and to my editor, Hugh van Dusen, for his enthusiasm and good judgment. I am also grateful to my wife, Cathy, who more than let me get on with it.

Shakespeare's
Philosophy

ONE

General Themes

In *Characters of Shakespeare's Plays*, published in 1817, William Hazlitt remarks (discussing Iago in *Othello*) that Shakespeare "was as good a philosopher as he was a poet."[1] In his discussion of *Coriolanus*, he observes that Shakespeare writes with "the spirit of a poet and the acuteness of a philosopher."[2] And the philosophical tenor of Shakespeare's plays has not gone unnoticed by other readers and audiences. We feel that large themes are at work in the plays, shaping the poetry and the drama. But little attempt has been made to identify and articulate these philosophical themes in any systematic way.[3] Critical studies tend to focus on issues of character, plot, and diction, as well as the social and political context of the plays, but the philosophical ideas suffusing them receive only passing mention. This is no doubt because those professionally involved in Shakespeare studies are not in general philosophers by training or inclination; they are literary scholars. Philosophy, perhaps, makes them nervous. It will be my contention in this book that an avowedly philosophical approach to Shakespeare can reveal new dimensions to his work, and that his work can contribute to philosophy itself. It is not my intention to *replace* poetic or dramatic treatments of Shakespeare, or even historical ones; I mean merely to supplement them with something more abstract. I want to look at Shakespeare's plays expressly from the point of view of their underlying philosophical concerns. This will, I believe, reveal the source of their depth.

The plan of the book is as follows. In this chapter I shall outline in a preliminary way what I take to be the main philosophical themes in Shakespeare's plays, with minimal attention to the text. I want to give the reader a sense of the issues themselves, before using them to interpret the plays. These issues are by no means antiquated, but have a continuing relevance. Then I shall move on to a close reading of Shakespeare's main plays, with these themes in hand, elaborating them as I go. At the end of the book I shall treat a small number of philosophical matters that are ancillary to my main themes. We shall see that Hazlitt was quite correct in his assessment of Shakespeare's talents.

Shakespeare is often commended for his "timelessness," rightly so, but of course he also wrote at a particular period in history—the end of the sixteenth century and the beginning of the seventeenth. For my purposes, the most relevant fact about this period is that it precedes the Scientific Revolution, so that science was in its infancy in Shakespeare's day. Very little that we now take for granted was understood—in astronomy, physics, chemistry, and biology. The achievements of Descartes, Leibniz, Galileo, Newton, Locke, Boyle, and other heroes of the Renaissance were still in the future. The laws of mechanics were unknown; disease was a mystery; genetics was unheard of. Intelligent people believed in witchcraft, ghosts, fairies, astrology, and all the rest. Eclipses were greeted with alarmed superstition. Scientific method was struggling to gain a foothold (Francis Bacon was laying the groundwork). The conception of the world as a set of intelligible law-governed causes was at most a distant dream. The most advanced learning available came from the ancients; intellectually things hadn't changed much in two thousand years. When Shakespeare looked up into the night sky, he had very little idea of what he was seeing, and the earth was still generally considered the center of the universe. Nor was much known about the extent of the earth and of other cultures (though global exploration had already begun). It can be hard to remember this when we are confronted by Shakespeare's sophistication in other matters. Nothing much was known about the natural world then, and this was known to be so; uncertainty and ignorance seemed man's natural lot. To give one striking example: so little was understood about the plague that devastated Europe in the late sixteenth century that orders were given in London to exterminate all cats and dogs—which were in fact the best enemies of the true carriers of the germs responsible, rats.

It was also a period of religious upheaval in which the source of divine authority was very much in doubt. The Protestant Reformation had challenged Catholicism, and the question of how we might know God was intensely real (you could die for taking the wrong view). Should believers rely on their own unaided reason to know God's ways, or must they depend ultimately on church dogma? How to interpret Scripture was a vexed question, with a great deal turning on it. Thus there was a strong interest in knowledge and how it might be acquired, but not very much that seemed to qualify as beyond doubt. It was an age of uncertainty, following a period (the Middle Ages) of dogmatism, and preceding the age in which human reason seemed to achieve undreamed-of understanding of the universe (the Age of Enlightenment in which we still live). It is fair, I think, to characterize Shakespeare's time as transitional—as one kind of authority (the church, monarchy) began to give way to another (science and human reason, a new social order). We might say, simplifying somewhat, that Shakespeare was "between cultures." Questioning is the spirit of this period, and a sense of shifting foundations. It would not be surprising, then, to find doubt and uncertainty running through Shakespeare's plays. And these aporias would run deep: the nature of man, his place in the cosmos, the very possibility of knowledge.

There are three areas in which I think this spirit of uncertainty pervades the plays: knowledge and skepticism; the nature of the self; and the character of causality. I shall consider these in turn.

Knowledge and Skepticism

Aristotle begins his *Metaphysics* with the terse sentence: "All men naturally desire knowledge." That sounds like a truism, but if it is, it is a truism with profound consequences. There are three parts to it:

that it is in man's *nature* to desire knowledge, part of man's essence, a condition of his being; that it is natural for man to *desire* knowledge, to seek it, to yearn for it, to value it highly; and that this desire is for *knowledge*—not just belief or probable opinion or faith. We could paraphrase Aristotle as saying that human beings have an innate propensity to seek and value true justified beliefs—and what they value above all is *certain* knowledge. We desire solid, reliable knowledge, a state of epistemological perfection, not false beliefs and shaky inferences. *Why* we desire such a thing is a further question, but Aristotle is surely right that we do. Ignorance is something we scorn and try to avoid. An enormous part of Western civilization (and others too) is founded on this desire—we are a knowledge-hungry species—and no teacher ever got very far by promising to fill you with error and groundless opinion. Men indeed naturally desire knowledge.

It was Plato who made the desire for genuine knowledge a central component of the good life. His whole philosophy is based on the premise that we need to penetrate the clouds of appearance and acquire authentic knowledge of reality. The parable of the cave is a warning that knowledge is not easily obtained, and that distortions and error are not readily detected by the knowing mind.[4] (Still, Plato firmly believed that knowledge was possible, that our epistemological desires can be fulfilled: we really can attain the desirable state of knowing truths about the world. In Plato's system, the pinnacle of such knowledge is knowledge of the Forms—those timeless, abstract, unchanging entities that Plato took to be the most real of things. The ultimate aim of life was to come to know these resplendent Forms— truth, justice, beauty, mathematics. Aristotle had a different view of what constitutes ideal knowledge—closer to the empirical science of today—but he too did not doubt that knowledge is possible, though the road to it may be arduous. For these founding thinkers, our epistemological desires are capable of fulfillment.

Socrates, the "gadfly," also valued knowledge, but he was acutely sensitive to impostors to knowledge. He demonstrated time and again how people overestimate their capacity for knowledge. The Socratic lesson is that ignorance is a lot more prevalent than we suppose—that we really don't know as much as we think we do. Thus Socrates advises caution and the suspension of belief; we shouldn't let our strong desire to know fool us into misconstruing erroneous belief for real knowledge. We are chronic epistemological overreachers, according to Socrates, always taking ourselves to be epistemologically richer than we really are. We can't even define our most familiar terms—such as "just" and "good"—let alone aspire to plumb the secrets of the universe. Socrates counseled epistemological modesty.

It was left to the Greek skeptics, notably Sextus Empiricus, to push the Socratic lesson to its conclusion: that knowledge, however desirable, is simply not within our grasp.[5] Plato's entire philosophy therefore founders, since it is just not possible to know anything worthwhile, let alone the nature of those impossibly transcendent Forms. Man does not have the capacity to satisfy his epistemological desires—he is too prone to illusion, error, and uncertainty. We cannot be sure that our senses are not deceiving us, or that our reasoning faculties yield sound inferences, even whether we are dreaming. Man is a small and feeble creature, epistemologically blighted, and not able to comprehend the universe. At its extreme, such skepticism claims that no belief has any greater justification than any other belief, so that belief itself is an irrational act (this is the school known as Pyrrhonism). The skeptics accepted Aristotle's dictum but argued that it is in man's nature also to be thwarted in his desire for knowledge.

What has this potted history of Greek thought about knowledge got to do with Shakespeare? First, these worries about knowledge, in the air since the time of the Greeks, would attain a new level of intensity in Shakespeare's day, given the growing awareness of how little human beings knew of the world. The questions were being asked—about what eclipses are, about what causes the plague, about witchcraft and astrology—but no clear answers seemed forthcoming. The crisis in church authority, the split between traditional Catholicism and the Protestant Reformation, in which the possibility of our knowledge of God's will became a subject for debate, only added to this sense of being epistemologically at sea. The ancient skeptics seemed to be roundly vindicated. Shakespeare would have absorbed these currents of thought; and they are manifest in several of his most important plays, particularly *A Midsummer Night's Dream, Hamlet,* and *Othello.* But, secondly, there is a more specific reason to link Shakespeare to skepticism: Michel Montaigne. Montaigne was born in 1533, Shakespeare in 1564, and the French aristocrat was a widely celebrated author when the English commoner was composing his most famous plays. Moreover, it has been established by scholars that Shakespeare had studied and absorbed Montaigne's writings (what had Shakespeare *not* absorbed?): there is, for example, a virtual quotation from an essay of Montaigne's in *The Tempest.* Montaigne was especially noted for his eloquent revival of Greek skepticism, particularly in his long essay "An Apology for Raymond Sebond."[6] Here he dwells with some relish on the limitations of man, his feeble senses, his preposterous overconfidence, his desire not just to obey God, but to imitate Him. In Montaigne's view, man is but a paltry animal, inferior to many animals in his acuity and good sense, far too fond of his Reason (John Locke, a century later, would argue much the same point). So Shakespeare would be exposed to full-blown philosophical skepticism in Montaigne's writings, and in a form I suspect he would have found especially appealing—since Montaigne is a dramatic, anecdotal, poetic, and powerful writer. Not for Montaigne the dry tomes of the traditional philosopher; his essays are personal, lively, and pungent. I myself, some five hundred years later, find them unusually persuasive and affecting, full of rugged wisdom and brutal honesty—the very characteristics, indeed, which leap from the page of Shakespeare. The word "unflinching" aptly describes the style of both authors—yet with a wry humanity. The great subject of death is never far from either writer, with a steady-eyed contemplation of its terrors and mysteries. But most of all it is Montaigne's contrarian skepticism that seems to have impressed Shakespeare—as it did so many of his contemporaries.

I shall be arguing in subsequent chapters that Montaigne had a profound influence on Shakespeare's works—or, to be more cautious, that many passages in Shakespeare echo passages from Montaigne.[7] In particular, a skeptical thread can be seen running through the plays, which draws upon the kind of skeptical thinking Montaigne revived from the

Greeks. What I think Shakespeare added to this ancient skepticism was a specific form of skeptical concern—the problem of *other minds*. This is a multifaceted problem, but its most straightforward statement is simply this: How do we know what other people are thinking, feeling, and intending? *Can* we know these things? The problem arises from a basic duality in human nature—the split between interior and exterior. It seems undeniable that all we observe of another person is his or her body—that is all that we can see and touch and smell. But another person's mind belongs to the interior aspect of the person—which we cannot see, touch, or smell. There is something *hidden* about other people's minds, which we can only infer from what is publicly available. People can keep their thoughts and motives to themselves, simply by not expressing them, and this puts us in a position of not knowing. We are all aware of this from our own case: we know that we can prevent other people from acquiring the knowledge of our own minds that we immediately possess. I may know that I have dubious motives in regard to someone else, but I also know that you do not know this—and I know that I can easily prevent you from knowing it. This is what makes deception possible—the asymmetry between my knowledge of my mind and your knowledge of my mind. There is a sense, then, in which my mind is private, and known to be so, while my body is public property.

The problem of knowing the external world strikes many people as a philosopher's problem—an abstract difficulty that takes some ingenuity to formulate and appreciate. It is not a problem that afflicts us every day, as a matter of course. But the problem of other minds seems far more immediate and commonsensical: we always seem to be having our nose rubbed in it. I really do know (I tell myself) that I am sitting in a chair right now, and it seems farfetched to object that I might just be dreaming that I am or hallucinating the situation; but I can easily be made to agree that I don't know what is really on other people's minds. (What *do* other people think of me?) The link between outward behavior and inner state of mind seems tenuous and fragile; and we really can be totally wrong about somebody we thought we knew quite well. Other minds actually are, in a quite everyday sense, extremely hard to know about, and radical mistakes are not only possible but also common. The philosopher's skeptical problem is thus rooted in mundane realities. I think Shakespeare was acutely conscious of this problem, and that it powers and structures many of his plays, notably *Othello*. He is working out the dramatic consequences of a philosophical problem, as this problem affects people locked into very real and intimate relationships. All our social relationships, from the most casual to the most intimate, as in marriage and family connections, are conditioned by the fundamental inaccessibility of other minds. Everything becomes a matter of *interpretation*, of competing hypotheses, with the perpetual possibility of massive error. Overconfidence is the besetting sin here, as people leap to unwarranted conclusions about the motives and thoughts of others. Tragedy can result. Anyone who has ever felt grievously misunderstood, or has gotten away with murder (perhaps literally), knows that the mind is not something that is exhibited out there for all to see; its concealment is essential to its nature. This is *the* fundamental fact of social relations, and hence of what it is to be a conscious being.

The skeptic, we might say, is a kind of tragedian about knowledge: he admits that Aristotle's dictum is correct—people do desire to know; they are not indifferent to knowledge—but he claims that this desire is necessarily thwarted. Thus a basic value in human life is declared unrealizable, and this is our tragedy. Other values may be brought in to make up for the fate of that one: acquiescence, epistemological stoicism, modesty, clear-sightedness. But it is admitted that the Good of knowledge is unobtainable; like Socrates, we must accept that our best knowledge is simply the knowledge that we are ignorant. I shall suggest that Shakespeare's tragedies often revolve around the tragedy of knowledge itself. It is a tragic fact that one of our deepest desires must go unfulfilled, and from this tragedy other tragedies ensue. Shakespeare's tragic figures are always coping with their ignorance—their inability to know what they need to. For example, Lear is tragically ignorant of the motivations of those around him, as well as of himself; Othello is steeped in error and mistaken inference; even the astute Hamlet is slow to understand his predicament in the court of Elsinore.

The Self

Drama deals, evidently, in a number of selves engaged in some kind of interaction. Mere bodies are not enough; a story of insentient robots all acting together would contain little in the way of drama (as opposed to spectacle). Drama must concern conscious beings equipped with a suitably rich psychology (they can be aliens, as distinct from humans, but a tale of mere worms, assuming them sentient, isn't exactly dramatic). Drama also concerns the individual self as it exists over time, changing in some ways, staying the same in others; we must be made witness to the adventures of the *same* person over time, not a succession of discrete selves—we want to know what happens to *that* person. So there is really no escaping the question of the nature of the self and its persistence over time. I believe Shakespeare was very interested in this question, particularly in *Hamlet*. The question is connected to the matter of personality or character: What gives an individual the personality or character he or she has? What *constitutes* personality? Can personality be separated from someone's outward circumstances? What is meant by speaking of the "real person"? The body has a collection of physical traits that give it the specific form it has, but does the person have a range of mental traits that collectively define his or her personality? What is the nature of such traits? How precisely are action and character related? How constant is the thing we call personality? How easy is it for someone to know his or her own character? Is character a gift from God or nature or neither? How solid is it? Is it a metaphysical essence or a social construction? In *Hamlet* this kind of question is powerfully explored, with Hamlet himself the focus of personal indeterminacy: what *is* his personality, and how constant is it? He seems like an assertion of the elusiveness of the self rather than a fully fledged "character." In *Macbeth* too, the title character undergoes startling transformations, morphing before our eyes (the same might be said of Lear).

These questions become pressing once we consider some of the more drastic changes a person may undergo. Madness is a conspicuous concern of Shakespeare's: does madness negate the personality, putting an end to the self, or does it reveal some underlying person-ality that is more real—or does it just install a brand-new self (Hamlet, Lear, Macbeth)? Madness is a kind of psychological meta-morphosis, a radical alteration of form or nature, yet somehow emerging from what has gone before; and, like all metamorphoses, it raises the question of identity—do we have the *same* thing after as before? Sleep, which in dreaming is akin to madness, raises a similar question, and was also a preoccupation of Shakespeare: I say that it is I dreaming, but in what sense is this the same person as he who accompanies my waking body? Certainly I change dramatically in my dreams, doing things I never would in waking life, so is it clear that my dreaming self and my waking self are the same person? And which is the more real? And with what right do we presume that it is the same self I wake up with every day? Then again, there is death: if people can survive bodily death, commonly believed past and pre-sent, then they can persist in a completely new state of being—but what makes them the *same* person in the two states? It cannot be the body, since it disintegrates, so what is it that constitutes persistence of the self beyond bodily death? What makes the ghost of Hamlet's father really the ghost *of his father?* There has to be some kind of continuity here, but what kind is it? The self can seem on the one hand like the most resilient and robust thing in the world, but on the other the most variable and evanescent. It is the most puzzling of entities.

As I shall argue, Shakespeare is profoundly suspicious of the idea of the self as a kind of internal substance with a fixed and given nature—something you just find yourself with, whose nature is antecedently determined. It is not that you have a heart and kidneys and a brain and a *self*—as if this were just one more naturally consti-tuted object inside you. Nor can the self be the soul as conceived in some religious traditions—a supernatural entity, whole and entire, that carries a person's identity through what we regard as his or her life, a kind of fixed spiritual nugget. Instead, Shakespeare regards the self as *interactive* and *theatrical*. The self is interactive in the sense that it makes little sense to ask what personality someone has inde-pendent of the social interactions in which he engages: to be generous is to be generous *to someone*, to be irascible is to be prone to anger at *other people*, and so on. Also, the personality you display is a function of the other people you are interacting with: you are one way with your children, another with your drinking friends; one way at your place of work, another at play. Personality is essentially a matter of how you interact with others—how you affect them, and how they affect you. The self is also theatrical in the sense that it is best understood in terms of the *roles* a person *plays*. Shakespeare often compares the world to a stage and people to actors: I shall suggest that he means this in a quite literal sense—namely, that our personality (or many personalities) is analogous to the character an actor plays on the stage. Hamlet, in particular, is a creature of the theater, forlornly in search of a viable role to play, and Bottom simply *is* an actor. In a certain sense, we construct or create our personality, using the kinds of skills possessed by an actor. This idea will take some spelling out, but it will be familiar to some readers from Erving Goffman's writings on what he calls the *dramaturgical* conception of the self, notably his seminal work *The Presentation of Self in Everyday Life*. The essential idea here is that each person treats the other as an audience on whom he must make an impression; he must manage his behavior in such a way as to convey a particular personality. This makes personality not a given but a choice, not determined but free. Most of us can recognize the veracity of this conception by recalling adolescence, in which unformed minds begin to "forge an identity": people try out one role and then another, until one seems to fit. Until then there is a kind of indeterminacy of personality, and a feeling of being lost. In its most extreme form the dramaturgical view of the self insists that there is nothing more to personality than a freely chosen dramatic role, or as many roles are there are audiences; there is no "real self" somehow lurking behind these freely chosen characters. I am what I make myself, according to my own aesthetic and practical standards. I am always acting a part, even in my most sincere moments (a person is a "poor player, that struts and frets his hour upon the stage," as Macbeth despairingly remarks). What I conceive as my authentic self—the core of my character—is just the one I have been acting the longest or the one that best suits my acting talents. It is not that I am always faking it, pretending to be something I'm not; rather, I have absorbed a role so completely that there is no sense to the idea that it is not my authentic self. Another way to put it is that society typically imposes a role on us and it is up to us to perfect that role—good son, dutiful father, regal monarch, beetle-browed intellectual, preening pimp. Personality, accordingly, is like the clothes you wear—a function of prevailing expectations and free choices, not something like the color of your eyes or your height. So suggests the theatrical theory of the self that Shakespeare appears to endorse.

I also believe that Shakespeare regarded the mind as subject to hidden and mysterious forces. It is not that everything that affects a person is transparent to her awareness, so that she always knows why she is doing what she is or feeling the way she does. Not everything in the psyche is subject to the person's rational control. The imagination, in particular, is vulnerable to this kind of irrational influence; we can become victims of our own imagination, as befalls Macbeth. Because of these extra-rational forces, the self can become divided and fragmented, losing its usual—but superficial—unity. In many of Shakespeare's most interesting characters there is a sense that the character is a "stranger to himself," that he is coexisting with a part of his psyche that is subject to unruly forces. The self is not always a harmonious whole, running on rational principles, but often a *mélange* of conflicting forces, the source of which is unclear. We are as much victims of ourselves as we are of the world around us, with one part of the psyche in rebellion against the rest. Accordingly, we can be mysteries to ourselves, bewildered by our feelings and actions; the conscious rational will has limited sway. This is why Shakespeare is so interested in abnormal states of mind, such as hallucination, dreaming, and insanity: they show the mind at its most unruly, as an agency with its own agenda, tangentially related to our conscious wishes. The mind can be at war with itself, and the self correspondingly fractured. Self-knowledge, therefore, like knowledge of other selves, is not always reliable; a person can be quite wrong about his character, and the way his mind operates. Self-knowledge, when possessed, is a hard-won achievement, not a given;

it tends to come to Shakespeare's characters only toward the end of their ordeals (as with Lear). Skepticism begins at home, with the problems of self-knowledge. What a Shakespearean character says about himself, even at his most sincere, is not always a reliable guide to the truth about that character; the character may be self-deceived, or just plain ignorant of himself. Several of Shakespeare's main characters seem to me to fall into that category (Othello, Macbeth, Lear).

Causality

How does the world work? What governs the flow of events? One thing gives rise to another, generating yet another, and so on indefinitely; but what principles lie behind this causal unfolding? What explains the causal sequence of the universe? One view is that a rational intelligence organizes the causal relations that characterize the way the world evolves—as it might be, the Christian God. There is a reason for what happens, even if it may be inscrutable: events are planned, designed a certain way, with foresight of some sort. Whenever one thing brings about another you can ask what explains this causality and expect there to be an answer in rational terms—it was *in order* that something be so. The world is an intelligible place, and causal relationships manifest that intelligibility. The universe is like a clock designed by a supreme intelligence: everything in it has a place, a function, and the whole has a purpose. According to this type of view, it is generally assumed that there is an *ethical* purpose behind what happens: some sort of cosmic justice controls the sequence of events, so that things happen "for the best." If a battle is won by a particular side, it was because the universe intended it; it was part of a large cosmic plan, an instance of divine justice. This view is naturally associated with the conviction that the universe was created by an intelligent and just God, and He imprinted His nature on the world. He may work in mysterious ways, but He is always working. Even the smallest causal interaction is an instance of the divine plan and carries its own quantum of cosmic justice. History, especially the affairs of man, is likewise controlled by such a supreme intelligence, always with the greater good in mind. Causality is never blind, always purposeful. Death itself is a part of this rational and ethical order.

We can call this the *teleological* view of causation—the idea that there is a purpose to what happens, a meaning. Clearly, it goes along with a theistic view of the universe. In its simplest formulation, it holds that *causation is moral*: what actually happens ought to happen. Set against the teleological view, we have the conception generally associated with the eighteenth-century skeptical philosopher David Hume, that causation is simply brute temporal sequence, with nothing rational underwriting it at all.[8] No rational principle connects a cause to its effect, according to Hume; causation does not have its basis in *reason* at all. As it is sometimes put, causation is just one damn thing after another—merely the conjunction of intrinsically unrelated events. There is no meaning to any of it; it is simply nature blindly following whatever laws govern it, with a large dose of randomness thrown in. Hume was an atheist and his view of causation fits that worldview perfectly: nothing confers meaning or rationality on causation; the process is essentially mindless. In principle, anything can cause anything—it is just a matter of what actually happens in nature, not some preconceived ideal of intelligible order. Rationality belongs only in human minds, and that to a limited degree; there is no rationality in nature itself. A person's death, say, is not the unfolding of a divine plan, but a mindless event not different in kind from any other instance of causation—a raindrop falling, the sun setting. In particular, causation is *morally neutral*: there is no cosmic justice governing the way causation works out, no redeeming explanation of apparent catastrophe. Right and wrong exercise no hold over causation whatsoever. Morality comes only from rational agents; it has nothing to do with the course of nature considered in itself.

I shall suggest that Shakespeare's plays involve themselves in this debate over the nature of causation, particularly *King Lear*. The play is concerned with why things happen as they do, and how one thing leads causally to another. *Macbeth* explores the way causation operates across time in the mind, and the causal connection between action and character. The causes of romantic love come in for skeptical treatment in *A Midsummer Night's Dream*. I shall argue that Shakespeare is inclined to the nonteleological view of causation: he rejects the idea of cosmic justice, and the rationalist view of causation that goes with it. He sees causation as unruly, unpredictable, unintelligible, blind, weird, and even paradoxical. The universe is not a place of rational harmonious order, but of jarring and improbable accidents, bizarre conjunctions. To this extent his worldview is atheistic, at least as theism is traditionally understood. The bleakness of his tragic vision is principally a matter of rejecting the notion of an immanent rational order in which moral ideas play a governing role. That is why his plays are so disturbing and challenging to comforting myths about how the world operates. Shakespeare shocks us out of our causal complacency.

Let me now sum up this quick overview of the themes I shall be exploring in Shakespeare's plays. According to an orthodox philosophy, we are rational beings capable of knowledge of the world, not signally prone to error; we also enjoy a constant identity over time, a unitary self that persists in its given nature over the course of our existence; and we live in a fundamentally rational universe in which justice is done and events make sense. In my interpretation, Shakespeare rejects that comforting picture entirely, and his plays are patterned by this rejection. With church authority crumbling and science not yet established, Shakespeare held a view of man and the universe that has no established name but that is approximated by such labels as "pessimism," "nihilism," "skepticism." Part of my aim in this book is to work out exactly what his view was, insofar as it is represented in the plays. If I were to award him a single label, it would be "naturalist," in somewhat the sense that one speaks of a student of natural history: he is a clear-eyed observer and recorder, sensitive to the facts before his eyes, not swayed by dogma or tradition (and naturalists have often returned from their observations with a "pessimistic" streak). He is simply saying, *This is the way things are, like it or not.* He is a detached, supremely sane student of human beings and their world, intent on descriptive accuracy. There is not a sentimental bone in his body. He has the curiosity of a scientist, the judgment of a philosopher, and the soul of a poet. He gives one the sense that he is ruthlessly peeling back the layers of self-delusion and wishful thinking that cloud our view of human affairs, exposing the bloody beating heart (and intestines) of man. He is a beady-eyed naturalist of raging human interiority and social collision. And his naturalism counsels a proper skepticism about human pretensions to knowledge, distrust of the notion of the substantial self, and rejection of the teleological interpretation of causation.

Keats famously spoke of a particular quality "which Shakespeare possessed so enormously—I mean *Negative Capability*, that is when man is capable of being in uncertainties, Mysteries, doubts without any irritable reaching after fact and reason."[9] This expresses what I am calling Shakespeare's naturalism quite well: the naturalistic observer puts himself to one side, accepting whatever mysteries and doubts the world offers to his faculties of investigation. He has no desire to explain things away, to paper over difficulties, to oversimplify, to settle for easy answers, to fit everything into some overarching theoretical framework. Montaigne too had this quality in his examination of himself—unsparing, exact, and fearless. You feel he is giving you reality, not doctrine; life, not literature. In both Montaigne's and Shakespeare's work, there is a kind of appalling, but exhilarating, candor. And some of that ruthlessness is philosophical: the determination to expose reality for what it is, to undermine dogma and complacency. In the end, of course, this is nothing other than a dedication to the truth.

TWO

A Midsummer Night's Dream

Persons of the Play

Theseus, Duke of Athens

Hippolyta, Queen of the Amazons, betrothed to Theseus

Philostrate, Master of the Revels to Theseus

Egeus, father of Hermia

Hermia, daughter of Egeus, in love with Lysander

Lysander, loved by Hermia

Demetrius, suitor to Hermia

Helena, in love with Demetrius

Oberon, King of Fairies

Titania, Queen of Fairies

Robin Goodfellow (or Puck), a sprite

Peaseblossom, a fairy

Cobweb, a fairy

Mote, a fairy

Mustardseed, a fairy

Peter Quince, a carpenter

Nick Bottom, a weaver

Francis Flute, a bellows mender

Tom Snout, a tinker

Snug, a joiner

Robin Starveling, a tailor

In a famous passage from his *Meditations*, published in 1641, Descartes writes:

> How could I deny that these hands or that this body is mine, unless perhaps I think that I am like some of those mad people whose brains are so impaired by the strong vapor of black bile that they confidently claim to be kings when they are paupers, that they are dressed up in purple when they are naked, that they have an earthenware head, or that they are a totally hollowed-out shell or are made of glass. But those people are insane and I would seem to be equally insane if I followed their example in any way. Very well. But am I not a man who is used to sleeping at night and having all the same experiences while asleep or, sometimes, even more improbable experiences than insane people have while awake? How often does the nocturnal quietness convince me of familiar things, for example, that I am here, dressed in my gown, sitting by the fire, when I am really undressed and asleep in my bed? But at the moment I certainly see this sheet of paper with my eyes open, the head I shake is not asleep, I extend and feel this hand carefully and knowingly; things which are as clear as this would not occur to someone who is asleep. As if I do not remember having been deluded by similar thoughts while asleep on other occasions! When I think about this more carefully, I see so clearly that I can never distinguish, by reliable signs, being awake from being asleep, that I am confused and this feeling of confusion almost confirms me in believing that I am asleep.[1]

Montaigne raised the same skeptical question around 1580: "Our rational souls accept notions and opinions produced during sleep, conferring on activities in our dreams the same approbation and authority as on our waking dreams: why should we therefore not doubt whether our thinking and acting are but another dream; our waking, some other species of sleep?"[2] Descartes would have known Montaigne's writings, so it is entirely likely that he was influenced by Montaigne, the most famous French skeptic before Descartes (though Descartes, in the end, took himself to have refuted the skeptic, unlike Montaigne, by invoking God's benevolent nature).

It is improbable, though chronologically possible, that Descartes ever saw a production of Shakespeare's *A Midsummer Night's Dream*, written around 1595, but if he had he would no doubt have recognized the theme of dream skepticism in that play. For the play is all about the difficulty of distinguishing dreaming from wakefulness, illusion from reality, what is merely imagined from what is veridically perceived. It deals, broadly speaking, with the power of fantasy, and the interactions of belief and fantasy. And it is notable that this is generally acknowledged to be the only play by Shakespeare that is wholly original, not based on any previous drama or story; notable too that it is regarded as his first great play, in which his peculiar talent began to reach its fullest expression. We might conjecture, then, that it provides the key to his major preoccupations. While similar in some respects to *Romeo and Juliet*—the two plays were written around the same time—it is far less conventional in structure, significantly freer in style and theme, and conceptually more intricate. We should not be misled by the fact that it is, nominally, a comedy; it has its dark moments, and it operates at a high conceptual altitude. In it we see Shakespeare flexing the muscles of his newly mature artistic vision. And I see philosophy at work.

The play begins on a characteristically stark note, with the prospect of two forced marriages. Theseus, the powerful Duke of Athens, is about to wed Hippolyta, Queen of the Amazons, but this is not to be a voluntary marriage: "I wooed thee with my sword, and won thy love doing thee injuries," Theseus dryly observes. What kind of love can be won, or granted, by injuries and the sword? It could only be a forced love, which is no kind of love at all. Hippolyta refers to the future wedding as "our solemnities," not exactly a joyful phrase, and Theseus can only manage to qualify his marriage-by-sword story by declaring: "But I will wed thee in another key—with pomp, with triumph, and with reveling"—no mention of love there either. Evidently, this is to be a marriage of political expediency, and maybe lust. Egeus then enters to complain about his daughter Hermia: "Full of vexation I come," he announces. His complaint is that Hermia is in love with Lysander, not Demetrius, the man preferred by Egeus (for no apparent reason, since Demetrius and Lysander seem almost interchangeable). Egeus's motive appears to be simply the desire to control his daughter's fate; he wants her to do what *he* wants, however arbitrary that may be. Lysander, he asserts, "hath bewitched the bosom of my child" and "stol'n the impression of her fantasy." His request to the duke is that, if she refuses to marry Demetrius, he be allowed to exact his punishment upon her: "I beg the ancient privilege of Athens: As she is mine, I may dispose of her, Which shall be either to this gentleman/Or to her death, according to our law immediately provided in that case." Theseus is quite prepared to enforce this harsh law, though he offers Hermia a third option—to become a celibate nun for life. Her wishes in love cannot be given any weight in the matter. "I would my father looked but with my eyes," she says; but Theseus responds with: "Rather your eyes must with his judgment look." The theme of looking with alien eyes, and of the interaction between seeing and judging, will become strongly stressed later in the play. For now, we have a contrast between the demands of authority and law and the promptings of personal emotion. Clearly, we are invited to sympathize with Hermia and deplore the violence of Egeus and Theseus, siding with true love over paternal power. But the rest of the play will cause us to question the inviolability of love. What is this precious thing that we value so highly? Is it worth dying for? Demetrius, it seems, though now in love with Hermia, had only recently declared his devotion to Helena, who now dotes on him. Might Lysander not switch his affections too? In any case, we have here a conflict between power and love; and it is not surprising that the pair decide to escape Athens to avoid the penalty exacted by cruel Athenian law.

Throughout this opening scene of harsh reality in collision with human emotion are dotted references to dreams. The second line of the play has Hippolyta say: "Four days will quickly steep themselves in night, Four nights will quickly dream away the time." Lysander speaks of love as "Swift as a shadow, short as any dream," and Hermia herself, dilating on the theme of true love never running smoothly, accepts the "customary cross" the two must bear—"As due to love as thoughts, and dreams, and sighs, Wishes, and tears, poor fancy's followers." Their escape into the wood outside Athens can easily be interpreted as an escape into the world of the dream, love's natural habitat—a world of primordial nature, away from power, authority, and human society. In this secluded place the distinction between sleeping and waking, dreaming and perceiving, becomes blurred and unstable, and love is able to follow its own logic, carving out its own strange shapes. But it is not a paradise, a heaven of romance and bliss; it is a place of queasy shifts and disturbing fantasies, capricious and tyrannical in its own way—another world of intrigue and the struggle for power, as well as total absurdity. The world of love, then, can be as much a nightmare as a wish-fulfilling fantasy. What happens in the wood is a kind of bad dream of love.

In this enchanted wood are also to be found "the mechanicals," a group of amateur actors, who are rehearsing a play about—guess what?—a pair of star-crossed lovers, Pyramus and Thisbe, as well as assorted fairies and sprites, themselves locked in a romantic drama of sorts. Peter Quince is the figure of authority among the mechanicals, constantly challenged by the unruly Bottom; and Oberon is the imperious king of the fairies, vying with Titania for possession of a child (for obscure reasons). Thus the actors in the wood are engaged on an imaginative project, and the supernatural characters are imaginary figures themselves—creatures of fantasy. To enter their world is to enter a world of illusion, as becomes quickly apparent when Oberon orders Puck to find a magic herb he can apply to Titania's eyelids to make her fall in love with the next animate thing she sees. From now on, the line between sleeping and waking, between dream and reality, will prove permeable and unclear, and insanity will never be far away. The consciousness of the lover is itself a strange blend of dream and wakefulness, prone to illusion, close to madness—so the wood represents this "altered state of consciousness." If romantic love is a waking dream, then the wood is the place for such dreams to unfold: it is the place for dreaming and waking to become one, for these parts of the characters' lives to bleed into one another. Accordingly, it is a place where reality and illusion, truth and error, become hopelessly confused, where the senses cannot be trusted and

reason seems eclipsed by fantasy. It is, in short, the ultimate
Cartesian nightmare. How can genuine knowledge be gained in such
a world? Everything is subject to doubt; nothing is certain. As
Hermia cries, awaking to find a now distant Lysander by her side:
"Help me, Lysander, help me! Do thy best/To pluck this crawling ser-
pent from my breast! Ay me, for pity. What a dream was here?
Lysander, look how I quake with fear. Methought a serpent ate my
heart away, And you sat smiling at his cruel prey." What a mixture of
fantasy and reality these lines contain! There is metaphorical truth to
her dream, given Lysander's change of heart, and the dream seems to
be leaking into her waking consciousness, making her still believe
herself the victim of a snake. In such a state only extreme skepticism
about appearances would be rational—since things are seldom as
they appear in the dreamworld. What is dreamed may prove real
here, and what seems real may be just a dream.

The following passage from Montaigne expresses the conception
Shakespeare is invoking:

> Those who have compared our lives to a dream are right—per-
> haps more right than they realized. When we are dreaming our
> soul lives, acts and exercises all her faculties neither more nor less
> than when we are awake, but she does it much more slackly
> and darkly; the difference is definitely not so great as between
> night and the living day: more like that between night and
> twilight. In one case the soul is sleeping, in the other more or less
> slumbering; but there is always darkness, perpetual Cimmerian
> darkness. We wake asleep: we sleep awake. When I am asleep I do
> see things less clearly but I never find my waking pure enough or
> cloudless. Deep sleep can even put dreams to sleep; but our wak-
> ing is never so wide awake that it can cure and purge those raving
> lunacies, those waking dreams that are worse than the real ones."[3]

He then goes on to state the skeptical dream hypothesis that I
quoted at the beginning of this chapter. If Shakespeare encountered
this passage in his study of Montaigne—and I find it hard to believe
he did not—he would certainly have seen the conceptual founda-

tions of his own play in Montaigne's words. What Montaigne refers to as "the unruliness of our minds" is amply attested by the action of Shakespeare's *Dream*. The night in the wood is like nothing so much as a fitful night of fever in which the sleeper keeps waking up and then dozing off again, with dreaming and waking merging together into a tangle of impressions that are impossible to unravel. It is not just, as Descartes insisted, that a dream may seem to us just like real life; dreaming and waking can become so intertwined that the distinction becomes moot. And in romantic love dream and waking consciousness become completely inseparable: love *is* a waking dream, a fantasy of the conscious subject. As Helena remarks: "Love looks not with the eyes, but with the mind, And therefore is winged Cupid painted blind." As we are blind in sleep, yet filled with visual experience, generated from our imaginative resources, so the lover weaves his fantasies around the object of his affection—in effect, he dreams his beloved into being. No wonder love is widely spoken of as the original site of *dis*-illusion.

And what is the cause of this love-dream? What brings love into being? In Shakespeare's *Dream* it is certainly not reason or even social convention; it is a magic potion, a chemical applied to the eyes. In this way Demetrius comes to love the formerly despised Helena (and apparently loved her once before already); Lysander loses his love for Hermia, whom he now finds repulsive, while doting on Helena (who mistakenly thinks she is being ridiculed by her new suitors); and Titania falls in love with Bottom transformed into an ass (at least down to his neck). The comedy of the play arises from the disparity between the way these lovers conceive their love and the way we know that it was caused: they think it is based on objectively perceived traits of the beloved, as if any reasonable person must feel as they do, while we see that it has a wholly irrational cause, a mere physical application. This is what we would nowadays speak of as hormonal causation—unknown physical causes in the body that influence the mind in ways that are not transparent to the person influenced. So the love that Hermia and Lysander prized so highly when Egeus threatened to thwart it turns out to be little more, in its basis, than a chemically induced trance, masquerading as the highest of evaluative faculties. The characters are victims or puppets of a fairy king whose mischief involves manipulating their affections: their emotions are shaped by forces outside their conscious will, with their reason bypassed and ridiculed. The irony in these words of Lysander is transparent, as he finds himself now in love with Helena: "Not Hermia but Helena I love. Who will not change a raven for a dove? The will of man is by his reason swayed, And reason says you are the worthier maid." Nothing could be further from the truth, of course. Love is a mirage in the wood, a convulsion brought on by chemical stimulation. It is left to Bottom, the wise fool, to note, in reply to Titania's sudden passion for him: "Methinks, mistress, you should have little reason for that. And yet, to say the truth, reason and love keep little company together nowadays—the more the pity that some honest neighbors will not make them friends." (Only "nowadays"? What about "always and everywhere"?) Nor are these illusions all righted by the end of the play and the characters' exit from the enchanted wood: Demetrius remains in love with Helena, and hence under the influence of Oberon's spell, and we are not to take this as in some way undermining the sincerity of his affections. Love is a chemically induced hallucination, as far as *Dream* is concerned. This is not the fey romanticism about love that is often associated with *Romeo and Juliet*; it is, as it were, the dark and skeptical side of that famous love story, which itself has its dark and skeptical side. It is love seen from the outside, as an alien naturalist might describe it.

Particularizing the general philosophical theme of dream skepticism in the shape of the romantic love of concrete characters is a very characteristic Shakespearean technique. The notion that dream and reality merge together in love, instead of being hermetically sealed parts of our lives, enables Shakespeare to dramatize the skeptical problem—to give it an urgency and human form that no abstract formulation can. The question of illusion and reality, fantasy and perception, has a particular vividness and power in the phenomenon of romantic love, because here dreaming and waking seem at their closest, and most easily confused. We may dream of the beloved at night and take our fantasy experiences to be veridical—but we also, in daytime hours, see her through the eyes of a dreamer. Not for nothing do we speak of the "dream man/woman." And isn't the gaze of the lover proverbially a dreamy gaze? But dreams are sources of error and delusion, our epistemological enemies. The illusions of love are thus a rich source of skeptical material—cases in which our epistemological confidence can be drastically misplaced. This is not necessarily to be a complete cynic about love—and I don't think that Shakespeare is—but it is a warning about the errors into which it may lead the unwary. It is a reminder of our fallibility, of "the unruliness of our minds." People speak of the "scales falling from their eyes," and this aptly expresses the delusory appearances that can so easily deceive us. This theme of appearance versus reality runs through Shakespeare's later plays; in *Dream* it is present in a particularly vivid and forthright way. We *see* the delusions of these epistemologically troubled characters.

The theme of personal transformation is equally pronounced in the play. People do not remain steady and the same; they mutate and sprout new selves at the drop of a hat. At the very beginning Lysander disdainfully refers to Demetrius as "this spotted and inconstant man," noting his earlier infatuation with Helena before Hermia took his fancy. Once in the wood the characters' identities become as fluid as can be, with one person merging into another, and the notion of distinct and continuous selves becomes moot. Both Lysander and Demetrius are transformed from lovers of Hermia to lovers of Helena, and since they were mainly defined at the outset by the object of their affections, this amounts to a virtual annihilation of their previous identities (they were never very distinct from each other to begin with). Bottom is transformed into an ass (an apt transformation in his case—a likable ass, though); yet he is recognizably the same Bottom we knew before. Titania becomes, alarmingly, sexually attracted to an animal—"Thou art as wise as thou art beautiful," she gushes, as she leads him seductively to her bower. She also promises to metamorphose her new love in due course (but not before she has him in her embrace): "And I will purge thy mortal grossness so/That thou shalt like an airy spirit go." The mechanicals transform themselves, by acting, into other beings, including a lion and a wall.

Hermia undergoes a startling transformation when she turns fiercely on her childhood friend Helena, accusing her of stealing Lysander from her, prompting Helena to observe: "O, when she is angry she is keen and shrewd. She was a vixen when she went to school, And though she be but little, she is fierce." This is Shakespeare noticing the transformations of character that rage can induce, and indeed in this scene Hermia suddenly loses the sweetness and balance she has displayed hitherto. All this shifting of identities is summed up in Hermia's response to Lysander's abrupt transformation: "Hate me—wherefore? O me, what news, my love? Am not I Hermia? Are not you Lysander? I am as fair now as I was erewhile. Since night you loved me, yet since night you left me. Why then, you left me—O, the gods forbid—In earnest, shall I say?" The repetition here of the first-person pronoun, and the questioning as to whether she is Hermia and he Lysander, underline the sense of doubt about personal identity that pervades the play—the question of who is the real Lysander becomes palpable. In dreams such shifts of identity are commonplace, as one person's soul enters the body of another—and we are here firmly in the realm of dreams. The play is all about becoming someone else, for reasons that are obscure—as if the characters are all hovering over the brink of some startling metamorphosis. The self seems fluid and indefinable, elusive and insubstantial.

Nor are such transformations confined to the realm of fantasy. Sleep itself is a dramatic daily transformation in the self. Shakespeare wrote a lot about sleep, and was well aware of the profound transformation of consciousness it brings about. Helena says: "And sleep, that sometimes shuts up sorrow's eye, Steal me a while from mine own company." In other words, sleep will take her away from herself, giving her daytime self a welcome respite. In her dreams she will exist as a mere alter ego. Bottom's physical transformation occurs during sleep; it is as if he becomes an ass in his dreams, and then wakes to find he really is one. When he says, "I have an exposition of sleep come upon me," his malapropism is apt, since a dream precisely is a kind of exposition of sleep—a story told by the sleeping mind. Titania is also transformed in her sleep, as are Demetrius and Lysander. They are actually transformed into what they might merely dream about themselves. What

Oberon calls "the fierce vexation of a dream" is a mutation of the self in which strange passions flow and dominate. Insanity, too, so akin to the dream, is a state of personal transformation, of turning from one person into another. Titania's love of Bottom seems just like psychotic delusion, a bizarre obsessive attachment to man/ass hybrids—yet she slides into it as if into a new suit of clothes. Shakespeare is dramatizing the transformations that we normally take for granted, and highlighting their implications for the solidity of personal identity over time. And love, source of much delusion in the play, is also a kind of transformation of the self: the lover feels he has become a new person; his world changes, his emotions flow differently, his identity merges with that of the beloved ("my heart unto yours is knit, So that but one heart we can make of it," Lysander declares to Hermia). The self is not some static essence, holding steady through all life's experiences, but a dynamic and variable thing, endlessly malleable (we shall see much more in this vein when we come to consider *Hamlet*).

Sex also transforms—in the sexual act it is as if another self is unleashed (adolescence is when this new self is born). This, I think, is the way to understand Titania's passion for Bottom: he has become animalistic, literally, and this arouses her desire. The potion has made her a changed being, amorous and sexually charged up; there is nothing chaste about her desire for her semi-animal lover—in contrast to the coy distance Hermia maintains from her beloved Lysander when they must sleep together in the wood. Clearly, the sexual union between the fairy queen and the man/ass is anything but conventional and accepted, and corresponds to the subversive character of much human sexuality—the way sex will break taboos with its own invincible force. It is also a clear case of the female partner assuming the position of dominance. The eroticism of their connection is palpable, and is only heightened by its "perversity." But it is, at least, voluntary: they both *want* to do it, even though their desires have been chemically manipulated (well, Bottom seems more along for the ride, as obliging as he knows how to be). Their (potential) sexual union is quite different from two others hinted at earlier in the play—between Hermia and Demetrius, and Theseus and Hippolyta—for these are cases in which the wife-to-be is quite clearly being forced into a marriage. This, of course, means being forced into a sexual relationship—which is not so far from legalized rape. For Hermia to marry Demetrius would be for her to enter into a sexual relationship with a man she not only doesn't love but seems to dislike quite intensely. To put it bluntly, her father is insisting, with the threat of death for disobedience, that she submit herself to rape by Demetrius—or something not so distant from that. Surely Shakespeare was aware of the contrast he was setting before us: the outrageous perversion of a fairy queen having sex with an animal, on the one hand, and the entirely conventional situation of an arranged marriage, on the other. And just as surely he is inviting us to consider the question of which is better. This is a subversive invitation on Shakespeare's part, as shocking now as it must have appeared then. The topic of sexual freedom and sexual slavery is being forthrightly addressed, however obliquely. To put it differently: if Titania loves Bottom, in his "mortal grossness," with the head of an ass, who are we to disagree and forbid? By contrast, it is hard to condone the kind of forced sexual relationship Egeus so harshly proposes. It may be folly on Titania's part, and funny too, but it is not evil in the way Egeus's command surely is.

Acting is another kind of personal transformation—one person intentionally becomes another. It is a transformation involving imagination: the actor imagines herself as someone else. And it takes imagination to process acting—to pretend that the person on the stage is this or that character. It is therefore appropriate that a play about the power of the imagination should contain a play within a play and feature actors as characters. Peter Quince and his players propose to put on a play for the duke, but their thespian talents seem somewhat in doubt—they are merely a group of tradesmen who fancy themselves actors. A good deal of comedy is derived from the mismatch between their rough manners and the characters they intend to portray. Flute pleads, "Nay, faith let me not play a woman. I have a beard coming"; Bottom assures us that he will "move stones" to tears, and frets that his lion part will so frighten the ladies that he will need to "roar you as gently as any sucking dove." But they propose, as Bottom puts it, to "rehearse most obscenely and courageously," in order to imbue their parts with maximum verisimilitude. When they come to perform the play, it is no doubt an amateurish production, with Snout the tinker as the wall with a chink in it, and much crude melodrama; but the wonder is that it hits its mark—the audience is carried along, despite their heckling mockery. "This palpable-gross play hath well beguiled/The heavy gate of night," Theseus says; and Hippolyta expresses her critical opinion thus: "Beshrew my heart, but I pity the man." Even these ham-fisted players, with their poor script and their sad props, can manage so to transform themselves that a critical audience is carried away, accepting the transformation. Their little drama works.

How do they manage it? They do so by means of the transforming power of the imagination. Hippolyta remarks: "This is the silliest stuff that ever I heard." Theseus replies: "The best in this kind are but shadows, and the worst are no worse if the imagination amend them." Hippolyta's retort is: "It must be your imagination, then, and not theirs." The point here is that the best actors are merely surrogates ("shadows"), and that all the work of creation is performed by the imagination—initially the actors', but crucially the audience's. The play of Pyramus and Thisbe works because the audience's imagination has been recruited, almost against its will, by the actors, despite their ineptitude. For we really can imagine that a man is a wall. Such is the extraordinary power of fantasy—a theme developed throughout the play. If the lover creates her beloved by means of her imagination, so the theatergoer creates the character by means of his imagination. We accordingly see people as we imagine them; imagination informs perception. We engage in *imaginative seeing* (a topic revived by Wittgenstein some four hundred years later in his explorations of "seeing-as" in *Philosophical Investigations*).[4] The interaction between perception and imagination is one of the central themes of the play. Seeing is not just an affair of the senses; it incorporates elements from the faculty of imagination.

Theseus may employ some dubious courtship methods, but he is given the definitive statement of the play, a kind of psychiatric diagnosis of what has gone on with the lovers in the woods:

Lovers and madmen have such seething brains,
Such shaping fantasies, that apprehend
More than cool reason ever comprehends.
The lunatic, the lover, and the poet
Are of imagination all compact.
One sees more devils than vast hell can hold:
That is the madman. The lover, all as frantic,
Sees Helen's beauty in a brow of Egypt.
The poet's eye, in a fine frenzy rolling,
Doth glance from heaven to earth, from earth to heaven,
And as imagination bodies forth
The forms of things unknown, the poet's pen
Turns them to shapes, and gives to airy nothing
A local habitation and a name.
Such tricks hath strong imagination
That if it would but apprehend some joy
It comprehends some bringer of that joy;
Or in the night, imagining some fear,
How easy is a bush supposed a bear!

I extract three theses from these pregnant words: first, that love, lunacy, and poetry all employ the same human faculty, viz imagination, so that they form a psychological natural kind (he might have added dreaming to the list); second, that this faculty, in excess, can lead to error, making us see things that aren't there; and third, that an overactive imagination results from a "seething brain"—as if the materials of the brain were bubbling like boiling water. The last thesis is no doubt scientifically crude, but it is interesting that Shakespeare offers us a neurological hypothesis to explain a psychological phenomenon—an advanced thought in his day. If we ask *why* the faculty of imagination is prone to these excesses, then the answer lies in brain chemistry—and not, say, in demonic possession or witchcraft or astrology. Here we see Shakespeare the empirical naturalist, the proto-scientist: he is linking the mind to the brain, suggesting a physical explanation of mental abnormality. The second thesis is a statement about human cognitive fallibility: that we are so built, psychologically, that error is natural to us. We are not perfect epistemic machines, governed by pure reason, but are flawed beings, often victims of our own wayward minds. Just as the body can let us down when engaged in some task, so the mind can let us down—and there isn't much we can do about it. The senses, in particular, are not reliable guides to truth. The first thesis is the basic plaint of *Dream*: art, romantic love, and madness belong together as manifestations of human fancy. And each may shade into the other, with madness the precipice to be avoided. The thought that romantic infatuation is akin to madness is familiar, but Shakespeare here seems to be warning that the poet, too, has his unstable side—with his eye "in a fine frenzy rolling." Never the sentimentalist, he alludes here to the darker side of artistic creation, as if art is madness controlled and domesticated. There is also the thought here that the poet is occupied with "airy nothing"—that his task is to convert vapor into something concrete and particular. He is trying to transform what is abstract, universal, and elusive into an entity that the senses can detect and respond to—speaking characters on the stage, in Shakespeare's own case. To do this he must glance between heaven and earth, between the ideal and the real, which is imagination's natural dwelling place: art is a kind of bridge between the two realms, an attempt to link the "forms of things unknown" to the details of concrete existence. The lover and the madman also dwell in this mysterious zone—between the ideal world of Plato and the concrete world of Aristotle, we might say. It is the imagination that links the world of the senses to the world of abstractions, meanings, and values. As such, it determines the essential form of the human mind.

Bottom too is awarded some keen psychological insights. Upon waking, now restored to zoological normality, he muses:

I have had a most rare vision. I have had a dream past the wit of man to say what dream it was. Man is but an ass if he go about t'expound this dream. Methought I was—there is no man can tell what. Methought I was, and methought I had—but man is but a patched fool if he will offer to say what methought I had. The eye of man hath not heard, the ear of man hath not seen, man's hand is not able to taste, his tongue to conceive, nor his heart to report what my dream was. I will get Peter Quince to write a ballad of this dream. It shall be called "Bottom's Dream," because it hath no bottom, and I will sing it in the latter end of the play, before the Duke. Peradventure, to make it more gracious, I shall sing it at her death.

In this muddle there is acuity, Shakespeare's. The first point to note is that it wasn't in fact a dream that Bottom had: he really was converted into a man/beast and did sleep with the queen of the fairies—so he is misidentifying a waking experience as a dream experience. This is the converse of the kind of error feared by Descartes—thinking that what is only a dream is real life. Bottom thinks that his real-life experiences of the night in the wood were just a dream. Of course, the distinction becomes moot in the wood, and at a metaphorical level the whole thing was a dream. But we did see Bottom and Titania locked in a lovers' embrace, with Bottom zoologically transformed. Bottom finds this "dream" ineffable; he can't tell us, or even himself, what it was about. He is baffled by his own experience, descriptively nonplussed. His dream strikes him as an unfathomable mystery; it has no "bottom." That is a thought familiar from Freud: that dreams are systematically elusive, tough to penetrate, teasingly mysterious. But Bottom makes no attempt to "interpret" his dream, or even to describe its content; he accepts its mystery without comment, as a simple fact of life. Yet he tells us he will enlist the aid of his artistic director to write a ballad of his dream—which presumably will require an act of communication between the two of them. Perhaps he will supply hints and leave it to the estimable Quince to fill in the details. But he is wisely cautious about trying to give premature shape to something so bizarre and shapeless; he senses that there is something beyond words in what he has experienced. Dreams, he seems to be saying, belong to the mysterious part of our psychological nature, and there is no point trying to reduce them to something familiar and manageable. This is why he expresses his puzzlement in terms of synesthesia—eyes hearing, ears seeing, hands tasting, tongues conceiving. The strange and paradoxical nature of his experience is captured by these conceptual collisions (compare Hippolyta's comment, "I never heard/So musical a discord, such sweet thunder"). He repeats this paradoxical mode of description when playing Pyramus: "I see a voice. Now will I to the chink/To spy an I can hear my Thisbe's face." Synesthesia is itself an act of imagination: a visual stimulus, say, suggests an imaginative association with the sense of hearing—so that we might imagine red, say, as like the sound of a trumpet, even experiencing it that way. This is a puzzling phenomenon, not readily explained, but Shakespeare is willing to present us with such oddities, in the spirit of a naturalist observing what the world offers, strange and contradictory as it may seem. Bottom himself has that "negative capability" that Keats ascribed to Shakespeare: he can live with uncertainty and ignorance—he feels no compulsion to explain away or deny what he cannot comprehend (and it is easy to see Bottom as the author's emissary or counterpart in this play).

The epilogue to the play, spoken by Robin Goodfellow (Puck), reminds the audience of its own role in imaginatively generating the play it has just witnessed, and toys with precisely the dream skepticism invoked by Descartes and Montaigne: "If we shadows have offended, Think but this, and all is mended: That you have but slumbered here, While these visions did appear; And this weak and idle theme, No more yielding but a dream, Gentles do not reprehend. If you pardon, we will mend." Robin is suggesting that the audience has itself been dreaming—and how, indeed, can they be certain they did not dream the whole thing? Surely, as Descartes would insist, it is logically possible to dream that you have been watching a play about dreaming, taking it to be reality. Just as the characters in the play find it difficult to distinguish waking from sleeping, so the audience has the same problem—for by what internal mark can they be distinguished? We have only our experience to rely on, a succession of sensory appearances, and it is unable to decide the issue. But Robin is also making another point, about the nature of dramatic art: namely, that the audience has been in a dreamlike state, by virtue of its imaginative engagement with the play it has just witnessed. As the poet (or playwright) uses his imagination to construct a work of art, so the audience must use *its* imagination to process a work of art—to respond to it *as* a work of art. And this imaginative response is akin to dreaming. The strange events that have taken place in *Dream* are themselves dreamlike, and the audience has registered that fact, thus entering a sleeplike state of mind. The imaginative involvement on the part of the audience, combined with the dreamlike character of the materials of the play, has produced in that audience the very dreamlike state with which the play has been dealing. Thus the play is as much about the audience as it is about Theseus, Hermia, Bottom, Oberon, and the rest. The power of fantasy is present in the very act of watching the play (as the embedded play reminds us). In that sense, the play is about itself and the way the human mind receives it.

Bottom is the most clearly delineated and distinctive character in *A Midsummer Night's Dream*, and the most likable. Only he, among mortals, can see the fairies. He is (at one stage) part ass, part human, and potentially a fairy himself—certainly he is most intimately related to fairies (as Titania can attest). He is a protean figure. He is also, notably, an actor, and never so happy as when he is playing a part; indeed, he is greedy to play *all* the parts in the play his troupe is to perform. He is *theatrical* through and through, sliding effortlessly from one role to the next. He is a weaver by trade and also a weaver by vocation—of tales, of imaginative constructions. His imagination sometimes runs away with him, taxing his linguistic abilities (which are comically off kilter). He is a master of transformation, always on the alert for what he can become, ready to accept any role that is offered to him. He is, in an important sense, a self-created being. In this respect, he is a close cousin of Hamlet, also deeply theatrical in nature, whom I shall consider in the next chapter.

THREE

Hamlet

Persons of the Play

Ghost of Hamlet, the late King of Denmark
King Claudius, his brother
Queen Gertrude of Denmark, widow of King Hamlet,
   now wife of Claudius
Prince Hamlet, son of King Hamlet and Queen Gertrude
Polonius, a lord
Laertes, son of Polonius
Ophelia, daughter of Polonius
Reynaldo, servant of Polonius
Horatio, friend of Prince Hamlet
Rosencrantz, friend of Prince Hamlet
Guildenstern, friend of Prince Hamlet
Francisco, soldier
Barnardo, soldier
Marcellus, soldier
Valtemand, courtier
Cornelius, courtier
Osric, courtier
A sailor
Two clowns, a gravedigger and his companion
A priest
Fortinbras, Prince of Norway
A captain in his army
Ambassadors from England

> *Players,* who play the parts of the Prologue, Player King,
>   Player Queen, and Lucianous, in *The Mousetrap*
> **Lords, messengers, attendants, guards, soldiers, followers**
>   **of Laertes, sailors**

In *A Treatise of Human Nature,* published in 1739, David Hume
writes:

> There are some philosophers, who imagine we are every
> moment intimately conscious of what we call our SELF; that we
> feel its existence and its continuance in existence; and are cer-
> tain, beyond the evidence of a demonstration, both of its per-
> fect identity and simplicity . . . If any impression gives rise to
> the idea of self, that impression must continue invariably the
> same, thro' the whole course of our lives; since self is suppos'd
> to exist after that manner. But there is no impression constant
> and invariable . . . For my part, when I enter most intimately
> into what I call *myself,* I always stumble on some particular per-
> ception or other, of heat or cold, light or shade, love or hatred,
> pain or pleasure. I never catch *myself* at any time without a per-
> ception, and never can observe anything but the perception . . .
> But setting aside some metaphysicians of this kind, I may ven-
> ture to affirm of the rest of mankind, that they are nothing but
> a bundle or collection of different perceptions, which succeed
> each other with an inconceivable rapidity, and are in a perpet-
> ual flux and movement . . . The mind is a kind of theatre, where
> several perceptions successively make their appearance; pass,
> re-pass, glide away, and mingle in an infinite variety of postures
> and situations. There is properly no *simplicity* in it at one time,
> nor identity in different; whatever natural propension we may
> have to imagine that simplicity and identity.[1]

Hume wrote these powerful words as a young man in his early
twenties, when questions of identity might be uppermost in his

mind. He is wondering what he *is*—what he means when he says "I"—and he discovers that he means nothing but a flux of varying perceptions, with no solid core he can call his *self*. There is no substance to which these perceptions belong, in which they inhere and which persists over time—only a bundle of mental states and events, more or less tenuously associated. We *speak* as if there is a unifying self that sustains us over a lifetime, or from day to day, but really, when we look candidly inside ourselves, we encounter nothing but this mental flux; honest introspection fails to turn up the supposed metaphysical substance of the simple and continuing self. There is nothing of that sort *in* there. This is an unnerving thought, because it makes us seem very much less substantial than we presumed: there is no *solidity* to the self, just a kind of perpetually moving array of psychological states. The notion of the self seems to dissolve before our eyes, like a chunk of ice melting into liquid. The *body* is a solid entity, observably enduring over time, and possessed of material integrity at any given time; but the thing we are pleased to call the self seems like a variable medley of distinct perceptions. Bluntly put, there is *no self*, at least as we naively suppose; and this, according to Hume, is apparent as soon as we introspectively search for it.

Hume does not say so explicitly, but the same observation can be made about the notion of character or personality. If we think that each person has something called a character that defines his identity—makes him the person he is—then we must ask whether such a thing can be encountered by introspection. But surely we never encounter any such entity; we only find particular conscious occurrences—sensations, emotions, thoughts, and so on. What we call character is not a datum of consciousness but a kind of hypothetical construct: it is supposed to somehow "lie behind" what transpires in our consciousness, while not itself being a constituent of consciousness. But perhaps this idea of character is an illusion: there is just the varying flux of mental events, with no fixed character underlying them. Our ordinary talk of character is really just a way to sum up certain patterns in the flux and should not be reified. And what do we mean by "character" anyway? What *gives* someone a particular character? Is the self the same thing as character, or does the self *have* a character? The more you reflect on these notions, the more puzzling they become; the only indisputable reality here seems to be the flux of conscious occurrences that assail us from moment to moment. We are tempted to suppose that this variable flux is supported by some continuing constancy, but maybe this is a metaphysical mistake.

Montaigne, writing more than a hundred years earlier, expresses a strikingly similar skepticism about the constancy and solidity of the self: "What varied thoughts and reasons, what conflicting notions, are presented to us by our varied passions! What certainty can we find in something so changeable and unstable as the soul, subject by her condition to the dominance of perturbations."[2] Later he writes: "To conclude: there is no permanent existence in our being or in that of objects. We ourselves, our faculty of judgment and all mortal things are flowing and rolling ceaselessly: nothing certain can be established about one from the other, since both judged and judging are ever shifting and changing."[3] He even goes so far as to suggest that a person is not the same from morning till night, and that a so-called single life contains many deaths, as one self is replaced by another. "We are entirely made up of bits and pieces," he says, "woven together so shapelessly that each of them pulls its own way at every moment. And there is as much difference between us and ourselves as there is between us and other people."[4] Clearly Montaigne, as much as Hume, regards the traditional notion of the self as a myth: there is no nugget of selfhood holding our lives together, just a mutable jumble of feelings, thoughts, and sensations. Both authors invite us to look inward and acknowledge that our identity is not the simple, fixed, and constant thing we suppose. The self is more like the beads on a string than the string itself.

It is against this philosophical background that *Hamlet* is best understood. This is fundamentally a play about the constitution of the self. The play begins with the brief line "Who's there?" as one sentinel questions the identity of the other. "Stand and unfold yourself," Francisco demands. Barnardo refuses, evasively responding,

"Long live the King!" To Francisco's "Barnardo?" the other simply replies, "He." There is uncertainty and reluctance with regard to personal identity in this deceptively simple exchange. The opening question could easily have been asked by Hume or Montaigne, as they gaze into themselves in search of the self; and, as I shall suggest, it is preeminently Hamlet's question about himself. The question could hardly be deeper or more general: it is the question, "What is the human soul?" When Horatio comes on the scene, there is a similar uncertainty as to who he is: "Say—what, is Horatio there?" Barnardo asks, and Horatio laconically replies, "A piece of him," as if only wishing to vouch for a particular temporal segment of himself. He is an entity of separate pieces, just as the passage from Montaigne quoted in the previous paragraph declares. And a similar doubt comes up in an early exchange between Hamlet and Horatio, when Hamlet says, "I am glad to see you well" upon meeting Horatio, and then puzzlingly adds, "Horatio—or do I forget myself." Horatio replies: "The same, my lord, and your poor servant ever." Hamlet knows perfectly well that it is his good friend Horatio, but he feigns a kind of ignorance, with the same doubt instantly directed toward his own identity—"or do I forget myself." Since Hamlet's basic question is "Who am I?" all this is grist for the mill—thematic stage setting.

The question of personal identity is immediately raised by the issue of the ghost's identity. The soldiers have witnessed an apparition, which they cautiously refer to as "this thing" and "it," not sure if what they have seen is even a person. When the apparition reappears Barnardo hesitantly describes it as "In the same figure as the King that's dead," and Horatio agrees that it looks like the king. "Is it not like the King?" Marcellus asks, to which Horatio judiciously responds, "As thou art to thyself," explicitly framing the question of personal identity. But such similarity does not imply strict identity: perhaps it is some impostor from another world made to *appear* like the king, a supernatural double. How can they establish the identity? Even after Hamlet has spoken to the ghost, a doubt remains, which will haunt Hamlet's decision to avenge his father's murder: "The spirit that I have seen/May be the devil, and the devil hath power/T'assume a pleasing shape; yea, and perhaps, Out of my weakness and my melancholy—As he is very potent with such spirits—Abuses me to damn me. I'll have grounds/More relative than this." Nor is this reaction irrational on Hamlet's part: how *can* he know that what he has seen is the genuine article? More deeply, how can flesh-and-blood people remain the same person in immaterial form anyway? How can a person in the afterlife be literally identical to a once living person? What *constitutes* the identity? With so much hanging on the veracity of the ghost's assertions, the issue of his identity is crucial—and elusive. The question "Who's there?" acquires additional weight.

Hamlet is in many ways a very strange and mysterious play, full of accidents and reversals—the miscalculated killing of Polonius (wrongly suspected of being Claudius), the baffling relationship between Hamlet and Ophelia, the apparent ease with which Gertrude married Claudius, the bizarre manner of King Hamlet's death, the perfidy of Rosencrantz and Guildenstern, to mention only a few. At the heart of the play's mystery is the mystery of Hamlet's character: who or what is he? He strikes us as a complete enigma, to himself as well us to others. At one moment he is a bookish, indolent dreamer, unable to carry out a clearly mandated act of vengeance; at another he is a rash and brutal murderer (as when, precipitously, he stabs Polonius behind the curtain and shows not a shred of remorse). He can be tender and loving, sensitive and refined, and then crude and cruel, callous and indifferent—as with his varying behavior toward Ophelia. Does he love her or not? There is really no saying. Then there is the question of his madness. He begins by feigning madness, as a result (he says) of his profound melancholy, but his melancholy seems to transmute into genuine madness; certainly, he becomes psychologically unhinged—only to recover himself by the final act. His dazzling verbal brilliance works together with his gift for satire and biting wit; yet he is given to verbal tics and grandiloquent insecurity, to self-recrimination and self-loathing. He is the most playful of men, but also the most serious—and these traits are inextricably interwoven. Is he a comedian or a tragedian? Does he love life or hate it? Is he likable or detestable? Is he the hero of the play or one of its villains? He is a poet and a philosopher, a man of high ideals and a sensitive soul; but he is also a soldier and man of action, capable of unreflective acts of violence. His extensive reading does not preclude impressive fencing skills. He lives by language, but can be contemptuous of words. On some occasions he is stricken with an overactive conscience; on others he has no conscience at all. Action seems farthest from him when he contemplates it most intensely; the more he knows he *must* do something, the less able he is to carry it out. He is a man who loves the theater, yet finds it impossible to occupy a clear role for himself. He yearns to die, but finds the prospect of death utterly intolerable. He is stranded midway between a weary stoicism and an excess of self-righteous activism. He is, in short, a mass of conflicting impulses, or perhaps a man in whom (what we think of as) ordinary human impulse is replaced by soaring intellect and imagination; at any rate, he is impossible to pin down. He cannot be encapsulated; he cannot be reduced to type; he defies all classification; he resists comprehension. To speak of Hamlet's "character" is already to misrepresent him. Hamlet is not so much a human being as a universe—though in an all-too-recognizable human form. We feel we know him, but he eludes our understanding. He contains everything, but consists of nothing. He approximates to the condition of paradox.

As with many Shakespearean characters, Hamlet's first words in the play are revealing of his nature. When Claudius refers to him as "my cousin Hamlet, and my son" (already a paradoxical dual identity), Hamlet replies, enigmatically, "A little more than kin and less than kind." There are multiple puns here: first on the verbal similarity between the words "kin" and "kind," and then the play on two meanings of "kind"—either a type of thing or a disposition of character. His condensed utterance slyly insults his uncle (and now stepfather), by suggesting that his biological kinship should not be interpreted as a similarity of character, still less a well-meaning disposition toward him. Words are used as a double-edged weapon here, but a disguised weapon. When Claudius inquires, "How is it that the clouds still hang on you?" Hamlet responds, "Not so, my lord, I am too much i'th' sun." Again, there is the verbal cleverness, and the covert insult (the irony of "my lord"), but also the pun on "sun," which when spoken is ambiguous between "sun" and "son." He doesn't like to think of himself as Claudius's son, a status Claudius is trying to foist upon him, and treats it as an affliction, like sunstroke. What is notable here are the multiple meanings, the evasiveness, and the indirection. Hamlet will not be reduced to any simple formula, to some conventional cliché of mourning; there is pride in his own originality of being, his indecipherability. He quickly drives the point home with his response to his mother's questioning of his grief about his father's recent death. "Why seems it so particular with thee?" she asks, as if Hamlet should be able to brush off his loss more easily. He replies: "Seems, madam? Nay, it *is*. I know not 'seems.' 'Tis not alone my inky cloak, good-mother, Nor customary suits of solemn black, Nor windy suspiration of forced breath, No, nor the fruitful river in the eye, Nor the dejected haviour of the visage, Together with all forms, moods, shows of grief/That can denote me truly. These indeed 'seem,' For they are actions that a man might play; But I have that within which passeth show—These but the trappings and the suits of woe." Again, there is the bitter irony of "good-mother," and the rejection of summary encapsulation; but there is also a claim to a deeper vision—he knows the "*is*" of things, not merely the "seems." And there is the contrast between the outer forms of grief, which may be dissimulated by mere acting, and the inward reality, which cannot be captured by those outer forms—that which "passeth show." He is warning us that we cannot rush to hasty judgment about what is going on in his soul, because this reality cannot be expressed in any outward mode or manner. He is making an epistemological point, about the radical inaccessibility of other minds, and he is hinting that he senses a mystery in himself—a profound elusiveness that can only be expressed by the unspecific word "something." The question at issue is what is the nature of the self, once it has been distinguished from external trappings and signs. Hamlet is insisting on his own transcendence of the aspect he presents to the world—that he *is* more than he seems.

He makes a similar protest to Guildenstern later in the play: "Why, look you now, how unworthy a thing you make of me! You would play upon me, you would seem to know my stops, you would pluck out the heart of my mystery, you would sound me from my lowest note to the top of my compass; and there is much music, excellent voice in this little organ, yet cannot you make it speak. 'Sblood, do you think I am easier to be played on than a pipe? Call me what instrument you will, though you can fret me, you cannot play upon me." This is pure Hamlet, truculently comic, condescending and dismissive, imaginative, mocking, tragic, and stubbornly insistent on his inner opacity. He is saying to dimwitted Guildenstern, *Don't even try to understand me!*—and indirectly instructing the audience similarly. And the question he is implicitly raising for us is whether ultimately we are *all* mysteries—his distinction being that he realizes it, in virtue of his superior intelligence and insight. He has looked within, as Hume did later, and found not a coherent, substantial self but a mysterious chasm, a gap where the simple self ought to be—a kind of throbbing nothingness. This is the self as systematically elusive, at once everything and nothing, an illimitable flux, disorderly and contrary.

Hamlet does seem clear about one thing: that he is melancholy. That is the overwhelming reality of his being as an embodied consciousness. As soon as he is alone he gives vent to this pressing reality: "O that this too too solid flesh would melt, Thaw, and resolve itself into a dew, Or that the Everlasting had not fixed his canon 'gainst self-slaughter! O God, O God, How weary, stale, flat, and unprofitable/ Seem to me all the uses of this world!" Why does he refer to his body as "this too too solid flesh"? Because his body, in its solidity, fails to reflect his fluid and mercurial soul: it mocks his inner indeterminacy. The body gives an *illusion* of robustness to the self; but the self is more like dew than a solid chunk of flesh—and as susceptible of swift evaporation. And what is the source of his melancholy? His own statement, which we are not bound to accept at face value, is that his mother wed his uncle within but a month of his father's untimely death (he doesn't yet know that it was his uncle who murdered his father): "O most wicked speed, to post/With such dexterity to incestuous sheets!" His mother has thus betrayed his father, and this has moved him to his painful melancholy. Our response to this declaration may be: Yes, but why the existential angst—why the spreading gloom, the indiscriminate disappointment at the universe? Why the wish to *die*? The response seems out of proportion to its cause. Is there not some deeper principle at work? Isn't the betrayal by his mother just a specific expression of some more free-floating melancholy? Isn't it life itself that strikes Hamlet as so painful and pointless? And if so, what exactly does he have against it? Does he even know quite what troubles him so? His despair seems existential, not occasional, a matter of how he looks at the world rather than what the world throws specifically in his direction.

Hamlet's elusiveness here seems designed by Shakespeare, part of the anti-portrait he is painting. I am struck by the following passage from Montaigne:

> What is commented on as rare in the case of Perses, King of Macedonia (that his mind, settling on no particular mode of being, wandered about among every kind of existence, manifesting such vagrant and free-flying manners that neither he nor anyone else knew what kind of man he really was), seems to me to apply to virtually everybody. And above all I have seen one man of the same rank as he to whom that conclusion would, I believe, even more properly apply: never in a middle position, always flying to one extreme or the other for causes impossible to divine; no kind of progress without astonishing side-tracking and back-tracking; none of his aptitudes straightforward, such that the most true-to-life portrait you will be able to sketch of him one day will show that he strove and studied to make himself known as unknowable.[5]

Since we know that Shakespeare studied Montaigne, it is easy to imagine this passage forming the seed that became the character of Hamlet. Hamlet is a man for whom no course of action can command full assent; no thought comes unqualified; nothing escapes the corrosive power of reflection. His personality seems to shimmer and wobble before his (and our) eyes. He is the victim of his own formlessness. And Shakespeare wants us to see that this is part of human reality, perhaps a much bigger part than the old reassuring idea of the fixed and immutable essence of the self.

Hamlet clearly dislikes his condition, as in this famous self-laceration:

> O, what a rogue and peasant slave am I!
> Is it not monstrous that this player here,
> But in a fiction, in a dream of passion,
> Could force his soul so to his whole conceit
> That from her working all his visage waned,
> Tears in his eyes, distraction in 's aspect,
> A broken voice, and his whole function suiting
> With forms to his conceit? And all for nothing.
> For Hecuba!
> What's Hecuba to him, or he to Hecuba,
> That he should weep for her. What would he do
> Had he the motive and the cue for passion
> That I have? . . .
> Yet I,
> a dull and muddy-mettled rascal, peak
> Like John-a-dreams, unpregnant of my cause,
> And can say nothing—no, not for a king
> Upon whose property and most dear life
> A damned defeat was made. Am I a coward?

The vacuum he finds within himself prevents him from carrying out what he regards as his plain duty. If only he could act with the conviction of an actor! I suggest that this comparison between himself and an actor provides the key to the play and to Hamlet's elusive character. Hamlet is facing the problem of the nothingness of the self, and his way out of this nothingness is through an essentially theatrical construction of a self (recall my discussion in chapter 1 of the theatrical conception of the self). We are nothing apart from the parts we play, to put it crudely. There is no antecedent substantial self that we can encounter in introspection; there is only the self that we creatively construct, as an actor creates a role. The self is not

something *given*, as the body is—just a piece of ontological furni-
ture, so to speak; it is something that has to be created, adopted, cho-
sen. Hamlet's interest in the theater, marked throughout the play, is
at root an interest in the construction of the self—which is to say,
finding something to fill the abyss he feels within. He is a bit of an
actor himself, we learn, and he inserts some lines into the play by
which he hopes to expose Claudius. He sees in the Players an escape
from the hesitation and indeterminacy he finds in himself (as many
a professional actor confesses). The play is shot through with the-
atrical conceits—a play within a play, the pretense and deception of
the Danish court (Claudius must act the part of an innocent man),
the prevalence of spying, of hidden audiences—but the most basic
theatrical element is the construction of Hamlet himself. He is a
born performer (Horatio seems like his straight man much of the
time), verbally and otherwise, sometimes acting the part of a mad-
man, sometimes lover, treating everyone as his audience. Without a
stage to act on he lapses into despondency and uncertainty—which
is why he loses fixity in his soliloquies, entertaining thoughts of
nothingness. His identity, such as it is, is essentially theatrical, a mat-
ter of adopting an imaginatively conceived role (not unlike Bottom
in *A Midsummer Night's Dream*).

As I noted in chapter 1, Erving Goffman introduced the idea of
the *dramaturgical* conception of the self in his influential book *The
Presentation of Self in Everyday Life*. In any given social interaction, a
person must act so as to give an impression to the audience of a par-
ticular self: she must convey, by means of her overt behavior, verbal
and otherwise, a certain identity. This management of behavior in
the project of conveying a self is akin to the skills employed by an
actor in filling a role: it is a matter of intentionally giving a certain
impression—say, of being a caring physician or a high-powered
lawyer. But, according to the dramaturgical conception, this is not
merely a matter of the impression of self that is conveyed to others; it
a matter of what the self *is*—of what *constitutes* the self. We consti-
tute ourselves as having a particular identity *by* envisaging and
enacting certain roles. And the plural here is important: there is not
a single personality, lurking somehow behind the others, but a whole

range, depending upon the audience. Think of the adolescent, unsure of the kind of person he or she wants to be: the process of acquiring an identity consists in playing a role, and hence involves theatrical skills. It is as if the person *absorbs* the role he or she plays. *You are what you act,* in a slogan. Goffman quotes the following well-known passage from Jean-Paul Sartre's *Being and Nothingness*:

Let us consider this waiter in the café. His movement is quick and forward, a little too precise, a little too rapid. He comes toward the patrons with a step a little too quick. He bends forward a little too eagerly; his voice, his eyes express an interest a little too solicitous for the order of the customer. Finally there he returns, trying to imitate in his walk the inflexible stiffness of some kind of automaton while carrying his tray with the recklessness of a tightrope-walker by putting it in a perpetually unstable, perpetually broken equilibrium which he perpetually re-establishes by a light movement of the arm and hand. All his behavior seems to us a game. He applies himself to chaining his movements as if they were mechanisms, the one regulating the other; his gestures and even his voice seem to be mechanisms; he gives himself the quickness and pitiless rapidity of things. He is playing, he is amusing himself. But what is he playing? We need not watch long before we can explain it: he is playing at being a waiter in a café. There is nothing there to surprise us. The game is a kind of marking out and investigation. The child plays with his body in order to explore it, to take inventory of it; the waiter in the café plays with his condition in order to *realize* it.[6]

Thus Sartre's waiter, so confident of his identity as a waiter, employs theatrical skills in constructing a performance for an audience: the café, in effect, is his stage. The point Goffman and Sartre are making is that this waiter is really a hyperbolic version of what is common to humanity: social life is the acting of parts, and what we call the self or personality is really a dramatic construction. The self must be willed and chosen, and it must be built up in some way.

Imitation can play a large part in this, so that each person becomes an observer of other persons, an audience of the universal theater of life.

I take it that this is a familiar enough conception and don't propose to labor it further. I am interested in applying it to Shakespeare's play. When Hegel remarked that Shakespeare's characters are "free artists of themselves" he had in mind this idea of self-creation by theatrical means.[7] Shakespeare's Hamlet is someone who is intensely aware of the dramaturgical nature of the self—a kind of seventeenth-century Goffman. He exemplifies the transition from formless consciousness to personal determinacy, or the closest he can get to that. It is not that Hamlet's character *unfolds* during the course of the play, with his "real self" finally revealed by the end; it is rather that he finally succeeds in forging a self from the dramatic materials at his disposal—*he finds a part he can play*. He eventually pins himself down theatrically, more or less. Accordingly, he mutates in the course of the play, as he veers from one role to another. Claudius tellingly remarks to Rosencrantz and Guildenstern: "Something have you heard of Hamlet's transformation—so I call it, Since not th'exterior nor the inward man/Resembles that it was. What it should be, More than his father's death, that thus hath put him/So much from th'understanding of himself, I cannot deem of." Claudius speaks here of Hamlet's apparent descent into melancholy and madness, in which it becomes a moot point whether he has become what he set out merely to simulate; but Hamlet seems to transform himself almost every time he appears on the stage, so variable is his temperament. Hamlet is passing through a succession of dramatic roles, or they are passing through him.

This general conception helps to explain one of the key puzzles of the play: the cause of Hamlet's delay in acting, his notorious procrastination (if that is not too loaded a word for a condition so mysterious). Even once he has become fully convinced of Claudius's guilt, and Claudius has confessed it to heaven (so that we also are in no doubt), and he has Claudius at his mercy, he cannot bring himself to exact the necessary vengeance. Claudius is alone, kneeling at prayer, and Hamlet knows he has a perfect opportunity, but he dodges the issue, saying, "Now might I do it pat, now he is praying," only to lapse into inaction as he draws his sword, telling himself that Claudius will go to heaven if killed now, instead of to the hell he deserves. This has seemed to everyone like a rationalization rather than a genuine reason; he simply cannot bring himself to do it. Yet in the final act of the play he has no difficulty in intentionally stabbing Claudius with a poisoned sword, no hesitation whatever (and his prompt killing of Polonius is under the impression that it is Claudius he is doing way with). The difference between the two occasions is theatrical: there is no audience on the first occasion, so there would be no performance in which Hamlet was playing a part—and the stabbing would also lack a dramatic and aesthetic shape. But on the second occasion, of competitive fencing, Hamlet *is* playing a role, acting a part, with an audience—and the poison thematically echoes the way his own father died. Shakespeare's stage directions here reiterate the words "They play," and Hamlet himself says, "I'll play this bout first." The difference is thus that on the first occasion Hamlet cannot act an appropriate part, but on the second he can. He can now play the role of dutiful avenger; he can stand in an established dramatic tradition. As he fights he has "the pitiless rapidity of things" (in Sartre's phrase), he is on theatrical autopilot, while before he was still without a clear role to play. He is like someone who has adopted and absorbed the role of military man, and can now perform actions that were beyond him before he came to define himself by that role. Hamlet's delay in acting is fundamentally a delay in forming a self. To act he must act in character, but earlier in the play he has no character, so all decisive action is beyond him.

There is no doubt that Hamlet suffers from weakness of will. When the Ghost appears to him for the second time, Hamlet says, "Do you not come your tardy son to chide, That, lapsed in time and passion, lets go by/Th'important acting of your dread command?" and the Ghost speaks in reply of Hamlet's "blunted purpose." Weakness of will has been much discussed by philosophers, because of its puzzling and paradoxical nature.[8] A person judges that he should perform a particular action, and that no contrary consideration counts against the action, and yet he persistently fails to perform it. The intention is there, as clear and strong as anyone could wish, the decision has been made, but no action comes of it. Why? It seems utterly irrational, mysterious, and incomprehensible. Plato even thought that genuine weakness of will is impossible, since no one could fail to act on what they knew they had to do: if you judge that such and such is your moral duty, and there is no fear of untoward consequences, how can you fail to carry out the act? Shouldn't the indicated action follow immediately? Thus Hamlet's inaction strikes us as perplexing. I think Shakespeare is well aware of the puzzle raised by Hamlet's inability to act, but he sees, as a naturalistic observer of human behavior, that weakness of will is not only possible but also quite common. We often, in fact, fail to do what we know we ought to do, even when the action is in our self-interest, and can say little or nothing to explain our failure. Weakness of will is easy; it is explaining it that is hard. What Hamlet primarily needs to perform his act of vengeance is a way to fit it into a dramatic context: it needs to issue from a coherent character playing a part in a drama.

But there is also his melancholy, and his mania—which can seem like two sides of the same coin. Sometimes he seems gloomy and becalmed; at other times he is almost Tourettish in his speech ("I humbly thank you, well, well, well," he ejaculates to Ophelia, and soon blurts out "Ha, ha? Are you honest?"). Montaigne has some interesting remarks in this connection. In "On Sadness" he writes: "The force of extreme sadness inevitably stuns the whole of our soul, impeding her freedom of action. It happens to us when we are suddenly struck with alarm by some piece of really bad news: we are enraptured, seized, paralyzed in all our movements in such a way that, afterwards, when the soul lets herself go with tears and lamentations, she seems to have struggled loose, disentangled herself and become free to range about as she wishes."[9] If we take Hamlet at his word, then the shock and grief he feels at his mother's betrayal, and then his father's murder, work to stun and paralyze him in the way Montaigne suggests. There is no use asking *why* his will becomes paralyzed by such a shock—as if some rational ground could be given for this; it is just a fact of human psychology that this is so. In another passage Montaigne could almost be speaking of Hamlet when he writes:

Is it not true that the soul can be most readily thrown into mania and driven mad by its own quickness, sharpness and nimbleness—in short by the qualities which constitute its strength? Does not the most subtle wisdom produce the most subtle madness? . . . Spirits without number are undermined by their own force and subtlety. There is an Italian poet, fashioned in the atmosphere of the pure poetry of Antiquity, who showed more judgment and genius than any other Italian for many a long year; yet his agile and lively mind has overthrown him; the light has made him blind; his reason's grasp was so precise and so intense that it has left him quite irrational; his quest for knowledge, eager and exacting, has led to his becoming like a dumb beast; his rare aptitude for the activities of the soul has left him with no activity . . . and with no soul. Ought he to be grateful to so murderous a mental agility?[10]

There is no doubting Hamlet's mental agility, his studious nature, his brittle brilliance—but these work to immobilize him and throw him into a state akin to madness. If we combine these two observations of Montaigne's, then we get Hamlet's predicament: a mixture of grief and brilliance leading to confusion and inaction. Hence his famous lines:

I have of late—but wherefore I know not—lost all my mirth, forgone all custom of exercise; and indeed it goes so heavily with my disposition that this goodly frame, the earth, seems to me a sterile promontory. This most excellent canopy of air, look you, this brave o'erhanging, this majestical roof fretted with golden fire—why, it appears no other thing to me than a foul and pestilent congregation of vapours. What a piece of work is man! How noble in reason, how infinite in faculty, in form and moving how express and admirable, in action how like an angel, in apprehension how like a god—the beauty of the world, the paragon of animals! And yet to me what is this quintessence of dust?

On the one hand, he can hymn man and the universe with rare eloquence; on the other, he can avow that it all leaves him cold: his mind can see clearly enough, but his heart isn't in it. What Shakespeare is giving us is a psychological syndrome—a picture of grief, intellectual power, melancholy, and paralysis. This may not fit a Platonic model of the mind as a super-rational agency, always equipped with reasons for action (or inaction), but it is a recognizable psychological profile nonetheless. We must avoid an oversimplified and reductive account of Hamlet's nature, or one that tries to expunge his inherent mystery. As Montaigne says: "Those who strive to account for a man's deeds are never more bewildered than when they try to knit them into one whole and to show them under one light, since they commonly contradict each other in so odd a fashion that it seems impossible that they should all come out of the same shop."[11] It is important that we can recognize the human reality of Hamlet, but that is not the same as trying to make him intelligible, if this means imposing some simplistic or traditional model on his subtleties and shadows.

We are now in a position to examine the most famous speech in the play, and possibly the most famous passage in all literature. "To be, or not to be," it resoundingly begins; not, note, "To live, or not to live." The question employs the most primordial of philosophical concepts, and the most basic metaphysical contrast—that between being and nonbeing. It is stripped down, monosyllabic, and gives the impression of concerning much more than the matter of Hamlet's individual life. It is a question God might ask Himself about whether to create a universe: should there be being or nonbeing? It is also a question you can imagine someone asking *before* he comes to exist, paradoxically enough: should I come into being or should I not? Is existence worth it? Descartes' *Cogito* is similarly pared down and powerful: "I think, therefore I am"—I have a mind, therefore I have being. Descartes thinks he can prove indubitably that he exists; Hamlet wonders whether this existence is worth a candle. Hamlet is a philosophy student, remember, and he expresses himself with philosophical generality: he finds in his own life a reflection of the most general of questions. Hamlet is confronted by his own being, as every reflective consciousness must be, and hence he can consider its absence. There is no more primal thought: I have being, but my being is contingent. Here is the passage in full:

> To be, or not to be; that is the question:
> Whether 'tis nobler in the mind to suffer
> The slings and arrows of outrageous fortune,
> Or to take arms against a sea of troubles,
> And, by opposing, end them. To die, to sleep—
> No more, and by a sleep to say we end
> The heartache and the natural shocks
> That flesh is heir to—'tis a consummation
> Devoutly to be wished. To die, to sleep.
> To sleep, perchance to dream. Ay, there's the rub,
> For in that sleep of death what dreams may come
> When we have shuffled off this mortal coil
> Must give us pause. There's the respect
> That makes calamity of so long life,
> For who would bear the whips and scorns of time,
> Th'oppressor's wrong, the proud man's contumely,
> The pangs of disprized love, the law's delay,
> The insolence of office, and the spurns
> That patient merit of th'unworthy takes,
> When he himself might his quietus make
> With a bare bodkin? Who would these fardels bear,
> To grunt and sweat under a weary life,
> But that the dread of something after death,
> The undiscovered country from whose bourn,
> No traveler returns, puzzles the will,
> And makes us rather bear those ills we have
> Than fly to others that we know not of?

Thus conscience doth make cowards of us all,
And thus the native hue of resolution
Is sicklied o'er with the pale cast of thought,
And enterprises of great pith and moment
With this regard their currents turn awry,
And lose the name of action.

This passage slides fitfully from one topic to the next, following the mercurial flow of Hamlet's turbulent mind. He quickly interprets his own opening question as about the choice between stoicism and activism (not an obvious interpretation of it, by any means): should he accept his troubles in serenity, or should he act so as to overcome them? This is a question about what sort of person to be, what sort of character to cultivate; and it is notable that Hamlet sees it as a choice, not a piece of fate. But he rapidly moves sideways to the question of whether death is preferable to life. In his melancholic mood he cannot see much advantage in life—his list of life's routine trials and torments is as cogent today as it was then—and his resistance to dying concerns a merely epistemological doubt: how can we know what death is really like? Maybe death is a type of dreaming in which one nightmare succeeds another, so that it is worse than life. Hamlet is expressing a kind of skepticism, to the effect that death might be a lot more disagreeable than we assume—not because of the threat of divine justice but because we have no evidence about what it is really like. Maybe suicide is not the end of a tormented life but the beginning of a new type of torment. We should fear death not because it is the end of something valuable but because it might be a dreadful new beginning. How can we know one way or the other? Descartes worried that our life now might be a dream, but there is an even more unnerving skepticism to contend with once we follow Hamlet's train of thought: that our experience might be just a dream we are having *after death*. How do I really know that I am not *dead* and dreaming? If death is a kind of sleep, it can be accompanied by dreams; but couldn't these dreams simulate ordinary waking life, inviting belief in their illusions? Descartes assumed that we are alive and possibly dreaming in his radical skepticism, but an even more extreme skepticism questions that first assumption: if death and dreaming are compatible, then dream skepticism can extend to the heady possibility that we are all *dead dreamers*. If we were, we would have the same beliefs as we do now, since the appearances would suggest such beliefs; but all these beliefs would be false, including the belief that we are alive. I don't say that Hamlet explicitly raises this extreme brand of skepticism in the quoted passage, but he has the materials with which to raise it—the idea is in the conceptual vicinity. If we add the dream skepticism of *Midsummer Night's Dream* to Hamlet's speculations about a dreaming death, then we reach the radical skeptical possibility of our being under the mistaken impression that we are living, perceiving beings. That is a highly vertiginous thought.

For Hamlet, our ignorance of the nature of death is what deters us from seeking it. It is our consciousness ("conscience") of our ignorance that prevents us opting for death as a way of avoiding the trials of life. This is a very grand form of despair—as if only a fool would not choose death if he could be assured that it was really the end of consciousness! It should be observed how very extreme this despair is, and it is hard to see how Hamlet's actual circumstances can objectively justify it. We could be forgiven for supposing that he is *playing* with despair here—acting the part. For this is the despair of a man who sees nothing positive in life, for whom consciousness itself is an intolerable burden. It is difficult to avoid the impression that his thinking at this point is not altogether sane, that his depressed imagination is running away with him. There is wisdom in his words, to be sure, but there is also madness. We feel sympathy for a man capable of such profound pessimism, but also some puzzlement. We must not forget that Hamlet's voice is not to be identified with Shakespeare's, and that he is certifiably sick in the head. What he offers as wisdom is by no means necessarily what the playwright regards as wisdom: Hamlet is just one character among others, not an infallible oracle (Polonius, despite his confident sententiousness, is full of dubious dicta). This famous speech is as much an expression of Hamlet's derangement as of the truth (according to William Shakespeare) about human life and death. Hamlet is a man troubled by his own thoughts, a victim of them, and his thoughts range into pathological territory at times. When Ophelia interrupts his reverie with "Good my lord, How does your honour for these many a day?" and he replies, "I humbly thank you, well, well, well," we must doubt his assertion of well-being and wonder at the distracted repetition of "well." This is not a man recently engaged upon sober logical reflection, which we as audience are intended to take to the bank, but someone in the grip of paralyzing confusion and grief. Magnificent as the "To be, or not to be" passage is, it must be seen in dramatic context and not excised as if it were Shakespeare's considered judgment on the Meaning of Life. I see it mainly as Hamlet's awareness of his own abyss, his ontological inconstancy, and his propensity to let words get the better of him. Or again, it is Hamlet the student of philosophy toying with possibilities, charting the limits of knowledge, without much regard for common sense or ordinary feeling. This is the man who, when asked what he is reading, dismissively replies "Words, words, words," and is capable of crudely joking to Ophelia of the "No thing" that lies "between maids' legs." He is not a model of discretion and sobriety, and is a master of irony and dissimulation. "These are wild and whirling words, my lord," Horatio says to him in another connection. We might take a leaf out of Horatio's book when interpreting the "To be" soliloquy.

I shall end this chapter by discussing some incidental lines in *Hamlet* that are philosophically interesting in their own right. One of the most frequently repeated lines in the play is: "There are more things in heaven and earth, Horatio, Than are dreamt of in our philosophy." By "philosophy" here we are to understand the full range of human knowledge, including science. The import of the statement is thus that the universe contains more than we can understand, or even than we can imagine. This is an expression of what philosophers call *realism*—the idea that reality is not limited by the possibilities of human knowledge. Knowledge has its limits, and on the other side of it are things unknown. It is not, then, that reality is determined by what we can know, understand, experience, or conceive; reality, in its intrinsic nature, is quite independent of our epistemological capacities. This is, indeed, the reason that skepticism is a genuine threat: our epistemological faculties can only be inadequate to discovering the world if the world itself is not constituted by those faculties. Knowledge can have limits only because there is something out there that it cannot encompass—facts it cannot reach. We are small creatures in a rich and complex cosmos, and there is no reason to suppose that our "philosophy" can bring everything within its scope, even in principle. Of course, in Shakespeare's time—when knowledge was very restricted—this realist conviction would have sounded a very plausible note to his audience. Hamlet is modestly confessing to the depth of human ignorance.

So Hamlet is a realist—but is Shakespeare? Certainly we cannot deduce the latter from the former, but I think Shakespeare's general outlook is realist, especially when it comes to the peculiarities of the human mind. He is willing to accept the existence of psychological phenomena that we find unintelligible: Hamlet's own nature is an instance of that willingness. As a naturalist, Shakespeare observes and records what nature contains, without regard to whether we can make sense of what we find there. In this sense, Shakespeare qualifies as what is now called a *mysterian*: he believes in the reality of things we cannot comprehend (Hamlet, as I noted earlier, at one point refers, somewhat boastfully, to his own "mystery").[12] He is receptive to the puzzling, the incomprehensible (which is not to say the supernatural). In this famous remark, then, Shakespeare is giving expression to a conception of reality as encompassing more than human minds can penetrate. We shall see later that this kind of realist perspective informs other of Shakespeare's plays. Shakespeare (like Montaigne) is not of the opinion that "man is the measure of all things," if that means that reality must conform to human conceptions.

At one point Hamlet remarks, "There is nothing either good or bad but thinking makes it so." Again, we must not simply assume that Shakespeare himself concurs with this claim about the nature of goodness and badness. Sometimes the line has been interpreted to mean that *moral* goodness or badness are constituted by our thinking, but the context makes clear that this is not Hamlet's intent. He is discussing whether Denmark is a prison, asserting, "To me it is a prison"; so he is speaking of *non*moral goodness—he is considering whether Denmark is a *good place to live*. And clearly Hamlet's statement is much more plausible in application to that question than it is when applied to ethics. For what *else* could make somewhere a good place to live, in the nonmoral sense, than its inhabitants *finding* it to be so? What could make food good to eat but the good effect it has on consumers? Again, Montaigne supplies the text for the line in his essay, "That the taste of good and evil things depends in large part on the opinion we have of them," which begins: "There is an old Greek saying that men are tormented not by things themselves but by what they think about them".[13] This is, in fact, an ancient and well-known philosophical question: the question of whether values inhere in objects independently of the mind, or whether they ultimately depend upon the mind's response to objects. The question matters because the latter view enables us to change the values of things. As Montaigne goes on to say: "If what we call evil or torment are only evil or torment insofar as our mental apprehension endows them with those qualities then it lies within our power to change those qualities."[14] This is a thought that might naturally occur to Hamlet, tormented as he is; and it shows that philosophical issues are not far from Shakespeare's mind in this play. Given that Shakespeare had read Montaigne, it seems to me highly likely that this line of Hamlet should bear the imprint of his reading. The point here, of course, is not that reality in general is constituted by our thinking of it in a certain way—that would flatly contradict the realism expressed in the line I discussed in the previous paragraph. It is the much more limited claim that the agreeableness of a thing or state of affairs is a matter of how agreeable we *find* it. To call something pleasant is to say that we derive pleasure from that thing, so there cannot be pleasant things in reality that no one takes pleasure in. But it is not that in general reality is constrained by our human response to it. I like to think that the work Hamlet is perusing when Polonius confronts him is Montaigne's *Essays*: he is, after all, a philosophy student at Wittenberg and might be expected to be up with the latest thing. If so, he is simply quoting Montaigne.

Polonius is the frequent butt of Hamlet's satirical wit; Hamlet mocks him mercilessly. And Polonius is indeed a fountain of verbose banality and spurious wisdom. Yet one particular line of his is regularly plucked out of context and paraded as a piece of "Shakespearean wisdom": "This above all—to thine own self be true, And it must follow, as the night the day, Thou canst not then be false to any man." These words trip easily off the tongue, but how wise are they really? Hamlet later utters another famous line: "That one may smile and smile and be a villain," in reference to Claudius. Claudius is undoubtedly false to many people, notably Hamlet: his entire conduct is an act (and a rather wooden act at that). But is he not true to himself? Does he not act out of his own nature in killing his brother? Being true to oneself, if that means acting in accordance with one's own nature, is simply no guarantee of truthfulness to others. The Shakespeare who created Iago could scarcely subscribe to Polonius's simple bromide: Iago prides himself on his fidelity to his own nature, and yet he is as false to others as anyone could be. So I can't see Shakespeare assenting to Polonius's pronouncement on this point, as on many others. Polonius is a master of smooth-sounding, but hollow, homilies, and this is one of them. Being true to oneself and being true to others are just very different things.

And there is a deeper point to be made: What *is* this notion of "true to oneself"? What might Hamlet, say, be true *to*? Surely, the entire content of the play contests any such simple idea of self or character. What might Hamlet attempt to be true to in his own nature as he begins his quest to exact revenge for his father's murder? He really doesn't *have* any character to be true to. He is a wavering flux of conflicting impulses, needing to cast himself in a role before he can acquire any meaningful determinacy. You can only be faithful to your given character if you have such a character to begin with. Shakespeare puts the line in the mouth of Polonius—a bumbling and phony courtier—precisely because of its superficial appeal: but it is put there ironically, I think, as hinting at a view of human nature that the play as a whole contests.

*   *   *

As Hamlet lies dying at the close of the play, he exhorts Horatio (his faithful interpreter and critic) "To tell my story." Is this a rather unbecoming concern with posthumous fame? Why is he so anxious to have his actions reported in this way? Why does he want an after-life in verbal form? I think it is because he sees how akin to fiction his life has been. He has created his character from nothing, like a playwright or novelist, and with it the actions and consequences that have ensued. Hamlet is the author and architect of his own being. Thus his life has been a kind of freely created story—a result of his imagination and theatrical talents. Horatio must tell his story because of the storylike character of his life. A play is a kind of story, and Hamlet has constructed himself as a character in a play (rather as Shakespeare constructed him). Or better, he constructs many characters for himself in the course of the play, ending as the aveng-ing hero he initially found it so difficult to enact. He can act only when he is *acting*—that is, when he can conceive of himself in fic-tional terms. He can *be* only when he occupies a role. He is consti-tuted by his own story.

Othello

Persons of the Play

Othello, the Moor of Venice
Desdemona, his wife
Michael Cassio, his lieutenant
Bianca, a courtesan, in love with Cassio
Iago, the Moor's ensign
Emilia, Iago's wife
A clown, a servant of Othello
Duke of Venice
Brabanzio, Desdemona's father, a Senator of Venice
Graziano, Brabanzio's brother
Lodovico, kinsman of Brabanzio
Senators of Venice
Roderigo, a Venetian gentleman, in love with Desdemona
Montano, Governor of Cyprus
A herald
A messenger
Attendants, officers, sailors, gentlemen of Cyprus,
     musicians

Before I engage directly with the text of *Othello,* it will be useful to set out in some detail the general form of philosophical skepticism, and particularly the so-called problem of other minds. This will set the stage (so to speak) for understanding the deeper themes of this play about error and epistemological anxiety. Shakespeare's concern with problems of knowledge, especially of the minds of others, is notably manifest in this story of deception and derangement. The character of Iago, in particular, is a locus of epistemological insecurity (even terror).

Epistemological problems arise from the basic facts of human cognition. They are not just farfetched theoretical doubts dreamed up by pedantically scrupulous philosophers. Skepticism is not the tedious insistence that "you can't be certain of anything in this world"; it is not merely excessive caution in the face of the necessity to believe. Rather, skepticism reflects deep *structural* truths about our faculties for knowing—particularly, the relationship between evidence and fact. Our reasons for belief can be alarmingly removed from what we believe in. In the case of beliefs about the past, say, our reasons relate to what is *presently* available in the form of memories and traces of past events; but the fact in which we believe is temporally remote from the present, sometimes very remote (as with our beliefs about dinosaurs or the Big Bang). How can we validly move from what is *now* the case to what *was* the case? Even more worrying, our supposed knowledge of the future involves a transition from what has been the case up to now to what *will* be the case: our reasons, again, concern times that are distinct from the times we have beliefs about. Thus Hume worried that we can never have any grounds for rational beliefs concerning the future, since all our evidence concerns times *prior* to the future: we seem to be leaping in the dark in trying to divine the future from the past (Macbeth, as we will see, suffers from ignorance of the future).[1] In the case of our knowledge of the physical world, our reasons seem to concern the *experiences* we have—the way the external world *appears* to us—but what we commit ourselves to are beliefs about the objects that (we suppose) *cause* those experiences. Again, we seem to be jumping from one kind of thing to something quite distinct—from states of our own consciousness to convictions about objects external to our consciousness. The worry that it might all be a dream is simply a way of expressing the point that experiences themselves bear no necessary, intrinsic relation to the world of real, physical things: you could in principle have all these experiences and there be no physical world "corresponding" to them (this is the skeptical possibility conjured up by *A Midsummer Night's Dream*). In each of these cases, the skeptic insists, we are rashly trying to exceed the bounds of the evidence—arguing from one kind of thing to something completely different. The point is not that we should be more cautious; it is that limitations of knowledge are built into the very structure of our cognitive faculties and our position in the world. In short, the facts we seek to know about transcend our means of access to them. We are condemned to make *inferences*, and these inferences are both fallible and structurally suspect.

This kind of problem is nowhere more pronounced than in the case of our supposed knowledge of other people's minds, the epistemological focus of *Othello*. It is disarmingly easy—almost second nature—to wonder how we can really know what is going on in someone else's mind. People's thoughts are not written on their forehead for us to read, nor are their motives always apparent. I can observe your outer behavior—what you say and do—but I have to make an inference as to what is true of your mind. You tell me that your intentions are honorable, but I have to take this on trust, since I can't observe your real intentions. Again, I have to make a transition from one kind of thing—a person's outward behavior—to another kind of thing entirely—his inward states of mind. And this inference is fraught with difficulty: the inference is not just notoriously fallible, but it seems to be structurally flawed, since states of mind are "private" while outer behavior is "public." The mind is "hidden" from everyone except its possessor. No one (except perhaps God) can peer into your mind and discern what is in there. Other minds are essentially impenetrable, concealed, and unknowable. So the skeptic insists, noting the logical gap between evidence and conclusion. When I gaze at another person, however fixedly, I must be struck by the obvious fact that I am at an epistemological disadvantage compared to him: I have only his behavior to go on in figuring out his mental states, but he doesn't have to follow this indirect route—he has "immediate access" to his states of consciousness. Iago knows quite well what is on his mind, but Othello can only guess—and consistently guesses wrongly. Knowledge of other people's states of mind is frustratingly indirect and prone to error.

We can look at this problem from both a first-person and a third-person point of view. From the third-person point of view, other people strike me as opaque: I look at them and sense their impenetrability—their minds hover somewhere out of my view. This is the way philosophers usually set up the problem. But we can also formulate the problem from a first-person point of view, as when I reflect that *my* mind is hidden from *you*. I am aware of my own mind and its contents and I know that you have no such direct access to it. Thus I am aware of *my* impenetrability to others—as I am aware of *their* impenetrability to me. I can think, "You don't know me," as much as, "I don't know you." In my view, the first-person version of the problem is the more primitive and powerful, because in it I am most aware of the *asymmetry* between my knowledge of my mind and your knowledge of my mind. It is surely a momentous day in a child's life when she realizes that her knowledge of her thoughts and feelings is not duplicated by other people's knowledge of her thoughts and feelings ("My mind is not open for all to see!"): for in that moment the possibility of *deception* becomes temptingly apparent. Iago is vividly aware that what is open to him is closed to others, and he seeks to exploit that fact. From the first-person perspective, I am aware of how much I am keeping back, how easy it is for me to mislead others, how privileged and exclusive my access to my own mind is. All they have to go on is my outward behavior, and that is at best an imperfect guide to my true state of mind. This gives me an extraordinary power—my impenetrability is something I can exploit. I have to choose how much I shall keep inside and how much I shall show the world.

Because of the gulf between outer behavior and inner consciousness, vast possibilities of concealment open up. These range from not boring people around me with everything that enters my head, to questions of tact and courtesy, to outright malicious lying in pursuit of my own nefarious ends. The arena of the mind is a zone of potential concealment, and how much I conceal is subject to my will, at least in large part (there can of course be involuntary revelations of inner states). If I have a lot of self-control, I can conceal much of what passes within; then I can trade heavily on my psychological impenetrability. I might become disingenuous, dishonest, mendacious, a pathological liar (like Iago)—all this arising from the very structure of human knowledge of other minds. Or, more positively, I might become someone who can keep a secret, be the soul of discretion, be able to withstand intense torture—I might use concealment for worthy ends. But all of this relies on the essential opacity of one human mind to others—the epistemological gap between the outer and the inner.

The role of language in the matter of concealment is significant. On the one hand, language can seem like the solution to the problem of other minds, since I can simply *tell you* what's on my mind: language vastly expands my repertoire for making my mental states known. Anyone who has ever tried to figure out what a cat wants when it meows can see the expressive limitations of the languageless. And the better a person is at using language, the better he will be able to transmit his states of mind to others. But, on the other hand, language opens up the possibilities of deception tremendously; for now we have a startlingly powerful resource for misleading others. We can *speak falsely*. We can use language as a barrier, not a conduit, a means of deception, not revelation. Language facilitates active concealment, and the better a person is at using it, the better he becomes at deceiving others. Again, Iago shows himself a master of verbal dissimulation, and Othello is woefully susceptible to linguistic manipulation. Language magnifies the problem of other minds, as well as sometimes reducing it. It can as easily function as a device for falsehood as for truth, in the wrong hands. Again, when a child recognizes that speech can be used to lie, and thus to misrepresent her actual state of mind, a milestone has been passed, and a whole new moral universe opens up. And, of course, the possibility of the lie can thwart the sincerest person's desire to reveal the truth within: you may want desperately to reveal yourself to another, and yet your sincere statements be suspected of intentional falsehood, no matter how much you insist on your truthfulness (Desdemona is the victim of this kind of opacity). It can be as hard to know that someone is telling the truth as that she is lying—and this is, again, because of the essential privacy of the mental.

It is because of the problem of knowing other minds that an indispensable element of *trust* pervades all social relations, especially those involving language. Othello repeatedly refers to Iago's honesty and trustworthiness, taking his words at face value. When I take your words at face value, I place my trust in you—that is the attitude I bring to the encounter. Since I cannot be *sure* that you are telling me the truth as you see it, I place myself in your hands, so to speak—I make a kind of leap of faith. The need for this attitude of trust shows that the encounter is fraught with epistemological danger, and a violation of such trust is accordingly felt as especially unethical. Since I *have* to rely on trust in forming my beliefs upon your say-so, given the inherent opacity of other minds, it is perceived as ruthless to exploit my helplessness in this regard. Without such trust being regularly well grounded, the opacity of other minds would undermine all social interactions of any importance. A convincing and systematic liar undermines the trust that is essential to human communication, and when that trust is destroyed, the problem of other minds prevents any further meaningful interaction. Trust is the solution we have come up with for dealing practically with the epistemological problem of other minds—but trust can be abused and violated.

Acting and deception are particularly closely associated. The consummate liar must be an expert actor; he must possess theatrical skills in generous measure. All social interaction involves theatrical skills in one sense, since we must intentionally manage our actions so as to make an impression on an audience—even when those impressions are as sincere and truthful as anyone could wish. In a sense, I must act myself, even when I am at my most "authentic." But if I am not being truthful—for good motives or bad—I must possess acting skills of another order; for I must be able to pretend to be something I'm not. I must act a person other than myself, projecting a state of mind I don't have. Acting and lying are closely related skills, the actor being a type of liar and the liar being a type of actor. Iago must be able to act the trustworthy subordinate, even as he lies through his teeth; he must be able to adopt a role that is alien to his underlying nature. Acting, like lying, depends on the structural opacity of other minds: if the actor's real state of mind were completely transparent to the audience (fretting, nervous, self-conscious, and so on), then there would be no possibility of acting another character entirely. Acting exploits the gap between the inner and the outer, just as lying does. In a certain sense, then, the liar must be a type of artist, since he must have the artistic skills of an actor—he must be able to construct his behavior as a kind of artifact. The liar, like the actor, is aiming for a certain kind of artistic perfection: to produce a performance that would fool the most skeptical of audiences—and to achieve this he must attend to detail and nuance. Lying, acting, and artistry are thus interwoven—and all are made possible by the problem of other minds. Shakespeare is well aware of the interrelations between acting, lying, and artistry, and in *Othello* he sets these against the structural epistemological problem posed by other people's interiority. The accomplished liar, like Iago, has an acute awareness of the gap between interior and exterior, and has perfected the talent of acting in such a way as to conceal the interior. Among other things, this gives him a level of self-consciousness not found in ordinary truth tellers. He possesses a specific type of psychological intelligence—as Iago indubitably does.

In my view, then, *Othello* is predicated on the philosophical problem of other minds, with all its ramifications—moral, personal, and metaphysical. It is thus a deeply philosophical play. This may seem a surprising claim, given the intensely human quality of the drama—a story of marriage, betrayal, jealousy, and race—but the problem of other minds is actually an intensely human problem. It affects the way we live our lives, our friendships, even (or especially) the relationship of marriage. It is not just a philosopher's abstract puzzle. Shakespeare's play is a living embodiment of this problem in epistemology. I could also say that *Othello* is an extended essay in the appearance/reality distinction, with the appearance of other people's minds as a special case. Appearances can mislead in general, but the appearance of others can be the most misleading thing of all; here the potential sources of error are manifold and perilous. Perhaps the most telling line in the play come from Iago, when Othello demands, "By heaven, I'll know thy thoughts," as Iago is planting the seeds of doubt in his mind: "You cannot, if my heart were in your hand; Nor shall not whilst 'tis in my custody." This is an outright statement of the problem of other minds: Iago is asserting that no amount of access to the physical nature of a person, even his "heart," will yield knowledge of what is going on inside his mind. Iago is also making a conceptual point when he says that Othello will not know his mind while it is in his "custody": a person's mind cannot, logically, ever be in someone else's custody, since that would make it *his* mind. But Iago's metaphor also suggests the idea of ownership or private property: no one else can gain access to his private domain, his inalienable self. He takes pride in this privacy, in the secrets of his soul. His privacy is the source of all his power: it is other people's ignorance of Iago's mind that makes it possible for him to control and manipulate them. He is standing right there before Othello, who has authority over him, and reveling in the power that comes from his psychological impenetrability. He knows that Othello's external scrutiny of him will never reveal his true designs, and he is vividly aware of the contrast between the reality of his mind and the appearance he presents to Othello. We can almost taste his cruel amusement at knowing that the reality, so close to the surface, is nevertheless hidden from Othello's desperate gaze; at any second he could choose to reveal it, but refrains from doing so, thus "pluming up his will." He delights in his own inscrutability, and in Othello's pathetic ignorance: he is excited by the asymmetry in epistemological power between them. Othello may be the general, and he the humble ensign, but in matters of knowledge he reigns supreme—and knowledge is power.

Once this theme is noticed it can be found everywhere in the play. Brabanzio says, when he learns of Desdemona's marriage to Othello: "Fathers, from hence trust not your daughters' minds/By what you see them act." Othello, questioning Desdemona about the lost handkerchief, says: "That handkerchief/Did an Egyptian to my mother give. She was a charmer, and could almost read/The thoughts of people." Lodovico, noting the dramatic change in Othello, comments: "I am sorry that I am deceived in him." Othello describes Desdemona as a "fair fiend," contrasting her outer beauty and inner (to him) corruption, saying of her: "This is a subtle whore, A closet lock and key of villainous secrets, And yet she'll kneel and pray—I ha' seen her do't." The general theme of deception occurs throughout the play. The Turks seek to deceive the Venetians with "a pageant to keep us in a false gaze." There is much talk of "proofs," as in these threatening words of Othello to Iago: "Villain, be sure thou prove my love a whore. Be sure of it. Give me the ocular proof, Or, by the worth of mine eternal soul, Thou hadst been better have been born a dog/Than answer my waked wrath." There is the deception practiced on Othello by means of the handkerchief, as Iago maliciously manipulates the appearances. The very blackness of Othello, and his allegedly unprepossessing appearance, belies his nobility of soul (Desdemona reports, "I saw Othello's visage in his mind"). The play is manifestly obsessed with the distinction between seeming and being, and with the elusiveness of truth. Error seems as likely as accuracy, falsehood as natural as truth, with delusion everywhere.

Nowhere is this pervasive error more powerful, and painful, than in the marital and family relations of the play. No one seems to understand anyone. Brabanzio is deceived by his beloved daughter, warning Othello: "Look to her, Moor, if thou hast eyes to see. She has deceived her father, and may thee." Othello clearly misjudges his wife, as he even more clearly misjudges Iago. But Desdemona also misjudges her husband, thinking him incapable of jealousy: "My noble Moor/Is true of mind, and made of no such baseness/As jealous creatures are." She also says, "I think the sun where he was born/Drew all such humors from him," in reply to Emilia's question, "Is he not jealous?" Less obviously, but no less profoundly, Iago and his wife, Emilia, deeply misunderstand each other. Emilia never suspects her husband of the wickedness of which he is capable, and is stunned to discover that he is the cause of Desdemona's death: "My husband?" she utters three times, in disbelief, when Othello tells her of Iago's plot. She was as clearly deceived by Iago's trick with the handkerchief as Othello, suspecting nothing sinister of her husband. His true nature is hidden from her, despite their years of marriage.

Equally, Iago is wrong about his wife's nature: he doesn't expect that she will reveal the truth about the handkerchief plot, thus unraveling his entire scheme and exposing him. She has more honor in her than he suspects, and his response to her honesty—and lack of marital solidarity—is to cut her down. Her love for her mistress is also much greater than he supposed.

So these are marriages with a deep ignorance at their heart—a lack of mutual comprehension. Without this ignorance the story could not unfold as it does; it is powered by human error. Othello has to be ignorant of his wife's real love from him in order to be persuaded by Iago. Desdemona has to be ignorant of her husband's weakness of character in order not to worry about the jealousy her advocacy of Cassio might inspire. So too must she be ignorant of Iago's character. Emilia must be ignorant of her husband's nature not to suspect him in the business of the handkerchief, and not to be wary that he might be plotting revenge on Othello for his lack of promotion. And unless Iago was ignorant of Emilia he would not be caught out as he eventually is: "Villainous whore!" he shouts at her, as if her truthfulness were an affront to his marriage. Iago has no idea of his wife's love for her mistress, and of her love of truth and justice—she could, after all, have saved herself and her husband simply by keeping quiet. The mutual ignorance of man and wife is here profound and shocking, as they stare at each other in utter incredulity, each striking the other as a total cipher. How could such ignorance thrive in a relationship of such intimacy? It is because of the essential impenetrability of the mind, even in situations of utmost proximity. The epistemological barrier between people cannot be surmounted even by the most intimate of connections. This is, in a way, the central tragedy of the play—the tragedy of knowledge itself. We seek knowledge of each other—to know and be known—but we easily fail in that quest. The best we can do is to admit the limitations of our knowledge, not to pretend that it is better than it is. Montaigne, as always, puts the point vividly: "Those outside us see only events and external appearances: anyone can put on a good outward show while inside he is full of fever and fright. They do not see my mind: they only see the looks on my face."[2]

Accordingly, he goes on, "all those judgments which are based on external appearances are unbelievably unreliable and dubious, and why there is no more reliable witness than each man is to himself."[3] In *Othello* Shakespeare has written a play in which the ability to see only the physical body of others tragically limits what the characters can know of each other's inner workings. Some characters strive to make themselves known and fail, as with Desdemona; others try to keep themselves unknown and succeed, as with Iago. The soul of the other remains systematically elusive. If we seek union with others through knowledge of them, then we are destined to disappointment, because such putative knowledge is subject to extreme and corrosive skepticism. The characters in *Othello* are desperate for knowledge but frustrated in their attempts to achieve it.

Let us go through the play with these themes in mind, so that we can see how they are woven into the drama. The play begins with Roderigo, Iago's easy dupe, protesting, "Tush, never tell me!" This serves as a motto for the whole play, because Iago's acts of telling are the main engine that drives the story: if nothing is told, then no deception is possible; and Iago is a master at deceptive telling. He is always telling people things that are not true, using language to manipulate and warp. He next assures Roderigo of his hatred for the Moor, alleging the promotion of Cassio over him as the motive. Significantly, his complaint against the man Othello has preferred is that he is merely a "great mathematician," inexperienced in actual war, full of "bookish theoric" and "prattle without practice"— whereas he, Iago, a man of vast experience of war, of whose competence Othello's "eyes had seen the proof," is passed over. His complaint, then, is that Cassio's alleged erudition is a sham kind of knowledge, quite unsuited to the realities of battle; Iago, despite his lack of formal education, has superior knowledge of matters martial. Cassio is his cognitive inferior, he asserts—a judgment he passes on many others as the story progresses. Moreover, Othello has rejected the "proof" of his competence, thus refusing to believe what he has seen with his own eyes. It is not the promotion as such that rankles with Iago; it is the grounds on which it was defended—the underestimation of his grasp of military lore, his cognitive standing in the world. His grudge against Othello is basically that Othello has underestimated his cognitive powers—something he will redress as he employs his superior intelligence to entrap his military superior. The strategic skill Othello has prevented him from using in the field he will now use against the general, and against Cassio with his useless brand of "learning." This is to be a battle of minds, and Iago is confident of his superior understanding of the world and of man. Othello has insulted his pride as knower, and he must pay.

Iago's response to this affront will be to bide his time, not letting his true feelings be known. Not for him to be the loyal servant to an unworthy master:

> Whip me such honest knaves. Others there are
> Who, trimmed in forms and visages of duty,
> Keep yet their hearts attending on themselves,
> And, throwing but shows of service on their lords,
> Do well thrive by 'em, and when they have lined their coats,
> Do themselves homage. These fellows have some soul,
> And such a one do I profess myself—for, sir,
> It is as sure as you are Roderigo,
> Were I the Moor I would not be Iago.
> In following him I follow but myself.
> Heaven is my judge, not I for love and duty,
> But seeming so for my peculiar end.
> For when my outward action doth demonstrate
> The native act and figure of my heart
> In compliment extern, 'tis not long after
> But I will wear my heart upon my sleeve
> For daws to peck at. I am not what I am.

Here we have it in so many words: Iago will set out to deceive his master by acting contrary to his true feelings, the outward show being but a mask for the interior reality. The resulting schism in his being will make him other than what he seems; his secrecy will go very deep. Of course, he cannot be literally what he is not—that would violate the logical law of noncontradiction—but he will work to split the inner from the outer so thoroughly that it will be as if there are *two* Iagos instead of one. There will be the external Iago, dutiful and honest, trusted and esteemed, and there will be the internal Iago, malicious and deceptive, cunning and violent: *he* (internal) will thus not be what *he* (external) is.

When Roderigo and Iago rouse Brabanzio from his sleep, proclaiming that his daughter is now "covered with a Barbary horse" and that "your daughter and the Moor are now making the beast with two backs" (two bestial metaphors very characteristic of Iago's descriptive style), Brabanzio declares: "This accident is not unlike my dream; Belief of it oppresses me already." Here is a Shakespearean theme I have commented on in earlier chapters—the way dream can masquerade as reality, only this time getting it right. Is it a nightmare Brabanzio is having or is it reality? It is night and strange fantasies can take hold. He has in fact been deceived, though not by his dream, but by his daughter, his dream daughter—"O, she deceives me past thought!" Thus Roderigo is deceived by Iago, and Brabanzio is deceived by Desdemona, and Iago undertakes to deceive Othello— all in the first few minutes of the play. Iago sums up the mood when he states: "Yet for necessity of present life/I must show out a flag and sign of love, Which is indeed but sign." Everything so far has been "but sign," with appearance and reality following dramatically divergent paths.

Brabanzio is convinced that Othello has used magic or drugs on his daughter: "For nature so preposterously to err, Being not deficient, blind, or lame of sense, Sans witchcraft could not." In other words, he suspects that the alien Othello has put Desdemona under a spell that has overturned her faculty of judgment: she is suffering the *illusion* that Othello is worthy of her love, it being otherwise incomprehensible that she should run to "the sooty bosom/Of such a thing as thou—to fear, not to delight." *She* has been deceived by Othello, he supposes, as she has deceived her father. Othello replies by detailing the course of their courtship, a "round unvarnished tale" with nothing false or illusory in it. His report ends: "She loved

me for the dangers I had passed, And I loved her that she did pity
them. This only is the witchcraft I have used." His reply, then, to the
charge of having deceived Desdemona, is that he spoke nothing but
the plain truth to her, and that she fell in love with that truth. He
gave her *knowledge* of himself; he revealed his soul to her as it is; he
concealed nothing. He made himself transparent to her, and she
responded to what she perceived in him. The scene ends with
Brabanzio's warning that she has deceived him and may now deceive
Othello (he seems to accept Othello's assurance that he did not
deceive her). The whole scene before the Venetian council is a quasi-
legal confrontation of truth and falsehood, with truth finally gaining
the upper hand. This truth between Othello and Desdemona will
quickly turn into error and darkness, as Iago works to subvert
Othello's trust in his wife. From mutual knowledge will emerge
mutual ignorance, and harmony will turn to discord: light will turn
to darkness, transparency will become opacity. The shared world of
the lovers will disintegrate into two enclosed and solipsistic worlds.

Iago is still playing his epistemological games when he reflects as
follows on his dastardly plans: "I hate the Moor, And it is thought
abroad that 'twixt my sheets/He has done my office. I know not if't
be true, But I, for mere suspicion in that kind, Will do as if for
surety." He doesn't really believe this malarkey, but is ready to *pre-
tend* that it is true. His own grip on truth and falsity is so fluid, so
subservient to his evil desires, that it matters little to him what is true
or false; so he is able to act *as if* something is true if that serves his
purposes best. Belief has become a creature of his will: he will treat
an unfounded suspicion as if it were a Cartesian certainty. His con-
tempt for people who are candid and trusting, who respect the truth,
is expressed thus: "The Moor is of a free and open nature, That
thinks men honest that but seem to be so, And will as tenderly be led
by th'nose/As asses are." Like an animal, Othello cannot see the dis-
tinction between appearance and reality; he is blind to the possibility
that a man might be otherwise than he seems. Great military leader
though he is, he can be led and steered like the most docile of ani-
mals—"tenderly" (a devastating word for Iago to use at this point).

But he is not the only one taken in by Iago: everyone is (only

Roderigo seems to have his doubts, and he is a deceiving scoundrel too). Cassio, Desdemona, and Emilia all credit Iago, taking him at his word. His persuasiveness is at its height in the scene in which he first suggests Desdemona's infidelity. He gives the impression of extreme reluctance in expressing his suspicions to *Othello*—"Think, my lord?" he repeats to Othello's inquiries, with many an "Indeed?" and much heavy hesitancy. "If thou dost love me, show me thy thought," Othello finally demands. Iago then brings Cassio under suspicion, remarking, "Men should be what they seem, Or those that be not, would they might seem none," no doubt relishing the irony and his cleverness. It is in this pivotal scene that he comments on the necessary invisibility of his heart when Othello exclaims, "By heaven, I'll know thy thoughts." He slyly reminds Othello of the fact that Desdemona deceived her father: "She that so young could give out such a seeming, To seel her father's eyes up close as oak, He thought 'twas witchcraft!" Riskily, he is reminding Othello of how easy it is for one person to deceive another—perhaps calculating that no one would have the nerve to make this point if he were himself in the middle of such a deception. With a sinking heart we hear Othello say to himself: "This fellow's of exceeding honesty, And knows all qualities with a learned spirit/ Of human dealings." He takes Iago to be a reliable source of knowledge, as if he passes some Cartesian test of indubitability. And yet, when he sees Desdemona again, he recovers his senses: "Look where she comes. If she be false, O then heaven mocks itself! I'll not believe't." The two are battling for Othello's beliefs, one wittingly, the other not: will he believe the truth or will he succumb to error?

It is the kind of question pressed by the skeptic: what *should* we believe, given that nothing is certain? This is not a straightforward matter, because there can be conflicting evidence, clashing appearances. Othello is in an epistemological quandary; he is racked by uncertainty. His fondly held conviction—that he has a loving wife—is crumbling under Iago's skeptical onslaught. The audience's question is whether he can hang on to the truth or whether he will submit to the forces of delusion. The drama is essentially a drama about his *beliefs*. As he says to Iago: "Thou hast set me on the rack. I

swear 'tis better to be much abused/Than but to know't a little."
Uncertainty is painful; felt ignorance is disturbing—especially on so
charged a matter. Here is where he demands his "ocular proof," an
end to his miserable uncertainty. Just as Hamlet wanted proof of the
ghost's veracity and his uncle's guilt, finding the uncertainty intoler-
able, so Othello wants proof of what Iago alleges: both are victims of
the agony of not knowing. And both resemble Montaigne and
Descartes, who also felt the force of skepticism and yearned for some
sort of reply to it: the fideism of Montaigne, in which we are to
accept the traditional teachings of the church without question; and
the proof of the existence of an undeceiving God in the case of
Descartes. The uncertainties of Hamlet and Othello mirror these
wider uncertainties of the age, giving them a human intensity.
"What do I really know?" is the overarching question, and the
answer "Nothing" is never dismissible *a priori*. Othello is caught in
the authentic skeptical bind when he says: "By the world, I think my
wife be honest, and think she is not. I think that thou art just, and
think thou art not. I'll have some proof." Iago cunningly retorts that
he lately slept in the same bed as Cassio and heard him mutter self-
incriminatingly of Desdemona, noting that this was "but his dream."
Othello replies, not unlike a professional logician, "But this denoted
a foregone conclusion," to which Iago responds, "'Tis a shrewd
doubt, though it be but a dream, And this may help to thicken other
proofs/That do demonstrate thinly." There is the whiff of the philos-
ophy seminar here, with students earnestly debating the merits and
demerits of a particular philosophical proposition—except that the
proposition in question concerns Desdemona's alleged infidelity
with Cassio. It is like a scholastic debate, but about marital infidelity.
And a lot hangs on these further proofs—"I'll tear her all to pieces,"
Othello declares, if the proofs go against her.

And what are these "proofs"? There are no proofs at all, except a
clever little setup involving a handkerchief. Iago lures Cassio into
giving Bianca Desdemona's handkerchief, a gift from Othello, which
Othello interprets to be a gift to her lover, Cassio. The whole situa-
tion is preposterous, and extremely risky for Iago, and yet Othello is
totally convinced by it; his jealousy has now gotten the better of him,

and he misconstrues what he observes, with disastrous conse-
quences. On the basis of this immensely shaky "proof" Othello
swears, "I will chop her into messes." He has lost all epistemological
responsibility by now. He will believe anything. His old eloquence
has fractured into incoherence. He literally breaks down in a fit. His
habitual martial restraint gives way to rash action. It is as if he will go
insane unless he believes *something*, and he is all too ready to resolve
his uncertainties in the wrong direction. Something must fill the
epistemological vacuum within, even if it is just a flimsy "proof" by
handkerchief. Nor is his newfound belief unconnected to action:
almost immediately he, unforgivably, strikes Desdemona without
explanation, prompting from her the pitiable and ominous line, "I
have not deserved this." Lodovico comments: "My Lord, this would
not be believed in Venice, Though I should swear I saw't." Cyprus
has unhinged the dignified and moderate general, to such an extent
that Lodovico finds it hard to believe his eyes—was he deluded in
what he just witnessed? No, the weight of error lies on Othello's side;
it is he that should be more skeptical of what appears before him.
The scene ends with Lodovico's remark, "I am sorry that I am
deceived in him."

I noted in the previous chapter Hamlet's use of the word "mystery"
to describe himself. The word occurs again in *Othello*, as Othello
instructs Emilia to warn him if anyone approaches the room: "Leave
procreants alone, and shut the door, Cough or cry 'Hem' if anybody
come. Your mystery, your mystery—nay, dispatch." The word seems
out of place in this context, until we note that in Shakespeare's time
"mystery" could mean "trade, profession or skill."[4] So what Othello
is saying, literally, is that Emilia must discharge her job properly—
her "mystery." But this is a one-dimensional reading of the text;
Shakespeare is surely trading on the dual meaning of the word—the
meaning it has in Hamlet's mouth (our contemporary meaning) as
well as this other obsolete meaning. We should note that Othello's
speech is quite fragmented by this stage, and phrases will be thrown
in that bear slender relevance to the surrounding utterances. I read
this passage as Shakespeare asserting the mystery of the characters in
the play, particularly perhaps Desdemona. Othello is baffled by

Desdemona, as well he might be given his peculiar state of belief; but we also sense mystery in the character of Iago, and in Othello himself. This is yet another way of expressing the impenetrability of others: they strike us as mysterious. Just before Othello utters these enigmatic (mysterious) words, he says to Desdemona, "Let me see your eyes. Look in my face," to which she responds, "What horrible fancy's this?" He doesn't follow up his request, immediately moving to his instructions to Emilia; but one can imagine him looking probingly into his wife's eyes and straining to see her soul, finding there nothing but mystery and elusiveness. The true reference, then, of "your mystery" would be not Emilia, but Desdemona, the two conflated now in Othello's deranged mind; and "nay, dispatch" accordingly takes on a far more ominous meaning. He will destroy her mystery; for once she is dead there will be nothing left that he fails to know about her. He will expunge what he cannot solve.

"Swear thou art honest," Othello commands, a futile gesture at this point, since no amount of swearing will make it so, and he knows that as well as anyone. She replies, "Heaven doth truly know it," which is actually not the same as the futile oath Othello is demanding. Othello rejects her protestation: "Heaven truly knows that thou art false as hell." Here we find truth and falsity jostling each other for dominance, with brute power the final factor in the encounter. Desdemona is desperate to reveal herself to her distraught and homicidal husband, but she cannot make herself transparent; she cannot put her heart in his palm and thereby make herself known. She is as much the victim of her opacity as Iago is the beneficiary of his. Othello's terrible response, "Ah, Desdemon, away, away, away!"—with its abbreviation of her name to what he believes she is, a demon—is an inarticulate expression of his frustration. Even now he is not completely sure of her guilt, but he cannot bear the uncertainty any longer—he must act to eliminate the source of all his doubts.

As the final scene of murder unfolds, Desdemona and Othello are each given lines that carry reflective generality. Desdemona remarks to Emilia: "Good faith, how foolish are our minds!" Othello, in reference to the murder of Roderigo, comments, like a would-be natural philosopher: "It is the very error of the moon, She comes more nearer earth than she was wont, And makes men mad." Both lines lament the instability of the human mind, and both have particular reference to the situation in which the characters find themselves. There is a recognition here of the waywardness of the mind, its proneness to error, delusion, and insanity. For, clever and persuasive as Iago is, Othello makes a willing victim in many ways: he is *given* to such instability of mind, unduly susceptible to Iago's suggestions, credulous and uncritical in his thinking. Here is Shakespeare commenting on the mind of man, very much in the spirit of Montaigne. When the problem of other minds combines with this kind of instability, tragedy can result. It is not just that other minds are intrinsically impossible to know; it is also that we are very *prone* to get them wrong, because of our own weaknesses and peculiarities. We lay traps for ourselves. The enemy lies within the gates. As Emilia rightly complains to Othello: "Thou art rash as fire/To say that she was false." The metaphor is apt: Othello consumed himself, and Desdemona, in his fire, and that fire came from within, raging and uncontrollable—Iago merely supplied the initial taper. Othello's enemy was as much his own unruly mind as the deceiver Iago.

Iago's final words in the play are fittingly epistemological: "Demand me nothing. What you know, you know. From this time forth I never will speak word." This is cryptic indeed, and does nothing to supply a motive where we might feel one to be lacking. I believe he is saying that there is nothing more to be known about him than what has emerged in the play (I will shortly return to the question of his motivation). He has no undisclosed grudge or grievance or quirk or injury. He did what he did for the reasons he has stated. At any rate, he refuses to be drawn into inquiries into his inner being; he wishes to remain as impenetrable as he has always been. It is as if he is saying: *Don't try to inquire any further; be content with the knowledge you have.* But his final sentence is also striking, since he has up to now been a consummate speaker, a master of language, a great verbal manipulator. He now abjures all speech, his prime power and talent. Is it that with the jig now up he has no interest in speech, because language for him has point only when it can be used to deceive? Or is it that he wants to deny his interlocutors the satisfaction of knowing the truth about him? He is promised torture, and it is easy to envisage him tight-lipped in the flames and stubbornly mute on the rack. He has demonstrated amazing self-control, and one feels that his pride would not allow him to speak what others wish to hear. He refuses to be a source of knowledge to anyone; his pride is in his power to instill error in others. As the play begins with Roderigo saying to Iago "Tush, never tell me," it draws to an end with Iago undertaking to tell no one anything ever again. The prospect of honesty so appalls him, apparently, that he would rather be tortured to death in silence than speak the truth.

Jealousy is an emotion, not a state of knowledge, but it has interesting relations to cognitive states. Jealousy comprises a powerful desire to know along with a distorted sense of evidence—curiosity combined with credulity. The jealous man, suspecting his wife of infidelity, becomes epistemologically voracious—he *must know*; hence the interrogations, the spying, the private detectives even. In this respect, jealousy resembles scientific curiosity—a burning desire to find out the truth on a certain matter. But, instead of the drive to know being accompanied by high standards of evidence and reasoning, the jealous man turns into an epistemological nincompoop. Scrupulous scientist he may be in the laboratory, but the jealous man is apt to become a credulous fool (this is Iago's phrase) when his wife's fidelity is brought into question. The emotion of jealousy upsets and clogs the epistemological machinery. Emilia, with her bracingly rough wisdom, expresses this point well, when Desdemona protests that she never gave her husband cause to be jealous: "But jealous souls will not be answered so. They are not ever jealous for the cause, But jealous for they're jealous. It is a monster/Begot upon itself, born on itself." (Earlier, Iago had spoken of his plot as a "monstrous birth.") Othello, it turns out, is a jealous soul—which is not unconnected to his social insecurity, which in turn traces back to his race and status—and he is ready to slide into error from his own psychological weak spot. Once Iago has kindled the flame of jealousy, Othello's own fire causes it to

spread and strengthen; soon he is the victim of "the green-eyed mon-
ster which doth/Mock the meat it feeds on." In other words, jealousy
is a potent source of irrationality, in which belief becomes detached
from reality. When a man is jealous his reasoning faculties desert him;
he becomes subject to error and delusion. As Iago says: "Trifles light
as air/Are to the jealous confirmations strong/As proofs of holy writ."
Jealousy dangerously lowers the threshold for belief.

The reason for the link between jealousy and irrational belief
appears to be that jealousy incites fantasy. Under Iago's expert
prompting, Othello imagines all sorts of lurid scenarios, and his fan-
tasies begin to dominate his mind, substituting for perceived reality.
When Iago refers to Desdemona and Cassio "as prime as goats, as
hot as monkeys, As salt as wolves in pride," he conjures in Othello's
susceptible imagination a pungent image of depravity, and this
image forces itself upon his consciousness with all the vigor of actual
perception. It is Othello's fevered imagination that does the work
that Iago's words merely trigger. Once he is imagining these scenes of
infidelity he is generating his own evidence for his erroneous beliefs.
Jealousy begets itself because it conjures fantasies that substitute for
reality. It is as if it creates dreams in the jealous person's mind, and
these dreams incite belief. Othello is a poet, as well as a warrior, and
his imaginative way with words betokens a mind given to fantasy
(certainly, he tells Desdemona some fantastic tales, though probably
true); the jealousy he feels excites his fantastic side, and this in turn
usurps his beliefs. Love, jealousy, fantasy, and unreason thus all
belong together (a point we also saw made in *A Midsummer Night's
Dream*). Othello is a kind of poetic dreamer, not equipped with a
powerful analytical intelligence, and as such he is susceptible to the
jealous fantasies Iago evokes in him. The result is that he is cogni-
tively deficient, easily gulled. It is not that he rushes headlong into
his jealous fantasies—Iago does put up a clever and suggestive
case—but at crucial moments he fails to question both himself and
his informer. He shows himself insufficiently skeptical, because too
dominated by fantasy.

And there is a connected area in which he appears cognitively
lacking: there is room for doubt as to whether he ever consummates

his marriage to Desdemona—if so, he does not "know" her. He seems only too willing to delay the moment of consummation, priding himself on his self-control and sense of civic responsibility. Thus he postpones acquiring carnal knowledge of Desdemona. It is a type of knowledge he seems strangely reticent to secure. He keeps himself ignorant in this crucial sphere. And since he has been a man of action, always engaged on military campaigns, we sense that his life has not been sexually very active. The omission is actually crucial, because Desdemona's real love for him would surely have shone through if they had enjoyed normal marital relations—he would have known her genuine physical passion for him. He might then have been more skeptical of Iago's insinuations, confident in the knowledge he had acquired of his wife from the marital bed. But this very sexual ignorance, hinted at in the text, which is largely self-inflicted, is what makes him susceptible to the errors planted in his mind by Iago; he has no firm knowledge to oppose to Iago's lies. He does not know his wife in the way he should—as an ordinary husband—and the consequence is a more catastrophic failure of knowledge. Othello knows about war and martial duty, but he remains critically ignorant about key areas of human life. His tragedy, again, is essentially epistemological.

The entire thrust of the play, therefore, concerns what we might call *epistemological anxiety*: the fear that we may not know what we think we do, that we may be the victims of massive error, that we may be vastly ignorant even of the minds of our closest intimates. Falsity begins to seem as natural and potent as truth. No force of nature, or divine assistance, will automatically turn our minds to the truth; they are just as likely to latch on to falsehood. Jealousy is a rich source of such error, a prime enemy of true belief. Othello is thus all of us in our worst nightmares: a victim of enormous, destructive delusion. Descartes conjured the possibility of an "evil demon" who systematically deceives us, and wondered how we could rule out such a possibility. Well, Iago is just such an evil demon—a seemingly all-powerful source of false belief, not just in Othello, but also in all those around him. If Descartes had ever read Shakespeare's *Othello*, I don't doubt that he would have seen his skeptical possibility embodied there in a peculiarly concrete form.

I have said very little so far about the nature of Iago's evil, a topic that has excited controversy throughout the play's history. Is such a man possible? Is his psychology realistic? Shakespeare anticipates the question in a pointed exchange between Iago and Emilia. Emilia, not yet knowing of her husband's part in causing Othello's jealousy, says: "I will be hanged if some eternal villain, Some busy and insinuating rogue, Some cogging, cozening slave, to get some office, Have not devised this slander. I will be hanged else." Iago, shrewd as ever, replies: "Fie, there is no such man. It is impossible." He thus asserts his own impossibility. Why does he seem impossible? Not because he has no motive to dislike Othello—he was passed over for promotion, his competence questioned—it is because his crime seems so disproportionate to the stated motive. His evil goes far beyond whatever legitimate grievance he might have. It is this excessive evil that challenges comprehension. He will not gain much, if anything, by Othello's destruction (and that of other innocents), so his evil actions seem gratuitous. He appears to be pursuing evil for its own sake, as opposed to what it might bring him; and this strikes us as puzzling, in need of some special explanation.[5] Certainly, the malice toward Othello is undeserved—Othello has done nothing to warrant the magnitude of Iago's evil design. The additional reason Iago cites—the suspicion that Othello has cuckolded him—is quite clearly manufactured, and anyway would scarcely merit the revenge Iago seeks (in which Desdemona too is to be destroyed, not to mention Cassio). There is no avoiding the conclusion that he is guilty of massive, unjustified evil. (Besides, he *reeks* of evil.) But is such evil intelligible? This question has seemed to many to pose a problem of credibility in the play's action.

Montaigne makes some interesting observations about evil in his essay "On Cruelty." Writing of the barbarities of the civil wars of religion in his time, he says:

If I had not seen it I could hardly have made myself believe that you could find souls so monstrous that they would commit murder for the sheer fun of it; would hack at another man's limbs and lop them off and would cudgel their brains to invent unusual tortures and new forms of murder, not from hatred or for gain but for the one sole purpose of enjoying the pleasant spectacle of the pitiful gestures and twitchings of a man dying in agony, while hearing his screams and groans. For there you have the furthest point that cruelty can reach: "That man should kill man not in anger or in fear but merely for the spectacle."[6]

He goes on to mention the human love of blood sports, watching animals tear each other apart, which bears witness to "an inborn propensity to cruelty." Iago himself speaks of the "sport" he enjoys in his machinations, which "plume up my will." Iago does not wish to kill Othello himself—his "sport" is not garden-variety violence and murder—but it is clear that he enjoys the spectacle of suffering he so imaginatively creates. There is something theatrical in his behavior: he must act a part himself ("honest Iago"), but he also is the director of a drama of his own devising—he is, in his way, an artist. He uses ingenuity, verbal skill, and psychological insight to manipulate his players, so that their wills become extensions of his will; he is the puppeteer, the hidden hand directing the action. He relishes the drama of it all, the suspense and tension, and congratulates himself on his part in producing it. He is an aficionado of suffering as sport and art—like those ingenious torturers Montaigne mentions. He likes the spectacle, the technique, and the power.

This idea that Iago's character, though extreme, is continuous with that of other human beings, in disturbingly large numbers, is endorsed by Hazlitt in his commentary on the play:

The character of Iago is one of the supererogations of Shakespeare's genius. Some persons, more nice than wise, have thought this whole character unnatural, because his villainy is *without a sufficient motive*. Shakespeare, who was as good a philosopher as he was a poet, thought otherwise. He knew that the love of power, which is another name for the love of mischief, is natural to man. He would know this as well or better than if it had been demonstrated to him by a logical diagram, merely by seeing children paddle in the dirt or kill flies for sport. Iago in fact belongs to a class of characters common to Shakespeare and at the same time peculiar to him; whose heads are as acute and active as their hearts are hard and callous. Iago is, to be sure, an extreme instance of the kind; that is to say, of diseased intellectual activity, with an almost perfect indifference to moral good or evil, or rather with a decided preference for the latter, because it falls more readily in with his favorite propensity, gives greater zest to his thoughts and scope to his actions. He is quite or nearly as indifferent to his own fate as to that of others; he runs all risks for a doubtful and trifling advantage; and is himself the dupe and victim of his ruling passion—an insatiable craving after action of the most difficult and dangerous kind.[7]

This strikes me as a fine summation of Iago's character, and it absolves Shakespeare of any charge of human implausibility. Iago is an adventurer, an enthusiast of extreme sports, and a risk taker—as well as being intrinsically nasty. He enjoys the game, the hunt, and he will make great sacrifices for this pleasure. He asserts his power over Othello, after enduring the sting of Othello's power over him, and he relishes the intellectual challenge he takes on. He enjoys duping the foolish Roderigo also, but he gets more of a charge from the bigger game represented by Othello. Cruelty for its own sake appeals to him (as it does, according to Montaigne, to many men), but what is more delightful to him is the harnessing of this enjoyment to his own powers of manipulation. He is an artist of the bold and audacious lie, and he is entranced by the aesthetics of his plotting.

Iago is not much given to reflecting on his motives, but at one point he does come close to diagnosing his own character. Speaking of Cassio, he remarks: "He hath a daily beauty in his life/That makes me ugly." He doesn't say, "makes me *appear* ugly"; he seems to think that Cassio's life *is* aesthetically superior to his. Cassio has the looks, the manners, the education, and the sophistication—while he is a rough soldier. Thus he suffers from simple envy of Cassio, an intelligible enough emotion. But there is a further dimension to this uncharacteristic episode of introspection, namely that Iago's plotting has itself an aesthetic quality. To be set beside Cassio's admitted beauty is Iago's own peculiar beauty—his beauty of evil, his beautifully woven tapestry of deceit. He cannot have Cassio's natural beauty, but he can contrive a beauty of his own, perverse as it may be. If Cassio is a talented mathematician, he can be a genius of deception, practicing his own brand of mathematical precision. He can match Cassio's intellectual artistry with his own. We never think of Iago as handsome and charming, but he can make up for these deficiencies by creating his own kind of aesthetic monument. His use of language is masterly, his timing expert, his performance of Oscar-winning caliber; he is a creative genius, in his own depraved way. He may be a second-rate soldier, an indifferent husband, and a charm-free companion—but he can be a brilliant liar, an inspired and peerless manipulator.

It is helpful to set Iago beside Desdemona: while he is unnaturally evil and despicable, she is unnaturally good and lovable. If there is a puzzle about him, then there is also a puzzle about her. Despite all of Othello's abuse, she never wavers in her love for him, protesting little at his outrageous statements and actions. ("Unkindness may do much," she says. "And his unkindness may defeat my life, But never taint my love.") She is a model of wifely obedience, propriety, and patience. She is almost *too good to be true*—as Iago has seemed to some too evil to be possible. Why is she so good? The answer is that she just is, as Iago simply is evil. She has no "motive" to be good; it is simply in her nature—as Iago has no "motive" for his evil. They are mirror images of each other, with her light corresponding to his dark. W. H. Auden astutely remarks that Iago is an "inverted saint," observing: "The saint and the villain have very similar psychologies. In both, ethics and aesthetics become almost the same thing. There is a similar detachment and similar freedom in both with respect to human relations, an absence of the usual scruples and motivations that govern or trouble most living."[8] Both Desdemona and Iago are, in one sense, unnatural, above the fray, as it were—they are not affected in the way normal people are, not weak in the usual respects. Iago seems preternaturally calm in tense and perilous situations, but so too does Desdemona—not quite human, one feels like saying. Desdemona contrasts with the sturdily commonplace Emilia in this respect—as when she protests that she really cannot understand how a wife could be unfaithful (Emilia has no trouble on the point). Desdemona is a saint, and Iago is her inversion. But *both* are incomprehensible in the same fundamental way, since neither shares the psychology of "normal" people: one is abnormally good, the other abnormally bad. But—Shakespeare is saying—abnormality happens.

To illuminate Iago's character, Auden quotes a well-known passage from St Augustine, in which he makes the following admission about his youth: "I had a desire to commit thievery; and did it, compelled neither by hunger nor poverty; but even through a cloyedness of well doing, and a pamperedness of iniquity. For I stole that, of which I had enough of mine own, and much better. Nor when I had done, cared I to enjoy the thing I had stolen, but joying in the theft and sin itself . . . Now, behold, let my heart tell thee, what it sought for there, that I should be thus evil for nothing, having no other provocation to ill, but ill itself. It was foul, yet I loved it, I loved to undo myself, I loved mine own fault, not that for which I committed the fault, but even the very fault itself."[9] Iago exemplifies this sort of moral inversion: evil is his good, vice his virtue. This is the *acte gratuit*, Auden suggests, a pure assertion of personal autonomy: it is choosing evil in order to demonstrate the radical freedom of the human spirit. Iago is asserting his free will by choosing the opposite of what is "natural" to man. He is insisting on the gap between morality and will—between what we ought to do and what we choose to do. He sees that nothing *forces* him to act morally; it is entirely up to him how he chooses to "plume up" his will. Iago demonstrates to us, alarmingly, the freedom to do evil. He thus inverts the motivation exemplified by Desdemona: her free choice is to do the good, even in the most difficult of circumstances, while he exerts his freedom in the pursuit of evil. She loves virtue as Iago (and the youthful Augustine) love vice. And she is no more comprehensible to him than he is to her.

Shakespeare, unblinking naturalist that he was, is pointing out to us that this sort of evil (and this sort of good) exists, difficult as it may be to make sense of it—mysterious as it may appear. We must not deny its reality just because it offends our natural sense of order. Human nature cannot always be slotted into comfortable, prearranged categories; and the irreducibly horrible can be just as real as the genuinely admirable, despite what we might wish to be so. Iago gets away with it for so long because no one is alert to the real possibility of a character like him; everyone is blinkered by wishful thinking. He thrives on his exceptionalness. But he is really just an extreme case of a recognizable type: the malcontent whose capacity for destruction is far greater than anyone suspects. Perhaps the most terrifying thought implanted by the play is the possibility that we might all have an Iago in our midst—an honest-seeming man, of no special qualities, but possessed of a virulent (and irrational) hatred, and enough cunning to put that hatred to devastating effect.

I wish briefly to mention two other aspects of *Othello* before leaving it. The first is the great variety of highly individualized characters that appear in the play: no two characters are the same, and the contrasts between them could hardly be sharper. Each sets up a very distinct image in the mind, a constellation of particular feeling. This matters to the action, because the variety of the characters, and hence the difference between them, is not so apparent to the participants in the action. They see only the outward face, not the inner being, and they underestimate how variable the other characters are in their essence. In particular, they tend to underestimate the characterological distance between themselves and whomever they are dealing with: for example, Othello cannot guess how far removed Iago is from himself, and no one, except perhaps Emilia, appreciates Desdemona's uniqueness. Shakespeare is, I think, acutely aware of the large differences that exist between people, and also of the human tendency not to notice and heed those differences. We tend to ascribe much more psychological uniformity to people than is warranted by the facts—because these facts are elusive, given the inaccessibility of other minds. In the action of *Othello* psychological variety and psychological opacity conspire together to generate interpersonal ignorance. People don't know how different other minds are from their own. This is a specific kind of cognitive deficiency.

The second point has to do with language and its power. The power of speech is conspicuous in the play, both with regard to Othello's courtship of Desdemona and to Iago's ability to deceive. Othello won Desdemona's heart, not by her witnessing the events of his life directly, but by hearing him report them, and very eloquently too: "She'd come again, and with a greedy ear devour up my discourse," he tells the court. Whether this was a sound basis for marriage may be debated, but it certainly places Othello's verbal prowess at the center of their relationship; which makes the later deterioration in his speech significant and lamentable. His nobility is bound up with his eloquence, but when the eloquence fragments into incoherence, the nobility goes with it. Othello's only serious rival for verbal skill in the play is Iago, whose power of language is the secret of his control over others. He can make a persuasive case for almost anything, like an ancient Sophist, turning truth to falsehood, and conversely. He knows that a confident assertion, made with an unblinking eye, always carries weight. His ability to string Roderigo along is masterful, and he plays upon Othello's weaknesses like a psychological virtuoso. Words are almost magical in this play, and indeed the association between language and magic is explicitly made, as in Othello's defense of his courtship to the council. This association is also a central theme of *The Tempest*, as we shall see; I mention it now because already in *Othello* language and magic are connected. But the magic is really Shakespeare's, of course. As Othello bewitches Desdemona with his story, and bewitches the council in his report of bewitching her, so Shakespeare bewitches us with his description of all this bewitching.

FIVE

Macbeth

Persons of the Play

King Duncan of Scotland
Malcolm, Duncan's son
Donalbain, Duncan's son
A captain in Duncan's army
Macbeth, Thane of Glamis, later Thane of Cawdor,
   then King of Scotland
A porter at Macbeth's castle
Three murderers attending on Macbeth
Seyton, servant of Macbeth
Lady Macbeth, Macbeth's wife
A doctor of physic
A waiting gentlewoman
Banquo, a Scottish thane
Fleance, his son
Macduff, Thane of Fife
Lady Macduff, his wife
Macduff's son
Lennox, Scottish thane
Ross, Scottish thane
Angus, Scottish thane
Caithness, Scottish thane
Menteith, Scottish thane
Siward, Earl of Northumberland
Young Siward, his son
An English doctor

Hecate, Queen of the Witches
Six witches
Three apparitions, one an armed head,
    one a bloody child, one a child crowned
A spirit like a cat
Other spirits
An old man
A messenger
Murderers
Servants
A show of eight kings; lords and thanes, attendants,
    soldiers, drummers

On the surface, *Macbeth* is a play about ambition, murder, intrigue, sorcery, ghosts, and revenge. Macbeth, spurred on by the three witches he encounters on the heath, and with the encouragement of his wife, murders King Duncan in his bed, so as to acquire the throne of Scotland. Not content with that, he next has his ally Banquo murdered, because he wishes to prevent Banquo's children from taking up the throne when Macbeth is dead, as the witches had prophesied. Banquo duly comes back to haunt him. In addition, he deems it necessary to have Macduff's wife and child murdered by hired killers. He slays a minor character (Young Siward) in a sword fight toward the end of the play. Finally, Macduff kills him in a sword fight and severs his head, which he victoriously parades. Macbeth's wife has apparently slain herself because of the murders to which she was party. At the very beginning of the play, before Macbeth's downward spiral has begun, he is reported to have killed the rebel Macdonald: "Disdaining fortune, with his brandished steel/Which smoked with bloody execution, Like valour's minion/Carved out his passage till he faced the slave, Which ne'er shook hands nor bade farewell to him/Till he unseamed him from the nave to th' chops, And fixed his head upon our battlements." There is a great deal of talk of blood in the play, and much violent imagery. *Macbeth* is by far the shortest of Shakespeare's tragedies, and is packed with action and event. It might seem the least cerebral of his tragic creations, the most unphilosophical—an action-thriller, as we might describe it today, with supernatural chills added.

But this would be a superficial view of the play. It is true that it contains all the elements of action and violence, spiced with the supernatural, which might excite the groundlings (as the ordinary members of Shakespeare's audience at the Globe were known). The play has always been a crowd pleaser. There are none of the longueurs that some may find in *Hamlet* or *King Lear*, and the speeches tend to be short and pithy. But there are still substantial philosophical themes lurking beneath the surface, shaping the action. I shall discuss four: (1) the relationship between action and character, (2) the power of imagination, (3) the appearance/reality distinction, (4) the nature of time. Some of these themes we have encountered before, but some are new. They are woven closely into the action, not separated out into soliloquies or aphorisms. Here Shakespeare has succeeded in welding indissolubly the philosophical and the dramatic, the abstract and the personal.

The play is centrally concerned, at a dramatic level, with the effects of evil actions on the soul of the perpetrator. Macbeth does not begin the play as an evil man; indeed, he is something of a hero, and a markedly reluctant murderer. Nevertheless, ambition, stiffened by Lady Macbeth's promptings, causes him to murder Duncan, a helpless guest in his house. The result is an access of conscience, manifested in torments of the mind, even to the point of hallucination. But once the first murder is committed he finds it easier and easier to do away with people: he coldly has his erstwhile friend Banquo murdered, and shockingly has Macduff's entire family butchered. By the close of the play he is a vicious tyrant, loathed by his subjects, steeped in guilt and blood—an absolute bastard. The play is a chronicle of his moral decline, steep and precipitous as it is. His wicked actions have eaten into his soul, and consumed him whole. He is therefore not a static character, but an evolving one. In this respect he may be contrasted with Iago: Iago begins the action as an evil man and he ends in much the same state, but Macbeth makes the descent into evil. There is no transformation in Iago's nature, just a steady, unchanging viciousness. (Neither is there much change in the chief villain of *Hamlet*, Claudius.) In *Macbeth* Shakespeare has given us a portrait of the dynamics of evil—its evolution over time (time itself is a key preoccupation of the play). He wants us to see how evil actions, undertaken for self-interested reasons, have consequences for the psyche of the agent. Iago's evil actions do not change his soul, but Macbeth's turn him into something quite other than he was. He transforms himself, but in a negative direction. And this is a transformation he did not predict: it comes upon him, ineluctably, incrementally, as he becomes enmeshed in his own web of wickedness. His actions, unlike Iago's, are never simply malicious—he has no love of evil for its own sake (except perhaps at the very end)—but issue from means-end reasoning: assassination is just the shortest route to achieve his royal ambitions. He is unscrupulous rather than demonic—which is why his conscience catches up with him. There is never a hint of conscience in Iago—we sense that he had his conscience excised at birth—but Macbeth is overcome by conscience: it is his worst enemy. In a sense, then, Macbeth is a more complex character than Iago, and one that must strike us as more familiar. Iago seems not quite human, or at the remote edge of humanity, but Macbeth is thoroughly human, tragically so. Perhaps this is why audiences respond to him, if not with warmth, then at least with appalled sympathy—whereas Iago sends an icy chill down the spine. In these two characters Shakespeare has given us two types of evil, the pure kind and the self-interested kind. When Roderigo, stabbed by Iago, exclaims, "O damned Iago! O inhuman dog!," he expresses what we all feel (except perhaps for any budding Iagos skulking in the audience). But such an accusation of inhumanity seems inapposite in the case of Macbeth—his evil actions are all *too* human. Iago's interest in evil is inhumanly pure, whereas Macbeth's stems from simple self-advancement, the most human of failings.

*   *   *

It is natural to think of character as something fixed independently of action. A person has a certain character, conceived as an antecedently given condition, and action then issues from this fixed quantity. Character causes action, on this model; or action expresses character. Character is held to consist of a set of traits—notably, virtues and vices—and these traits operate together to generate action. More exactly, character leads to *choice*, and choice determines deed, which in turn determines external consequences. Action is an outcome of character in somewhat the way the behavior of a machine results from its internal configuration: given that configuration, the machine will function in a certain way as a consequence. It is not that the internal configuration is caused by the behavior; similarly, on this model, a person's character is not caused by his actions. Action, in this view, is the unfolding of character—it reveals what was there already. Over time, a person's actions will reveal more about his character—which is conceived as a fixed commodity—but the actions don't work to constitute character. The self is a determinate entity that brings about the person's actions, so that the self is constituted independently of action. You are what you are, whatever you may decide to do. The outer merely *evinces* the inner; it cannot *create* the inner.

I think *Macbeth* subverts this simple picture, as *Hamlet* had already done. Macbeth does not have Hamlet's extreme personal plasticity, to be solidified only by adopting a theatrical role, but the series of his actions operates to confer an identity on him that was not his to begin with. The action of murdering Duncan in his sleep—cowardly, perfidious, and vicious as it was—irrevocably alters Macbeth's character: he thenceforward mutates from man of honor to unprincipled blackguard. When Lady Macbeth hears from her husband of the witches' prophecy, she fears that he has not the will to do what must be done: "Yet I do fear thy nature. It is too full o'th' milk of human kindness/To catch the nearest way. Thou wouldst be great, Art not without ambition, but without/The illness should attend it. What thou wouldst highly, That wouldst thou holily; wouldst not play false, And yet wouldst wrongly win." In other words, he is of too good a character to do what, in Lady

Macbeth's view, needs to be done; he lacks the necessary ruthless-ness. He himself observes: "I have no spur to prick the sides of my intent, but only/Vaulting ambition which o'erleaps itself/And falls on the other." He goes to murder Duncan almost against his will, goaded by his wife, trying to distance himself from the deed he is about to perform: "I go, and it is done. The bell invites me. Hear it not, Duncan; for it is a knell/That summons thee to heaven or to hell"—as if it is the bell, not he, that is initiating Duncan's dispatch. Once the deed is done he says: "I am afraid to think what I have done, Look on't again I dare not." At this point, his deed is out of character; it comes from a wrenching of his will, not from a settled disposition. We might almost say that it issues from another self within Macbeth, a self of bare potentiality. But before long this type of action becomes entirely characteristic of Macbeth—it is no longer out of character but *in* character. His next murder, of Banquo, is no strain at all in comparison. "Is he dispatched?" asks Macbeth of the First Murderer. "My Lord, his throat is cut. That I did for him," the murderer replies. Macbeth responds, almost jocularly: "Thou art the best o'th' cut-throats." When the murderer reports that Banquo has "twenty trenched gashes on his head," Macbeth curtly replies, "Thanks for that." Here we see a degree of callousness not evident at the time of Duncan's assassination. Earlier Macbeth merely mur-dered—he committed the deed—but now he has *become a murderer*: he has absorbed that identity into his being. Murdering has become part of his nature.

The reason that his actions can have this kind of effect on Macbeth is that he is *self-aware*: a person is aware of the acts he performs—he knows what he has done. Macbeth tries to avoid this knowledge: "The eye wink at the hand; yet let that be/Which the eye fears, when it is done, to see." When he has committed the act he stares at his bloody hands and comments, "This is a sorry sight," and he does everything he can to protect himself from self-awareness. But he cannot: as a self-aware agent he knows what he does—he cannot dissociate himself from his actions, no matter how hard he tries. In this respect, a man is not like a machine, which has no awareness of what it does. It was *his deed*, and he cannot evade knowledge of that fact. But then, the deed will shape the agent of it, through such reflexive knowledge. Macbeth cannot *be* one way and *act* in another. To put the point in the theatrical mode: Macbeth cannot separate himself from the *role* he has chosen to play. If he will play the part of a murderer, then he will *be* a murderer, because there is no essence to a person beyond the roles he plays. His character doesn't control his actions; his actions control his character. Goethe said: "In the beginning was the deed." Macbeth exemplifies the truth of that dictum. In a certain sense, then, the will precedes character: by choosing to perform certain actions Macbeth becomes the architect of his own identity. It isn't that choice results from character; character can result from choice. Thus he is, in Hegel's phrase, "a free artist of himself"—he is his own creation. There is constant reference in the play to action—as in Macbeth's "If it were done when 'tis done, then 'twere well/It were done quickly"— because the significance of action is a prime theme of the play. We are constantly directed toward human *doing*—not emotion, not thought—because in this drama action is where character has its origin. Words are not the focus here either, as they are in *Othello*, and to a lesser extent in *Hamlet*; *Macbeth* is a play about the psychological power of the nonlinguistic action. This is a rather anti-Cartesian perspective, because the body is placed at the heart of the mind: the soul does not float free of our active bodies, as if its fate and the body's are quite distinct; instead, the mind and the acting body are inseparable. To put it in philosophical language: the essence of the human being is *embodied agency*, not some immaterial essence or transcendent soul. If Hamlet was too insulated from action, Macbeth is trapped in it: where Hamlet contemplates, Macbeth executes (in both senses of the term). Hamlet's being is nothingness; Macbeth's being is doing. When Shakespeare has Macbeth declare, "The very firstlings of my heart shall be/The firstlings of my hand," the contrast with Hamlet could hardly be more pronounced (at least in the early stages of the Danish play), and Shakespeare must have been keenly aware of the contrast. Hamlet is lost in an excess of thinking; Macbeth thinks not enough. He fails to think through the consequences of his actions, most particularly on his own psyche.

*   *   *

If Macbeth is a man of action (literally—that is what composes him), he is also, and equally, a man of imagination. This play is Shakespeare's great hymn to the power—the anarchic, uncontrollable power—of the human imagination. Macbeth's vulnerability to his own imagination is apparent very early in the play, immediately after his encounter with the three witches. Speaking of their prediction, he muses: "If good, why do I yield to that suggestion/Whose horrid image doth unfix my hair/And make my seated heart knock at my ribs/Against the use of nature. Present fears/Are less than horrible imaginings." He here reports a psycho-physiological fact about himself—that his images make his heart beat heavily. He is not their master, but their victim; they overwhelm him. His very first utterance of the play—"So fair and foul a day I have not seen"—is less paradoxical when understood in the context of his peculiar psychology: to his outer eye the day is fair, but to his inner eye it is foul. His mind's eye is exceptionally vivid, and it portrays the day as his emotions suggest, which is not what his outer eye reveals.[1] He is always seeing double, as it were, with his senses and with his imagination. When he later remarks, "My dull brain was wrought/With things forgotten," he is again reporting on his susceptibility to his imagination, now in the form of memory images. We sense in Macbeth a man out of harmony with his own psychological nature: his imagination is forever subjecting him to its assaults—surprising him, taunting him, unmanning him. To this extent, he is alienated from himself, persecuted by a part of his own mind.

This hyper-imaginativeness comes to a head in the famous scene of the fantastical dagger:

Is this a dagger which I see before me,
The handle toward my hand? Come, let me clutch thee.
I have thee not, and yet I see thee still.
Art thou not, fatal vision, sensible
To feeling as to sight? Or art thou but
A dagger of the mind, a false creation
Proceeding from the heat-oppressed brain? I see thee yet,
    in form as palpable

As this which now I draw.
Thou marshall'st me the way that I was going,
And such an instrument I was to use.
Mine eyes are made the fools o'th' other senses,
Or else worth all the rest. I see thee still,
And on thy blade and dudgeon gouts of blood,
Which was not so before. There's no such thing.
It is the bloody business which informs
Thus to mine eyes.

In this episode, Macbeth's imagination has attained the status of full-blown hallucination, as the planned murder of Duncan stirs it to greater heights than ever. The image comes unbidden and mutates before Macbeth's consciousness, quite out of his voluntary control. It is nothing like an ordinary daydream that can be controlled and is not mistaken for reality. It is more like a night dream that has entered Macbeth's fevered waking brain. He stands in appalled fascination before his imaginary dagger, as vividly real to him as any concrete dagger. He doesn't speak of being confronted by the *impression* of a dagger, or what philosophers might call the "sense-datum" of a dagger, conceived as a subjective entity; it is a concrete *dagger* that confronts him—nonexistent though it may be. His visual experience is just as it would be if it were a real dagger in his visual field. Nor does his experience seem like a mere mental image of a dagger: it seems to him just as if he is seeing an actual dagger. Here imagination has gained the power of reality, and it has the hold over Macbeth that reality does; it is as *convincing* as reality. Thus imagination, for Macbeth, can mimic reality itself. We should also notice that this is no mere memory image, since the deed has yet to be performed; it is an image of the future—an expectation-image, we might call it. Those gouts of blood anticipate the murder that will soon supervene. Macbeth intends to commit the murder, and his imagination supplies an enactment of it ahead of time. (In this drama of the supernatural, precognitive imagery is permissible; Macbeth's foresight here is analogous to that claimed by the witches.)

The other main manifestation of Macbeth's dysfunctional imagination is his sighting of the ghost of Banquo, murdered at his behest. Lady Macbeth reports, "My lord is often thus, And hath been from his youth," and Macbeth himself admits, "I have a strange infirmity which is nothing/To those who know me." Despite this piece of self-knowledge, he is ready to rail loudly at the ghost once he reappears (no one else can see him); he is only too ready to be taken in by his imagination—to him the apparition is real. Stage directions instruct the ghost of Banquo to enter, so that a real actor must supply the object of Macbeth's hallucination, whereas there is no such direction in the case of the dagger—thus suggesting that his confusion of fantasy and reality has reached new heights. In any case, the ability of imagination to masquerade as reality is emphasized. Nor is Macbeth alone in this: Lady Macbeth too is duped by her imagination, though in the more orthodox form of a dream. Her sleepwalking, and her talking in her sleep about the murder of Duncan ("Out, damned spot; out, I say"), reflect her imaginative excesses, and she is as persecuted by her imaginative faculty as her husband is. For both of them the imagination has a terrible reality.

In my judgment, Shakespeare is here making an emendation to the kind of "faculty psychology" common in his time, a conception of the mind as an amalgam of distinct faculties, various in nature, yet interacting. While traditional authors restricted themselves to the three faculties of Reason, Passion, and Will, Shakespeare adds the faculty of Imagination, to be accorded the same status as the classic three. The imagination is just as much of a force in the psyche as the other three, and cannot be reduced to some sort of "faint copy" of sense impressions (as Hume later tried to do).[2] Indeed, as we have seen, the imagination plays a powerful role in other plays of Shakespeare, particularly *A Midsummer Night's Dream* (though also in *Hamlet* and *Othello*). As a natural psychologist, Shakespeare is insisting on the centrality of the imagination in the human mind—with Macbeth an extreme case of something universal. This emphasis on the imagination did not really resurface until the Romanticism of the eighteenth and nineteenth centuries, with Coleridge, Blake, and others. It has yet to be fully appreciated in philosophical and psychological circles even today.

It will perhaps not come as a surprise that Montaigne also

stressed the power of the imagination, even writing an essay with that very title. The essay begins: "I am one of those by whom the powerful blows of imagination are felt most strongly. Everyone is hit by it, but some are bowled over. It cuts a deep impression into me: my skill consists in avoiding it not resisting it . . . I do not find it strange that imagination should bring fevers and death to those who let it act freely and who give it encouragement."[3] And he goes on to enumerate alleged instances (many of which are doubtless questionable) in which imagination has wrought amazing effects. In "On Experience" he also writes: "In my opinion that faculty [imagination] concerns everything, at least more than any other does: the most grievous and frequent of ills are those which imagination loads upon us."[4] We cannot know for sure whether Shakespeare's *Macbeth* was directly influenced by these writings, but they are certainly highly consonant with the play; those words from Montaigne could almost be a commentary on the play (though they were written earlier). If Shakespeare did not derive inspiration directly from Montaigne, then he could certainly have derived confirmation from him. Naturalistic psychologist that Montaigne was, he provides a perfect model for Shakespeare's own psychological naturalism.

It is not an accident, I think, that Macbeth's imagination is closely tied to his conscience. His guilt expresses itself in the form of unwanted imaginings. That is psychologically astute on Shakespeare's part: for some reason, a guilty conscience does manifest itself in just this way. *Why* it does so is harder to say. If we ask what other emotion has this kind of tie to imagination, the obvious answer is fear: when we are afraid of something we are prone to imagine it. Everything from anxiety dreams to a phobia of heights bears this out (in the grip of this fear we are apt to imagine throwing ourselves over). So we imagine what we are afraid of and we imagine what makes us feel guilty—does this suggest some commonality in the two emotions? Is guilt, perhaps, a particular type of fear—of retribution, of discovery, of God's judgment? Macbeth is very fearful of discovery, and this fear mingles with his guilty conscience in his wild imaginings. Fear, guilt, and oppressive imagination belong together, it seems. In any event, Shakespeare is right that conscience and imagery go naturally together; and no doubt

Macbeth's vivid imagery contributes to the sharp pangs of conscience he must endure.

But here we are approaching an area of the mysterious—the strange workings of conscience and imagination. A. C. Bradley, still perhaps the most acute commentator on Shakespeare, has some interesting observations under this head in his classic *Shakespearean Tragedy*:

> *Macbeth* leaves on most readers a profound impression of the misery of a guilty conscience and the retribution of crime. And the strength of this impression is one of the reasons why the tragedy is admired by readers who shrink from *Othello* and are made unhappy by *Lear*. But what Shakespeare perhaps felt even more deeply, when he wrote the play, was the *incalculability* of evil—that in meddling with it human beings do they know not what. The soul, he seems to feel, is a thing of such inconceivable depth, complexity, and delicacy, that when you introduce into it, or suffer to develop in it, any change, and particularly the change called evil, you can form only the vaguest idea of the reaction you will provoke. All you can be sure of is that it will not be what you expected, and that you cannot possibly escape it.[5]

This strikes me as a profound comment on Shakespeare's intentions in this play. When Macbeth says, somewhat puzzlingly, "To know my deed 'twere best not know myself," he expresses a deep truth about his predicament: he undertakes actions whose effects on his soul he cannot possibly calculate or predict (much the same is true of Lady Macbeth). The soul is a mysterious thing, as Bradley indicates, and Macbeth cannot fathom what he will do to himself by the actions he carries out. He is, accordingly, *surprised by himself*. He has "meddled" with something beyond his comprehension, notably his own moral sense, and it comes back to baffle and torment him. Changes occur in him that he cannot grasp; he can only stand back and marvel at what he becomes. He knowingly acts against his nature, but his nature is not the predictable mechanism he expects.

In some ways this problem of incalculability is even more obvious in the case of Lady Macbeth. Seized with overwhelming ambition, and willed ruthlessness, she summons the forces of evil to stiffen her murderous resolve: "Come, you spirits/That tend on mortal thoughts, unsex me here, And fill me from the crown to the toe top-full/Of direst cruelty. Make thick my blood, Stop up th'access and passage to remorse, That no compunctious visitings of nature/Shake my fell purpose, nor keep peace between/Th'effect and it." She is calling evil into the very marrow of her soul, but she has no idea what this might do to her—and she ends up half-mad, sleepwalking, and racked with inexpiable guilt. Moral psychology—with its joining of passion, imagination, and conscience—is not a simple mechanism that can be tinkered with at will; it is a mysterious and unpredictable human attribute that can be meddled with only at considerable peril. Macbeth has upset some sort of psychological balance within his soul, which is opaque to him (as well as to us), and his reactions are as bizarre as his soul is mysterious. When he exclaims, "O, full of scorpions is my mind, dear wife!" we pity him, but we also take note of the fact that his mind is, like the brew in the witches' cauldron, an unpredictable mixture of strange ingredients that may produce the oddest and nastiest of creatures. He is a victim of his own mystery.

The deceptive powers of the imagination link with epistemological themes we have encountered already in Shakespeare. Aside from hallucinations, delusions, and dreams, which raise the specter of skepticism about the external world, the problem of other minds is also registered throughout *Macbeth*, though more mutedly than in *Othello*; it is a backdrop to the action rather than its focus. Macbeth is as much a deceiver himself as he is deceived: he frames Duncan's servants by making it look as if they murdered their king; he deceives Banquo in his murder; and generally he pretends to an innocence that is not his—at the same time as he is being deceived by his imagination. But, in addition, sprinkled throughout the play, there are intimations of the essential opacity of other minds. Duncan declares himself deceived by the traitorous Thane of Cawdor, observing: "There's no art/To find the mind's construction in the face. He was a gentleman on whom I built an absolute trust." And yet he is quickly equally mistaken about his host Macbeth, whose real intentions are easily hidden from the overly trusting king. "Stars, hide your fires," Macbeth says, "Let not light see my black and deep desires," and he proceeds cloaked in his own show of goodwill. Lady Macbeth, perhaps skeptical of her husband's deceptive talents, upbraids him: "Your face, my thane, is as a book where men/May read strange matters. To beguile the time, Look like the time; bear welcome in your eye, Your hand, your tongue; look like the innocent flower, But be the serpent under't." One feels that she has no difficulty concealing her interior, and has an excellent grasp of the strategic necessity of hiding what lies within. Shakespeare, once again, is stressing the gap between inner and outer—the permanent possibility of error and deception about the minds of others. Macbeth takes his wife's advice to heart: "Away, and mock the time with fairest show. False face must hide what the false heart doth know." The phrase "false face" provides a terse formulation of the divide, always exploitable, between what the human frame offers and what the human soul actually contains. As Malcolm later remarks, "To show an unfelt sorrow is an office, Which the false man does easy." And Donalbain comments: "Where we are/There's daggers in men's smiles." Macbeth, addressing his wife, makes this suggestion: "Present him eminence/Both with eye and tongue; unsafe the while that we/Must lave our honors in these flattering streams/And make our faces visors to our hearts, Disguising what they are." By this point he seems rather more comfortable with the art of deception.

The richness and variety of Shakespeare's metaphors for the concealment of inner thoughts and motives suggests careful attention to the phenomenon described. The human ability to deceive and dissemble is indeed remarkable; it is one of the main distinguishing characteristics of our species. Animals can offer misleading appearances to other animals, for reasons of safety or predation, but it is in humans that the ability to mislead is brought to the level of high art (and the term here is suggestive). Language greatly facilitates this achievement, but our ability to control our facial expressions so as to give a misleading impression is also remarkable. We have an uncanny ability to act a false part, and the face is the main locus of that falsity. Shakespeare was acutely aware of this fact, and of its role in human interactions. I think there were two factors that made him especially sensitive to the point. The first is simply that he was an actor himself, involved with other actors: and a good actor simply is one who can convey a false impression with the greatest authenticity. A competent actor can arrive at the theater depressed and gloomy but be on stage ten minutes later as jolly as he is required to be: he can radically dissociate the inner from the outer—and in this lies the possibility of self-alienation and self-splitting. In general, as I have emphasized, we are a species of actors, forever putting on a front (*Homo dramatis*). But secondly, Shakespeare was living at an historical moment when concealment of the inner could be a matter of life or death—that is to say, a time of religious persecution. Catholics in the Elizabethan period had to conceal their true thoughts and emotions, acting the part of good Protestants, putting on a show of faith they didn't feel. And torture was there to penetrate the carapace of deception if necessary. If, as some scholars believe, Shakespeare was himself a convinced Catholic, he would be familiar with this routine form of concealment—making his face visor to his heart; certainly he would have witnessed it in others.[6] In any case, Elizabethan England, with its religious and political climate, held many an opportunity for practicing one's acting talents, projecting a false self to others. Was the theater so popular at the time, with Shakespeare as the star playwright, precisely because people were so familiar with acting a part from their daily lives? When a Shakespearean character compares the world to a stage, the audience of the time might nod their heads in silent agreement, knowing the amount of dissembling needed to get by. But it is not that things have radically changed even in our more tolerant society: social life is still very largely a dance of concealment, of calculating how much to reveal. Dissembling, in one form or another, is part of life. In any case, for Shakespeare, the split between face and heart would have been second nature.

*   *   *

No one can read or watch *Macbeth* without noticing the repeated references to time. The past and the future are constantly invoked, with the present a thin evanescent wafer between them. Shakespeare is clearly meditating on the essential temporality of human life. I could give multiple quotations to illustrate this point, but let me be selective. Lady Macbeth says to her husband: "Thy letters have transported me beyond/This ignorant present, and I feel now/The future in the instant." That question, of how the future relates to the present—is the former somehow contained in the latter?—is quintessentially philosophical. Macbeth is pondering the passage of time when he comments: "If it were done when 'tis done, then 'twere well/It were done quickly. If th'assassination/Could trammel up the consequence, and catch/With his surcease success: that but this blow/Might be the be-all and the end-all, here, But here upon this bank and shoal of time, We'd jump the life to come." Time unfolds and bears the consequences of our actions, no matter how much we may wish to confine them to the instant of action. Later he remarks: "Time, thou anticipat'st my dread exploits," personifying time to give it the active nature it has in the play. It is the medium in which he must live out his crimes, enduring their aftermath. In an aside, he notes: "Come what may, Time and the hour runs through the roughest day." The very first sentence of the play, uttered by the First Witch, is about time: "When shall we three meet again?" When Macduff finally brandishes Macbeth's severed head, he tersely observes: "The time is free"—but he might well have said that Macbeth is now free of time. Macbeth's fate is to be haunted by a past that ramifies into the present, threatening the future. He kills Duncan for a glorious future as king, but fears exposure, which requires the killing of Banquo, who later comes to haunt him. He acts to prevent the sons of Banquo from becoming future kings, instead of his own sons (significantly, he has no children). He is always referring to "tomorrow," as if this will provide refuge from the past and present. He has, in effect, mortgaged the past and present to the future, but he finds that the future cannot be dissociated from the past. He is stretched on the rack of time, tormented by his own temporally extended acts. The witches' predictions purport to annul time, finding Macbeth's future already settled in the present; and his hallucination of the dagger is a case of tempo-. ral leapfrogging, drawing the future into the present. It is as if Macbeth wishes to murder time, as he has murdered so much else (his soul, his marriage, the respect of others—not to mention several real people). But time cannot be disposed of so easily, and his attempts to thwart it only enmesh him further in its coils. He is engaged in an epic struggle with time—a struggle he definitively, and predictably, loses. The laws of time—of action, memory, and conse-quence—cannot be evaded. His own spiritual decay is simply the pas-sage of time making itself felt.

I have left till last (such is my timing) the most celebrated speech of the play, a forlorn poem to time. Macbeth, already in despair at what his life has become, receives word that his beloved queen is dead. He replies to the news as follows: "She should have died here-after. There would have been a time for such a word. Tomorrow, and tomorrow, and tomorrow/Creeps in this petty pace from day to day/To the last syllable of recorded time, And all our yesterdays have lighted fools/The way to dusty death. Out, out, brief candle. Life's but a walking shadow, a poor player/That struts and frets his hour upon the stage, And then is heard no more. It is a tale/Told by an idiot, full of sound and fury, Signifying nothing." Like Hamlet's "To be" speech, this one must be read in context, as uttered by a particular dramati-cally situated character; we cannot assume that it is Shakespeare speaking directly to us in his own person—as if the passage contained his "philosophy of life." Perhaps it is Shakespeare in some moods, as it might be many of us (though minus his eloquence), but it cannot be taken to be a simple statement of how the playwright thinks of human life, period. It is plainly a profoundly pessimistic passage, expressing the utter meaninglessness of human life, in particular its brevity and incoherence. We are fools trudging our way toward an early death, covering our despair with bombast, devoid of any signif-icance or value whatever. This certainly fits Macbeth's predicament, as all his ambitious plans for future glory and happiness have come to naught, except sleepless nights, hatred, and loneliness. The tomorrow that would contain his joy never came, and never will; his yesterdays have been foolish and wicked; his present is a living hell. This is not everybody's predicament, obviously, but it does serve to remind us all of the inescapably temporal character of human life—that we live in an inevitable sequence of yesterdays, todays, and tomorrows, with death the ultimate finality. That, we may safely assume, is an authentically Shakespearean sentiment. Macbeth, for his part, is now numbed and dulled, with death his only possible release; by this stage even his imagination seems spent. As he comments to his servant Seyton: "I have lived long enough. My way of life/Is fall'n into the sere, the yellow leaf, And that which should accompany old age, As honor, love, obedience, troops of friends, I must not look to have, but in their stead/Curses, not loud but deep, mouth-honor, breath/ Which the poor heart would fain deny and dare not." The "Tomorrow" speech magnificently captures this mood of apocalyptic despair; but we cannot assume that it represents Shakespeare's considered estimate of human life.

And there is that other frequent Shakespearean theme in this time-obsessed speech—the comparison of life to the theater. Look how much Shakespeare packs into that short description, "a poor player that struts and frets his hour upon the stage": the poverty of life, its brevity, its falseness, the way we posture and worry—trying to cover our unease with exaggerated gestures, playing a role that always feels somehow wrong, pathetically subservient to the applause of others. That, indeed, has the ring of awful truth to it. I certainly feel Shakespeare talking directly to us in that description, with Macbeth as his mouthpiece. Somehow it is the interaction of time and theatricality that seems particularly terrible here—"his hour upon the stage." Life is brief, a flickering candle soon snuffed, but worse it is taken up with *acting*—with concealment, artifice, the need to impress. If only we could live out our brief life span in some other mode, with more ... authenticity (but what exactly would that *be*?). The self is essentially a theatrical construct, so there is really no possible exit from our status as "poor player." We are condemned to perform the dramatic strut, fret as we may. Our short time on earth is taken up with trying to make ourselves into a convincing character, weaving some sort of coherent story around ourselves; and when, peremptorily, we vanish from the stage, having turned in a passable or poor performance, other players will come to strut and fret in our place—and so on, without end. That seems a bleak enough thought with which to end this section.

I will depart *Macbeth* with one observation about the manner of his death (notice how the two words rhyme). He is decapitated, his head brandished on stage while his body is left elsewhere. Thus he is finally presented to the audience in a bodiless state. It seems to me that this device achieves two dramatic aims in the play: it focuses our attention on Macbeth's mind, which has seethed before us in all its waywardness—his tormented, crowded cranium; but it also detaches that head from his criminal body and its terrible deeds. No longer can that body carry out violent actions: there is no more *doing* for Macbeth. As I noted at the beginning of this chapter, Macbeth has a dual nature—as a man of action, and as a man of imagination: the body represents the former, the head the latter. By severing head from body, Shakespeare accentuates Macbeth's dual nature, and at the same time makes the world safe from him.

SIX

King Lear

Persons of the Play

Lear, King of Britain

Goneril, Lear's eldest daughter

Duke of Albany, her husband

Regan, Lear's second daughter

Duke of Cornwall, her husband

Cordelia, Lear's youngest daughter

King of France, suitor of Cordelia

Duke of Burgundy, suitor of Cordelia

Earl of Kent, later disguised as Caius

Earl of Gloucester

Edgar, elder son of Gloucester, later disguised
   as Tom o'Bedlam

Edmund, bastard son of Gloucester

Old Man, a tenant of Gloucester

Curan, Gloucester's retainer

Lear's Fool

Oswald, Goneril's steward

Three servants of Cornwall

Doctor, attendant on Cordelia

Three captains

A herald

A knight

A messenger

Gentlemen, servants, soldiers, followers,
   trumpeters, others

How did the world originate? Is there any purpose to its existence? Is nature intelligible? Is it just? These are fundamental philosophical questions, belonging to what we call metaphysics or cosmology—the study of reality in its most general nature. Such questions revolve around two basic (and related) concepts: *creation* and *causation*. When we ask about the origins of the universe, we are asking about its creation—the processes that brought it into being. And once we frame that question, two sorts of answer present themselves: that the world was created from something, and that it was created from nothing. These two answers, we should note, are neutral with respect to the question of divine creation. If we suppose that God created the universe, we can ask whether He created it from something or from nothing; and if we reject the notion of divine creation, we can still ask whether the original creative event proceeded from something or from nothing. Cosmology is difficult, philosophically, because both kinds of answer lead to fairly obvious problems. If the universe as we know it was created from something, then there is the problem of what created *that*—and then we will have our original question all over again. We wanted to know what created *reality*, and it is no use to be told that reality was created by reality. Maybe the something that created the universe we know was of a very different nature from that universe, so that a real explanation would be provided by knowing how it happened; but this still does not address the question of how existence *tout court* originated—of how whatever created the world we observe was itself created. No matter what something we suggest to explain the existence of things, we can always ask about what created *it*. The alternative, then, appears to be that the world was created from nothing—with or without God's intervention. First there was nothing—not even empty space, but a total ontological void—and then the full plenitude of being came from this nothing. If so, God (if we bring Him into the picture) is like a craftsman who can fashion an object—a very big object—from zero raw materials. But this seems unsatisfactory, to put it mildly: How can something come from nothing? How can you take pure nothingness and convert it into substantial being? How is it possible for the existing universe to be brought into being from outright nonexistence? Nothing can come from nothing, one wants to say—nonexistence can only beget nonexistence. On the other hand, if existence begets existence, then we still have that first existence to explain—we never seem to get an explanation of the existence of *everything*. This is why cosmology is hard, *very* hard.

I have no intention here of trying to resolve any of these big, resounding questions. What I want to record is the constellation of concepts that revolve around these issues: they include creation, existence, nonexistence, causation, beginnings, everything, and nothing. These are elemental concepts, concerning the axes of being as such; it doesn't get much more general, or fundamental, than this. The concept of causation has some claim to be the most basic of them all, because the question of the origins of the universe is really a question about causation: what is it that *caused* things to come into being—was it something or was it nothing? The history of the universe is essentially a causal history, with one state of affairs bringing about another; and the question of origins inquires into the *first* cause. But there is also the issue of the nature of causation once the universe has been brought into existence. By what principles does the universe evolve? When one thing causes another, what kind of relationship is that? Again, this is a characteristically philosophical question, about which an enormous amount has been written. As I explained in chapter 1, there are two opposed positions on causation: one view regards the causal nexus as rational, intelligible, purposeful, predictable; the other sees it as brute, nonrational, purposeless, and unpredictable. The first view naturally goes along with the idea of a divine creator: the causal structure of the world exhibits intelligent design, rational order, a meaning, and some respect for man. Causation, thus, is both teleological and ethical: it aims at some end, and it is not indifferent to morality. In common parlance, "everything happens for a reason": when something occurs it was designed with a point in view, a plan that makes sense of it from a human perspective. In its simplest form, the view holds that everything happens for the best: causation is directed by God toward the Good. The universe is like a clock, designed by an intelligent being, where everything has its place and function, and things happen according to plan.

According to the opposed view, however, causation does not have this kind of rational structure: it is a mindless sequence of inherently unrelated events. David Hume developed a view of this type: causation, for him, is simply one thing following another, without any plan, reason, or even necessary connection.[1] There are natural laws that govern causal sequences, but these laws have no basis in an intelligent mind; they have no teleological dimension. Things do not happen to fulfill some sort of goal, and they are not morally sensitive. Causation does not tend to the Good; it is indifferent to human concerns; it has no directing intelligence behind it. The universe is therefore not intelligible, if that means that we can discover the *reason* that things happen as they do: they just happen, but there is no further *justification* for the way they happen. We must not ask *why* one thing leads to another, if that means wanting to know what rational plan the world exemplifies; we must content ourselves simply with observing that they *do* happen that way. The universe is not a machine designed with an end in view; it is just a brute assemblage of objects and events, held together by nothing more (and sometimes less) than regular sequence.

I have sketched these contrasting positions, noting the concepts that occur in them, to shed light on the philosophical substrate of *King Lear*, arguably the pinnacle of Shakespeare's tragic vision. The play is set on a cosmic scale, in a craggy pre-Christian England, and deals in the extremes of human emotion. It does not have the claustrophobia of Shakespeare's other great tragedies, but examines man in nature, and man at the limits of his being (and nonbeing). It is a play of sharp contrasts, of great forces arrayed against each other, of monstrosity, cruelty, of negations and reductions. The tragedy seems to echo through the universe itself, and not merely in the lives of the individual characters. It is not merely the characters that are tragic, but the stage on which they perform. The tragedy seeps into everything, leaving its stain. It is cosmic as well as human; or rather, the human becomes the cosmic, and the cosmic the human. The play thus possesses a kind of abstract grandeur, aided by the philosophical themes it exemplifies. In it, everything is out of joint; nothing happens in the way it should; inversions abound. Things turn into their opposites; evil springs from the unlikeliest of sources; nothing is as it appears. The very structure of the universe seems fractured and paradoxical. In short, it is the second, Humean conception of causation that seems to rule events.

Nothingness makes its resonant appearance early on in *Lear*. The king, wishing to retire, has decided to divide his kingdom into three parts, each part to be given to one of his three daughters. (There is no Queen Lear, nor is mention ever made of her: she is conspicuous by her absence, a giant nothingness at the heart of the play. We might even see the vacuum she creates as the source of all the nothingness that pervades the play.) With all the pomposity and presumption he deems proper to his regal position, Lear demands: "Tell me, my daughters, Which of you shall we say doth love us most, That we our largest bounty may extend/Where merit doth most challenge it?" Goneril and Regan acquit themselves well, turning in the obsequious performance Lear requires of them—dubiously sincere as it is. Cordelia, in an aside, expresses her misgivings: "What shall Cordelia do? Love and be silent": that is, love her father and yet say nothing. When Lear turns to her, with his preposterous question, "What can you say to win a third more opulent than your sisters?" her reply is the laconic: "Nothing, my lord." In other words, she can say nothing in order to gain something very substantial. Lear's irritated retort is: "How? Nothing can come of nothing. Speak again." All Cordelia can muster in response is: "Unhappy that I am, I cannot heave my heart into my mouth. I love your majesty/According to my bond, nor more nor less." This lawyerly response leads to Lear disowning her, thus setting the wheels of the tragedy in motion; but my concern at present is with the career of the concept of nothingness as it patterns the play. Lear's "nothing can come of nothing" echoes the theological and cosmological debates prevalent at Shakespeare's time and outlined at the beginning of this chapter: as God cannot create something from nothing, nor can Cordelia expect to gain something from the nothing of her silence. Nothing cannot cause something, in both cases. And yet, already at this stage, the nothing that is in the hearts of Goneril and Regan has caused them to be endowed with a substantial something: for them, something *has* come from nothing. Causation is behaving strangely, paradoxically, just beneath the surface. It has its own peculiar potency, its own negative vitality.

Lear invokes nothingness again in his discussion with Burgundy of Cordelia's dowry: "But now her price has fallen. Sir, there she stands. If aught within that little seeming substance, Or all of it, with our displeasure pieced, And nothing else, may fitly like your grace, She's there, and she is yours." She has been reduced in value to something approaching zero, in Lear's eyes, and is nothing but a "little seeming substance." She has moved from something to nothing, as a result of her own nothing. Lear's response to Burgundy's request for a dowry is a firm and stern, "Nothing. I have sworn." Cordelia is thus stripped both of father and husband, a drastic reduction in her state of being. She has abruptly descended from plenitude to nullity.

Gloucester, whose fate will mirror Lear's, has a brush with nothingness himself soon after this opening scene, in a conversation with his bastard son Edmund. Edmund is busy deceiving his father by pretending to have a traitorous letter from his brother Edgar. "What paper were you reading?" Gloucester inquires. "Nothing, my lord," Edmund replies. Gloucester proceeds: "No? What needs then that terrible dispatch of it into your pocket? The quality of nothing hath not such need to hide itself. Let's see. Come, if it be nothing, I shall not need spectacles." The point here is that the letter is indeed a piece of nothing, a mere fake, and so also is Edmund's affection for his father. Nothing does need to hide, and here we see it hiding. (Notice too Gloucester's reference to his sight, to be so viciously removed later, producing another kind of nothing—blindness.) Later in the same conversation, with Gloucester now wrongly convinced of Edgar's perfidy, he commands: "Find out this villain, Edmund; it shall lose thee nothing."

Nothing recurs in full force during Lear's conversation with his Fool. Lear declares, in response to a silly verse of the Fool's: "This is nothing, fool." The Fool retorts: "Then, like the breath of an unfee'd lawyer, you gave me nothing for't. Can you make no use of nothing, uncle?" Lear's impatient reply echoes his earlier statement to Cordelia: "Why no, boy. Nothing can be made out of nothing." Later the Fool says: "I had rather be any kind of thing than a fool; and yet, I would not be thee, nuncle. Thou hast pared thy wit o' both sides and left nothing in the middle." Of course, he speaks the bitter truth: Lear has rashly trusted his two villainous daughters, while banishing his virtuous daughter—and the result is a vast nothing at his core. Before long he will be reduced to a nothing even more extreme than the nothing he tried to inflict on Cordelia: he will make the transition from royal fullness to beggarly nothingness. As the Fool goes on to observe: "Now thou art an 0 without a figure. I am better than thou art, now. I am a fool; thou art nothing." When Lear rages against Goneril's rejection and ingratitude, asking, "Who is it that can tell me who I am? Lear's shadow?" he employs an apt metaphor; for a shadow is the closest thing to nothingness a person can be, without losing being altogether. A shadow is an absence of light, a mere blank trace, having no bulk or substance—and this is what Lear compares himself to. To be a shadow of one's former self is to be a nothing where once one was a something. Lear's ontological status is in the process of being stripped away, till he reaches the ultimate reduction.

Edgar, too, unjustly rejected by his father, feels the sting of nothingness, as he wanders the earth disguised at the beggar Poor Tom: "Poor Tuelygod, Poor Tom! That's something yet. Edgar I nothing am." And there are other references to nothingness scattered about the play, as if to remind us constantly of the abyss of nonbeing. In these invocations we have the impression of life reduced to the barest of oppositions, between being and nothingness.[2] I want to suggest that Shakespeare is mapping a personal, psychological matter onto a cosmological one. The stark opposition between existence and nonexistence when we try to contemplate the origins of the universe, and the puzzle of a causal upheaval of being from nothingness, is reflected in the being and nothingness that haunts human life. For we are under constant threat of reduction to nothing—as our rank, position, possessions, family, and dignity (not to mention our lives) teeter on the brink of extinction. Lear, Cordelia, Gloucester, and Edgar all suffer this ontological annulment—but especially Lear, as he sinks from resplendent kingship to naked beggardom. Death is one kind of nothingness that may overtake us, but there are also forms of living nothingness to fear. There are many ways our substance may be depleted, made "little." Thus the anxiety of nonbeing, of annihilation, hovers over the play. Gloucester exclaims at one point, "O ruined piece of nature! This great world/Shall so wear out to naught": he is making the eschatological point that all this being will one day revert to nothing. But people too can "wear out to naught," as he himself does, as well as the once great Lear. Indeed, Lear so describes Goneril to Regan: "Thy sister is naught." There is cosmic nothingness, and there is personal nothingness. Nothingness is a reality, an inescapable modality. In fact, in some respects nothingness is ontologically primary, the default condition of the world, since it requires some sort of creative effort to bring existence about: arguably, the natural state of things is Nothingness, which God (or Nature) must jump-start into Being; and man rises above animal nothingness only by dint of his outer trappings—his "accommodations." Tragedy may indeed be defined as the eruption of nothingness, the triumph of nonbeing over being. Tragedy is waste, loss, diminishment, ruin, death—and all these are types of absence. Reduction to nothing is the abstract shape of the tragic fact. In *King Lear* Shakespeare is distilling tragedy to its bare essence, purifying it almost.

Montaigne, pressing as always the limitations of man, declares in "An Apology for Raymond Sebond," "In truth we are but nothing," and speaks of "the emptiness, the vanity, the nothingness of Man."[3] His thesis is that we deceive ourselves: we rate ourselves much too highly, supposing ourselves far above the unclothed, "unaccommodated" animals; we puff ourselves up, trying to disguise our essential nothingness. Shakespeare in *Lear* seems to be reminding us that we are always just an inch away from being, in Lear's famous phrase, "a poor, bare, forked animal." Here again, we find a striking convergence between the two writers. Lear swings from the status of king to the status of animal, and in his descent we see vividly the truth about the human condition—that we are really beasts in disguise. To put it differently, there is nothing *intrinsic* to Lear that marks him out as a king: he can become a beggar and still be himself—only now without the illusions of transcendence. The nothingness was really always there, lurking behind the power and position; it simply took a bit of folly and a dose of villainy to bring it out into the open. Lear's true, intrinsic nature is revealed not in his royal court but out on the heath: here we see what he is really made of. The reduction to nothing is really an exposure *as* nothing. Only later in the play, after Lear has suffered every reduction in his material being, does he gain the fullness of thought and emotion that eluded him at the outset. Viewed in this light, *King Lear* is a kind of dramatic expression of Montaigne's thesis about the essential nothingness of man.

When we think of nothingness we think of naught or zero, that is, that number. Zero is the lowest the numbers can go before they dip into the negatives, if I can put it that way. Not accidentally, then, the play has arithmetical portions. Lear begins the action with a problem in division—how to apportion his kingdom into three parcels. Cordelia attempts to explain her disappointing answer to her father's question by suggesting that when she marries she will give half her love to her husband and leave half for her father (an oddly arithmetical way to think about love). Lear's initial point of contention with Regan and Goneril arises from their desire to reduce the number of his knights, and there is much talk of what the factor of subtraction will be. Lear says to Goneril, comparing her to Regan: "Thy fifty yet doth double five-and-twenty, And thou art twice her love" (an arithmetical approach to love seems to run in the family). Goneril matches his arithmetic: "What need you five-and-twenty, ten, or five, To follow in a house where twice so many/Have a command to tend you?" Division, subtraction, and addition thus figure in the play alongside zero and more-than-zero. I don't want to assign undue significance to this fact, but it does seem that Shakespeare is toying with the basic mathematics of the universe, noting our subjection to its laws (though it would be many years till Newton subsumed the universe under a set of mathematical equations). Land and emotions can be divided, additions of wealth and status can be effected, and vicious subtractions are also possible—with zero as the end point of all sub-traction. When the sisters propose halving or quartering Lear's ret-inue, they cut away at his being—they subtract from his royal super-fluity. There is a stark arithmetic to his loss. Being is a matter of quantity, and quantities come in degrees. Abstractly put, Lear suffers a decrease in his *quantity*, as do Gloucester, Edgar, and Cordelia—while Goneril and Regan have their quantity increased (until the end, of course). This mathematical imagery aids the play's effect of ren-dering the personal impersonal, and vice versa. And the rigidity of arithmetic seems to underlie the logic of the play's development. By instigating an ill-judged game of division, Lear begins a process of subtraction, which will eventually bring him to zero. He wants to compare the quantity of his daughters' love, and his own quantity in consequence suffers a drastic diminishment. The arithmetical motif is not exactly salient in the play, compared to the presence of the notion of nothing, but I think it does work to underscore the more abstract lineaments of the play's structure. It contributes to the extreme generality of the play's themes. And there is an almost math-ematical necessity about the way the tragedy unfolds once Lear has made his ill-fated request in the opening scene.

Upon the reunion of Lear and Cordelia, she ruefully observes, "We are not the first/Who with best meaning have incurred the worst," suggesting the inversions that causality permits—the best of motives leading to the direst of consequences. Lear responds, movingly, by inviting her to prison with him, speaking of what they will do there together ("pray, and sing, and tell old tales, and laugh/At gilded but-terflies"), adding: "And take upon's the mystery of things/As if we were God's spies." Here the cosmological theme is sounded loud and clear; and note it is the mystery of *things* Lear refers to, not minds. As I have observed, very little of the natural world was understood in Shakespeare's day: the cause of the plague was a mystery; eclipses were baffling; the nature of heredity was an enigma. Not surpris-ingly, astrology was invoked to deal with these puzzles, as when Kent speculates: "It is the stars, The stars above us govern our conditions/Else one self mate and make could not beget/Such different issues." Edmund, hardheaded realist that he is, rejects such explanations, dismissing astrology in these words: "Admirable evasion of whoremaster man, to lay his goatish disposition to the charge of stars! My father compounded with my mother under the Dragon's tail and my nativity was under Ursa Major, so that it follows I am rough and lecherous. Fut! I should have been that I am had the maidenliest star of the firmament twinkled on my bastardy." Lear, pondering the unfathomable wickedness of his daughter, envisages a scientific inquiry: "Then let them anatomize Regan; see what breeds about her heart. Is there any cause in nature that makes this hardness?" Reflecting on his abandonment, he notes: "Judicious punishment: 'twas this flesh begot/Those pelican daughters." At the beginning of the play, Gloucester dilates on the begetting of his bastard son, admitting that "this knave came something saucily into the world before he was sent for, yet was his mother fair, there was good sport at his making, and the whoreson must be acknowledged." The question of origins troubles and preoccupies these characters.

Clearly, then, there is a concern in the play with the nature of heredity, which is one species of causation—the causation of children by parents (and whatever other causal factors may be at work, such as astrological arrangements). This too can seem like getting something from nothing: so little in the way of original materials, and yet so large an outcome. The entire process, in Shakespeare's day, was a complete mystery. Moreover, the causation involved can seem startlingly unprincipled, even random. How did Lear produce those two abominable daughters, so different from him, and why was his third daughter so unlike her sisters? There seems neither rhyme nor reason to it. How did the consistently decent Gloucester give rise to the villain Edmund? No wonder people appealed to astrology to explain such things, since properties of the parents alone seem unable to account for the children that are their issue. Of course, with our knowledge of genetics such things begin to make sense, but in Shakespeare's day all this must have seemed like a giant enigma. Causation seems here to be operating lawlessly, unintelligibly. Scholastic principles of causation—such as "there cannot be more reality in the effect than the cause," that is, effects cannot exceed in their nature the causes that produce them—seem contradicted by the facts of heredity, since children are often vastly different from their parents. The world seems causally unruly, an unsolvable jigsaw of puzzling juxtapositions. Causation is not the well-behaved, rational matter that some philosophers suppose. Things can come from very different, even opposite, things, and sometimes something can come from nothing (and vice versa). Whatever produced Goneril and Regan from Lear seems neither intelligible nor just. "I gave you all," Lear says at one point to Regan, and now his ungrateful daughter is giving him nothing in return: his everything causes her nothing. Causation is not here respecting Lear's just deserts; indeed, it seems contrary to justice. To put it differently, nature, which is a causal system, is not an intelligible teleological order; it often behaves both inimically and randomly, without regard to reason or right. Hence Lear talks ingenuously to Cordelia of "the mystery of things," in which both are caught up.

Of particular significance, to my mind, are the words Cordelia repeats to Lear during their immensely affecting reconciliation. Lear is by this stage half-mad and scarcely recognizes his daughter—"Do not laugh at me, For as I am a man, I think this lady/To be my child, Cordelia." "And so I am," she replies, with characteristic terseness. Lear then compares her admirable behavior to that of his other two daughters, conceding that only she has "cause" to do him wrong. Cordelia's heartbreaking reply is: "No cause, no cause." The personal meaning of her laconic utterance is clear, but I think there are also more abstract undertones. Indeed, I see this simple sentence as encompassing the entire meaning of the play, concerned as it is with the perplexities of causation (*inter alia*). I don't wish to suggest that Shakespeare had foreknowledge of the worldview contained in quantum theory (!), with its causal fractures and bizarre conjunctions, but I do think that *Lear* similarly presents a universe in which the tidy logic of rational causation breaks down. History does not unfold by *a priori* intelligible principles, following a rational system, in which effects can be rigorously predicted from causes, but is rather a patchwork of incongruous associations, often paradoxical

and surprising. Indeed, it can sometimes seem that the best descrip-
tion of things would abandon the notion of causation entirely (as
some philosophers have recommended), replacing it with the idea of
brute association—in which case Cordelia's "No cause, no cause"
would sum the world up perfectly.

Cordelia's own death, so repugnant to audiences, is in fact an
illustration of the random character of causation. Edmund had
ordered that she be hanged in prison, but now repents—yet too late
to save her. Fittingly, but tragically, her body is carried on stage in
Lear's arms. This is a death that *should not* have happened in every
sense (except the tragic): it was a sheer accident, and not necessary to
the general outcome of the drama, as well as being awful in itself. It
has seemed to some critics like a gratuitous infliction on the audi-
ence's emotions by the playwright, as if Shakespeare were just piling
on the agony for the sake of it. But if I am right, it is integral to the
deeper meaning of the play: for it reflects the irrational, random,
unjust nature of causation. Hume described causation as "the
cement of the universe"; according to *Lear*, it is a type of cement
with some very untoward and alarming properties. It is less a princi-
ple of cohesion than one of chaos. It destroys as much as it creates.
"All's cheerless, dark, and deadly," as Kent mournfully says at the
story's end.

King Lear is a play about stark dichotomies—between good and evil,
being and nothingness, sense and nonsense. It also presents us with a
contrast between civilization and nature, exemplified by the royal
household and the wild heath. How does the play depict nature?
We see Lear in both habitats, obviously emblematic of man's relation
to both types of surrounding, and in neither is there much comfort.
Nature is no peaceful idyll from the hell of other people (to use
Sartre's phrase)—a pastoral paradise of stream and field, à la
Rousseau. But neither is home and family any respite from the smit-
ing forces of nature. Lear feels the whips and lashes of both, with
nowhere to shield him from the lacerations of life. Hobbes famously
described man's life in a state of nature as "nasty, brutish, and short,"

but that description equally fits the life of man within human society in the fallen world of *Lear* (or perhaps I should say "haughty, waspish, and fraught"). It is hard to tell whose fangs are sharper—the lion's or the sisters'. Indeed, Regan and Goneril are frequently compared to predatory wild animals in the play ("Tigers, not daughters," says Albany). Shakespeare is not elevating one of these above the other— as Rousseau and Hobbes in effect do—he is noticing their terrible symmetry. Ruthlessness and cold indifference are to be found in both society and nature.

Here is Lear railing against the storm: "Rumble thy bellyful; spit, fire; spout, rain. Nor rain, wind, thunder, fire are my daughters. I tax you not, you elements, with unkindness. I never gave you kingdom, called you children. You owe me no subscription. Why then, let fall/Your horrible pleasure. Here I stand your slave, A poor, infirm, weak and despised old man, But yet I call you servile ministers, That have with two pernicious daughters joined/Your high engendered battle 'gainst a head/So old and white as this. O, 'tis foul!" Two ideas are in play in this passage: first, that nature is not to *blame* for abusing Lear thus—it is showing no unkindness toward him, in contrast to his daughters; secondly, that there is nevertheless, in his mind, a kind of merging of hostilities between storm and daughters, as if they have colluded together (and these two ideas are in some tension with each other). The first idea is obviously correct—nature has no vicious intentions toward Lear; but the second is also natural in Lear's extremity—it *seems* to him that the entire universe is in a plot against him (a common enough feeling). It can *appear* that nature has it in for us, but of course it harbors no such ill will; rather, it is simply blindly indifferent—a somewhat worse thought, perhaps. The storm has no conception that Lear was once a king and is now suffering *in extremis*; it is simply playing out its own laws. Nature cannot be, literally, "nasty" or "brutish," since these adjectives suggest sentience and intention; it is something much scarier—entirely oblivious. The causality of nature is not teleological, intrinsically intentioned; it is merely mechanical. It is— though this is a dangerous way to put it—far too absorbed in its own drama to notice what it visits upon insignificant human beings. We are not in any way part of nature's *plot*—despite Lear's bout of animism.

A second striking passage is the following, as Lear addresses the wretched Edgar: "Why, thou wert better in thy grave than to answer with thy uncovered body this extremity of the skies. Is man no more than this? Consider him well. Thou owest the worm no silk, the beast no hide, the sheep no wool, the cat no perfume. Here's three on 's are sophisticated; thou art the thing itself. Unaccommodated man is no more but such a poor, bare, forked animal as thou art. Off, off, you lendings! Come on, be true." Compare this with the following passage from Montaigne's "An Apology for Raymond Sebond":

> We are, they say, the only animal abandoned naked on the naked earth; we are in bonds and fetters, having nothing to arm or cover ourselves with but the pelts of other creatures; Nature has clad all others with shells, pods, husks, hair, wool, spikes, hide, down, feathers, scales, fleece or silk, according to the several necessities of their being; she has armed them with claws, teeth and horns for assault and defense; and, as is proper to them, has herself taught them to swim, to run, to fly or to sing. Man, on the other hand, without an apprenticeship, does not know how to walk, talk, eat or do anything at all but wail.[4]

This is all part of Montaigne's campaign to disabuse man of his epistemological pretensions, to remind us that we are really part of nature, not gods; indeed, in some respects we are less sophisticated than other animals. For a man to be homeless, as Lear now is, is not just for him to lack a roof over his head; it is to be reduced to the vulnerable core of what a human being is—to be "the thing itself," a "bare, forked animal." If society will not protect us, then we shall have no protection at all; we cannot live outside society. We must have our clothes, our fires, our beds, and our kitchens—unlike other animals. The essence of human existence is therefore *fragility*. We feel this fragility constantly, with brutal nature standing just the other side of the rattling door that protects us from its ravages. And this existential fragility takes the form of *dependence*: we are depen-

dent on others for our necessary accommodations, as Lear is depen-
dent on his perfidious daughters. What *Lear* intimates to us is that
all this can be taken away in an instant, and then we are at the mercy
of oblivious nature. If Lear can be reduced to homeless nothingness,
wailing (like a child) in the storm, so can anyone. The play makes us
feel the storm raging against our paper-thin walls. We are fragile
beings, and our accommodations are fragile too. We are always one
step away from nothingness, with only our peculiarly forked frame
to support us.

It is not, however, that nature and society are entirely separate
realms. People are products of nature too. Regan, Goneril, and
Edmund are not opposed to nature; they are parts of nature. As
the play is at pains to record, they were begot by natural processes.
A character known only as First Gentleman observes to Lear: "Thou
hast one daughter/ Who redeems nature from the general curse/
Which twain hath brought her to." The evil sisters thus reflect badly
on the nature that spawned them; so their own nature must be seen
as part of nature at large. Human nature is part of nature. This is
quite a startling thought for someone of Shakespeare's time, since
man was so regularly assigned to another order entirely—the reli-
gious order of souls and of God's designs. But in *Lear* evil is credited
to nature, as if it were just one more turn of the great wheel of natu-
ral processes. When Edmund remarks, disconcertingly, given his
earlier total blackness of character, "Some good I mean to do,
Despite of mine own nature," he is expressing a related thought—
that he is evil by nature, not by intention. He was just *made that
way.* So the evil that erupts in the court—the very epicenter of civi-
lization, one might have thought—is in the end an evil that
emanates from the world of nature. The natural bleeds into the cul-
tural, bringing its blind causality. So, at least, the play appears to be
suggesting.

I should mention a famous line that may seem to contradict the
general picture of the play I am defending, namely Gloucester's: "As
flies to wanton boys are we to th' gods; They kill us for their sport."
Does this show that the play operates with a more teleological con-
ception of the workings of nature than I have allowed? Is it that the

deaths and disasters of *Lear* are held to be the result of the plans and
intentions of divine persons? Emphatically not, I would say. First, this
is a statement made by a particular character and cannot be read into
the general worldview of the play; indeed, these words come from a
character who earlier had expressed belief in astrology. He is a super-
stitious type, too ready to accept the explanations that tradition sup-
plies, however unsupported. Or, more charitably, he is not himself
speaking literally here, but employing what can seem like an unavoid-
able metaphor. It can sometimes *feel* as if we are the playthings of
cruel gods—but it is another thing to propose this as serious cosmol-
ogy. And there is no reason to suppose that Shakespeare himself is
endorsing any such view. He is, characteristically, offering us a variety
of viewpoints, emanating from different characters in the play; but
the general thrust of the play is against this kind of teleological per-
spective. After all, the real agencies of the play that create the evil are
Regan, Goneril, and Edmund, with some initial assistance from
Lear—all too human sources of destruction and viciousness. It is
these human beings that are responsible for putting out Gloucester's
eyes and other villainies, not some supposed band of mischievous
gods; no one *made* them do it. Gloucester's words are not, then, one
of those pieces of "Shakespearean wisdom" we often hear about, but
the words of a specific character with a particular point of view; the
deeper meaning of the play must be sought less directly. Unlike other
of Shakespeare's plays, there is no supernatural element to the
action—no ghosts or witches or soothsayers. The play is resolutely
naturalistic: its monstrosities and shocks are all of the natural order.
No supernatural realm is conjured up, so that we are presented with
the depredations and depravities of nature itself. The world of *Lear* is
a closed system of mindless natural causality—along with the malice
of all-too-human individual characters. There is nothing of the
uncanny or divine about it. The gods, in this play, are conspicuous by
their absence.

So far I have concentrated on some of the more impersonal themes
of the play, pursuing my philosophical purpose, but there are also

some less abstract matters that should be mentioned, mainly having to do with good and evil. The evil in other Shakespearean tragedies seems, though potent, relatively confined—to the personalities of Iago, the Macbeths, Claudius. But in *Lear* it appears rampant, elemental, part of the air the play breathes—in Regan, Goneril, and Edmund, obviously, but also in minor characters like Cornwall and Oswald. Equally, goodness seems powerfully and elementally present—in Cordelia, Edgar, Kent, and Albany, in particular. We have the impression of diametrically opposed universal forces working through individuals. This contributes to the grandly cosmic quality of the play. Shakespeare has arranged a formal opposition of good and evil, as if each force has its own representative battalions. And evil seems the stronger force—it has the greater causal heft. Moreover, the conspiracy of evil seems to generate a special potency—acting upon both the innocent and the guilty. Iago worked his evil alone, but in *Lear* several characters independently conspire to evil ends—and this produces a kind of superabundance of evil, an unstoppable wave of the stuff. Goodness operates more individually, and with less elemental force; there is a flimsy lightness to it, despite its capacity to compel admiration. We feel, accordingly, that Cordelia never really stood a chance, with her reticent and low-wattage goodness. Even the deaths of Regan and Goneril stem less from any force for good than from their own inherent viciousness.

It is a nice question which of these characters is the most evil. Though Iago no doubt has his own private chamber in hell, in among the elite of evil, the characters in *Lear* come close to his exacting standard. For my money, Regan tops the lot in her treatment of Gloucester. She begins the scene of his blinding by demanding, "Hang him instantly," but settles for the vicious blinding that Cornwall initiates. When one eye has been gouged out and stamped on, it is Regan who comments, with unimaginable viciousness: "One side will mock another; t'other too." She then proceeds to stab in the back a servant who protests at Gloucester's mutilation. It is she who insists on telling Gloucester that it was his own son who betrayed him into their hands. Once both his eyes have been plucked out, she delivers the bloodcurdling command: "Go thrust him out at gates, and let him smell/His way to Dover." Iago loved his evil plotting, his criminal artistry, but Regan revels in the direct cruelty of violent acts, accompanied by verbal viciousness—no pity, no compassion, no justice. Regan spits villainy.

Lear is never evil, though he is certainly foolish and unjust, rash and cantankerous. He is a good example of a type well described by Montaigne:

> Now there is no category of man who has greater need of such true and frank counsels as kings do. They sustain a life lived in public and have to remain acceptable to the opinions of a great many on-lookers: yet, since it is customary not to tell them anything which makes them change their ways, they discover that they have, quite unawares, begun to be hated and loathed by their subjects for reasons which they could often have avoided (with no loss to their pleasures moreover) if only they had been warned in time and corrected.[5]

Lear's character has suffered from his own power: his position has allowed the worst aspects of his personality to develop and intensify. He is arrogant, ignorant, unheeding, callous, vain, blinkered, childish, intemperate, and ludicrous. His treatment of Cordelia in the opening scene is unforgivable. Yet he does learn—he is deeply changed by his subsequent experience. He comes to see that he has treated Cordelia appallingly, and he even begins to appreciate the plight of those less fortunate than his erstwhile self: "Poor naked wretches, wheresoe'er you are, That bide the pelting of this pitiless night, How shall your houseless heads and unfed sides, Your looped and windowed raggedness, defend you/From seasons such as these? O, I have ta'en/Too little care of this! Take physic, pomp, Expose thyself to feel what wretches feel, That thou mayst shake the superflux to them/And show the heavens more just." In other words, he arrives at a better understanding of social justice: he can now put himself in the position of the homeless and poor. His grasp of reality has immeasurably improved, and with it his own moral character. This implies, in yet another paradox of causality, that his reduction to nothing has eventuated in an abundance of soul: he has lost all material things, all rank and station, but he has gained enormously in knowledge, moral and other. He is, in a sense, a richer man now than when he was undisputed king. Beneath his crown was an empty head; now, bareheaded, he carries a fullness of knowledge. He lived foolishly, but he did not die so. In a way, the whole play is about the education of King Lear, his torturous passage from confident igno-rance to hard-won insight. The tragedy is that he was so difficult to teach.

Nor is Cordelia entirely blameless, despite her manifest integrity. She must have known, knowing her father, what impact her initial silence would have on him, touchy and imperious as he was. Yet she was unwilling to bend to his—no doubt unreasonable—request. She refused to act the part he demanded of her, resolutely so. While this shows an admirable integrity and respect for the truth on her part, it perhaps also reveals a streak of stubbornness (Lear calls it pride): sometimes telling the plain truth to a parent is not morally what is required. In short, she seems quite willing deliberately to hurt his feelings. She refuses to accept the superior virtue of the white lie, as if not wanting to taint herself. This is, to be sure, a failing that flows from a virtue, but it is a failing nonetheless. She is more concerned with preserving her integrity than in protecting her father's feelings. By the play's end, when she replies "No cause" to her father's admission that she had cause to be resentful, she is no longer sticking to the literal truth come what may—for she *did* have cause. Now she understands that kind words can sometimes be better than true words. Perhaps she too had to be educated. To put it in the theatrical mode: she has learned how to put on an act for the sake of other people's feelings.

It could be said of both Lear and Gloucester that the scales fall from their eyes. Lear comes to see that Cordelia is his true and faithful daughter, not Regan and Goneril; and Gloucester recognizes that it is Edgar, not Edmund, who has been his dutiful son. These two paternal figures thus undergo large epistemological reversals, as if fathers are particularly prone to error. And they make their discoveries by way of the greatest losses in their cognitive faculties: Lear goes mad and Gloucester is struck blind. Lear, in great fear of madness, pleads: "O, let me not be mad, sweet heaven! I would not be mad. Keep me in temper. I would not be mad." But once the madness has overtaken him he suffers no reduction of knowledge, but sees things more clearly than ever; as Edgar remarks, "O, matter and impertinency mixed—Reason in madness!" He finds his clearest vision in his most deranged state. Gloucester, for his part, perceives the truth about his two sons at the very moment his eyesight is removed—"O, my follies! Then Edgar was abused." His blindness is the accomplice of his vision. With sane mind and seeing eyes these two men were ignorant of reality, but they see the truth just when they lose those faculties ("I see it feelingly," Gloucester says of his newfound vision of the world). This, again, is one of those paradoxes of which Shakespeare is so fond: the presence in absence, the something from nothing, the causal inversions. Just when we thought they had lost everything, there is a further reduction—of rational mind and of sight: their very faculties of knowledge are being negated. But this extra step toward nothingness is, paradoxically, accompanied by an increase in understanding. They swell inwardly, while diminishing outwardly. It is almost as if their outer trappings (including, now, their cognitive faculties) are being transmuted into a new kind of substance—insight, understanding, and compassion. If so, there is a strange kind of conservation at work here: what is lost in one form comes back in another form, essentially undiminished. Both men are larger figures at the play's end, grander, more substantial; yet this enhancement results from a drastic diminution in their outward attributes. The outer is being transformed into the inner, so that the nothing they have become turns out to be a new kind of something. Madness and blindness count as the end of something, but they are the beginning of something else—and something valuable.

Albany, too, comes to a new level of knowledge, about the nature of his wife, Goneril—he comes to understand how terrible she truly is. He delivers himself of these trenchant words: "Wisdom and goodness to the vile seem vile; Filths savour but themselves. What have you done? Tigers, not daughters, what have you performed?" Here is another Shakespearean inversion: to the vile good things appear vile.

Why? It is because, says Albany, the vile person can taste only her own nature. The vile—the evil—are so saturated in their own wickedness that virtue can only strike them as distasteful. If this is a sentiment of Shakespeare's, as well as Albany's, then I applaud his psychological insight: to the evil person goodness is indeed an irritant, a toxin, something to be shunned. This is why, like Iago, evil people always try to dismiss goodness as hypocrisy or dishonesty or concealed selfishness or weakness—it is an affront to their very existence. Regan never appreciated her virtuous sister, Cordelia; she actively disliked her. Cynicism is an invariable trait of the vile. This is Shakespeare bringing home to us the bitter truth about the world. (I am aware that, in saying this, I shall be accused of being an "old-fashioned moralist"; I accept the appellation, but at least I am in good company.)[6]

King Lear is more concerned with metaphysics than epistemology: it deals principally with questions of existence and causality rather than our ability to know reality. But epistemology is still present in the play, though in the thematic background. The villains of the piece are first and foremost deceivers, not just for the duration but also as a way of life: they are practiced dissemblers of their own intentions. Edmund's very first act in the play is to deceive his father into believing that Edgar is about to betray him—and Gloucester (like Othello) is too easily swayed by his deceptions. Regan and Goneril smoothly deceive Lear into believing in their love and good intentions toward him, and he too is excessively credulous. A touch more skepticism would have been in order for these rash believers. Notable too is the fact that two characters spend much of the play in disguise—Edgar and Kent—concealing their identity. They must deceive to survive, though both are virtuous men. Cordelia has Desdemona's problem: she cannot *reveal* enough of herself to the skeptical other. When she says, in frustration, "I cannot heave/My heart into my mouth," she is expressing the difficulty of making her inner self visible to her father—so as to quench his skepticism about her true feelings. She seeks transparency, while her sisters thrive on opacity: but both conditions depend on the gap between inner and outer. Thus, what is known of the characters by the characters is out of keeping with the internal facts, as the audience is aware of those facts. We, the audience, are aware of what the characters themselves don't know of each other. We are confronted by their errors and blindspots. And this itself is a lesson in epistemology.

Lear's ignorance is the most thoroughgoing: not only does he misunderstand almost everyone around him (a condition permitted by his royal position); he also fails in knowledge of himself. As Regan remarks of her father (beady-eyed realist that she is): "He hath ever but slenderly known himself." His self-ignorance is longstanding and deep-seated, and it leads to his ignorance of others. Socrates would have had a fine old time exposing his delusions, his lazy thinking, and his rashness in belief. He is a man in need of a complete cognitive overhaul—and the play gives him one. By the end he has shaped up, epistemologically. Earlier, he shows no cognitive responsibility, rushing from one belief to the next according to his whims. He is, literally, a fool (unlike his Fool). It takes madness to sober him up; and suffering, lots of suffering. Only from subtraction comes inward addition. He reveals his newfound epistemological modesty during his final reunion with Cordelia, in these touching words: "Pray do not mock. I am a very foolish, fond old man, Fourscore and upward, and to deal plainly, I fear I am not in my perfect mind. Methinks I should know you, and know this man; Yet I am doubtful, for I am mainly ignorant/What place this is; and all the skill I have/Remembers not these garments; nor I know not/Where I did lodge last night. Do not laugh at me, For as I am a man, I think this lady/To be my child Cordelia." The tone of caution, hesitation, and self-doubt stands in marked contrast to the arrogance of belief Lear demonstrates at the start of the action. The passage is full of epistemic verbs, all used negatively. Gone is the man who will brook no contradiction, smugly confident in his woeful ignorance. Now he knows that justified beliefs do not come easily (as the Greek skeptics were anxious to insist). He has learned that there is a folly of belief as there is a folly of action.

Shakespeare's heightened sensitivity to the problem of other minds shows in Albany's remark to Goneril: "See thyself, devil. Proper deformity shows not in the fiend/So horrid as in woman"; and, "Howe'er thou art a fiend, A woman's shape doth shield thee." Kent speaks of Lear's "dog-hearted daughters." Lear, giving his opinion of women's sexual appetites, observes: "Down from the waist/They're centaurs, though women all above"—as if they conceal their baser natures in a show of coy femininity. Albany calls Regan a "gilded serpent." The theme of the opacity of other people is nowhere near as pronounced in *Lear* as it is in *Othello*, but it plays a role, particularly in characterizing the dual nature of Regan and Goneril: they are cultivated ladies of the court on the outside—elegant, well-spoken, and controlled—but inside they are fiends, serpents, dogs. It is not just that their true intentions are hidden; they are actually different *kinds of being* beneath the silky surface, creatures of another species. Ferocious killers lurk behind the ladylike appearance, occasionally bursting to the surface with fangs flaring. It is the nightmare of the devil himself within the beautiful stranger—the ultimate demonstration of the problem of other minds. Albany really had no idea, before the events of the play, that his beloved wife was actually a fiend from hell in disguise. He, too, suffers a sharp epistemic shock.

I have said nothing so far about the most overtly philosophical passage in *King Lear*. It is a most curious passage, which takes some parsing. We are on the heath, with Edgar disguised as a deranged beggar blathering about the "foul fiend" pursuing him, and Lear hovering between sanity and madness. Suddenly, for no particular reason, Lear says, "First let me talk with this philosopher," referring to the incoherent Edgar (as Tom). "What is the cause of thunder?" Lear inquires. Edgar gives him no reply. "What is your study?" Lear persists. Now Edgar has an answer: "How to prevent the fiend, and to kill vermin," he says. Lear continues: "Let me ask you one word in private"; and, as the stage directions say, *"They converse apart."* About what, we are not informed. "Noble philosopher, your company," Lear then says, to be met with Edgar's "Tom's a-cold." Invited to step into the hovel for warmth, Lear responds, "I will keep still with my philosopher," calling Edgar "good Athenian." It is a complete nonconversation, in which nothing substantial is discussed, and no sense is made (a discursive vacuum). It begins with a straightforward question as to the cause of thunder (the kind of causal question I have been attributing to the play), but no answer is given to the question—and the answer was not known in Shakespeare's time. The exchange quickly devolves into nonsense, pauses, and indecipherable murmurings. What is Shakespeare telling us here? He is telling us that philosophy has *nothing useful to say*. That is, natural philosophy—what we now call science—is almost entirely ignorant of the workings of the universe. We can ask causal questions, but we cannot expect satisfying answers. This exchange between two deranged men is thus a kind of commentary on the themes of the play itself: it is saying that the enigma of the world is not resolved by those people calling themselves philosophers—that is, by those supposedly learned men who undertake to explain the hidden workings of nature. In other words, Shakespeare is warning his audience against what we would now call pseudo-science. It is better frankly to accept ignorance than to bandy pseudo-scientific explanations. Remember that Shakespeare was writing well in advance of the development of science as we now know it; his concern was with what was claimed to be knowledge of nature at that time. Like Montaigne, Shakespeare was more of a general skeptic than a believer in one or another cosmological theory. Alchemy, for example, was a pseudo-science of the period (Ben Jonson wrote a whole play about it, *The Alchemist*); and the babblings of Edgar as Tom are not much worse than its excesses. I think Shakespeare is slyly poking fun at such pretensions to understanding. It is not that he has no philosophy (in our contemporary sense)—this whole book is about his philosophical preoccupations—but he is skeptical of the kind of hollow and obscure pronouncements of people who think they have gotten to the bottom of things. Immediately after Lear calls Edgar a "good Athenian," Gloucester intervenes with the sturdy advice: "No words, no words. Hush"—which I think about sums up Shakespeare's position.

SEVEN

The Tempest

Persons of the Play

Prospero, the rightful Duke of Milan
Miranda, his daughter
Antonio, his brother, the usurping Duke
of Milan
Alonso, King of Naples
Sebastian, his brother
Ferdinand, Alonso's son
Gonzalo, an honest old counselor of Naples
Adrian, a lord
Francisco, a lord
Ariel, an airy spirit attendant upon Prospero
Caliban, a savage and deformed native of the
island, Prospero's slave
Trinculo, Alonso's jester
Stefano, Alonso's drunken butler
The master of a ship
Boatswain
Mariners
Spirits
The masque: spirits appearing as Iris, Ceres,
Juno, nymphs, reapers

If *A Midsummer Night's Dream* marks the beginning of Shakespeare's great mature period, then *The Tempest* marks its end, the play being generally agreed to be the last Shakespeare wrote without collaboration (written around 1610). The two plays are in fact remarkably similar, structurally. Both concern an imperious father seeking to arrange the marriage of his daughter (a common enough theme in Shakespeare). They take place mainly within an enchanted area, an island or a wood, in which magic is the norm. Prospero is the presiding magician of *Tempest*, while Oberon initiates the magic in *Dream* (neither character could be said to be especially sensitive to the desires of others). There are sprites and fairies in both plays, mischievously meddling in human affairs. Puck is the chief sprite in *Dream*, Ariel in *Tempest*. In both we are given a figure combining animal and human traits—Caliban the man-fish and Bottom the man-ass. There is much bewitched sleeping, and talk of dreams, and extremes of romantic love. Only by means of magic do things come out right at the end. The human beings seem lost and foolish most of the time, susceptible to the slightest influence; they are the subjects of outside forces they scarcely comprehend. They have delusions of personal autonomy, failing to realize the extent of their powerlessness. Both plays seem concerned with locating human action against a background of hidden and mysterious influences, embodied in supernatural agencies. And both operate on a dreamlike plane, with the audience cast as dreamer.

Thematically, however, there is a deep difference between the two plays. If *Dream* is concerned principally with the power of the imagination, *Tempest* is concerned above all with the power of language. It is the influence of language over human consciousness and conduct that primarily exercises Shakespeare in *Tempest*—what we might call the "natural magic" of speech (and writing). The play deals with sound in general—of a storm, of music—but speech is the type of sound that is highlighted and subjected to scrutiny. And language is connected expressly to magic, as if speaking itself were a form of spell-casting (we do, after all, refer to spellbinding speakers). Wittgenstein once said that philosophy is "a battle against the bewitchment of our intelligence by means of language,"[1] and that could serve as a motto for the theme of this play (though Wittgenstein and Shakespeare have, it must be said, different kinds of bewitchment in mind: Wittgenstein means the malign influence of superficial grammatical form in shaping our ideas of how language functions, while Shakespeare is interested in how speech affects and constitutes mind and self). It is sometimes wondered why Shakespeare called this play "The Tempest," when the storm that begins the play is such a small part of its content. I would suggest that the term refers to the storm of *speech* that constitutes the play—which, indeed, constitutes so much of human life. We live surrounded by a tempest of words, assailed and buffeted by language. Words can be menacing and dangerous, oppressive and noisy, as well as suspiciously seductive. And we as much need relief and protection from the tempest of language as we do from a literal tempest—we need the silence that is the absence of both.

The power of language is uncanny, mysterious. Of course, there is nothing very mysterious about sounds and marks: we produce sounds with our mouths and marks with our pens (or computers), and these are physical phenomena that have a causal impact on things like eardrums and eyes. But it is not sounds and marks that constitute the essence of language as a medium of communication: it is meaning. It is what sounds *mean* that determines their impact on the mind, not their acoustic or graphic properties. But the linguistic meaning that influences the mind is not some straightforward physical fact in the world; meaning is impalpable, imperceptible. As Wittgenstein would observe, the meaning of a sentence strikes us as a kind of magic aura around the sentence, a halo of significance—a kind of shadowy and sublime super-fact. It is not the sentence itself, as a sequence of sounds or marks, that enables it to operate on the mind; it is what philosophers call the *proposition* it expresses that is where the action is—the meaning that the words somehow convey. But this meaning, this impalpable proposition, is puzzling, ontologically problematic; and its ability to influence the mind can seem almost magical.[2] Thus it is not inappropriate for Shakespeare to associate speaking with sorcery. Language, we might say, is naturally magical, in that its very nature is to exercise great power by ethereal means—by the apprehension of this peculiar thing we call meaning. Even when I ask you for a cup of tea and get it, a small miracle has occurred: my meaning has penetrated your mind and made you act in a certain way. This is not the kind of causal influence we know from physics, but another kind of influence altogether (and philosophers of language today are still keenly debating how this influence works). Speech is a kind of immaterial causation, in which the thing doing all the work—the meaning—is essentially noiseless. You grasp meaning by virtue of the noises you hear, but what you thereby latch on to is essentially a silent thing—something that, as we think, lies behind mere words, giving them whatever semantic life they possess. Behind the raucous tempest of words lies an ocean of silence—what those words *signify*. And this realm of sense, seemingly abstract and imperceptible, carries with it a whiff of the supernatural—as if it resides in a nonnatural world of its own, tenuously linked to empirical reality. Some philosophers, indeed, have opted for a strong kind of Platonism about meaning, supposing that meaning really is something that resides in its own nonnatural realm, alongside numbers and geometrical forms.[3] Not surprisingly, opponents of these views have accused the Platonists of trafficking in magic. We need not enter into these debates here; for our purposes it is enough to note the natural way in which meaning and magic can become connected—as Shakespeare connects them in *Tempest* (not that he was thinking explicitly in terms of semantic Platonism).

A further linguistic theme of *Tempest*, buried deeper within the play, concerns the power of language, not merely to reflect the world and enable us to communicate about it, but also to *create* its own world. I mean this in two ways: first, to create fictional worlds, of the kind Shakespeare himself creates, and thus to bring fictional characters into being; but secondly, to create human nature as we experience it—to make us what we distinctively are. It is not that language merely mirrors an antecedent reality; it can also generate vast and intricate fictional worlds, and it works to confer upon us the kind of consciousness we have. When our biological ancestors first learned how to speak, a profound transformation took place—they entered another ontological plane. I think that Shakespeare presents us with a parable of this ascent in the form of Caliban, a creature who makes the transition from mute to loquacious, and who reminds us of our prelinguistic selves. Language is an architect of reality, notably mental reality, not merely a representation of it. From some perspectives, indeed, language can seem like an evolutionary development that got out of control—that has far more power in it, constructive and destructive, than anyone ever bargained for. Shakespeare is keenly aware of that awesome power (he was probably its greatest human conduit, after all), and his play is an ambivalent tribute to it. Hence he gives the play its allusive and self-referential title, *The Tempest*.

I shall now go through the play with this interpretation in mind. The play begins with a stage direction: "*A tempestuous noise of thunder and lightning heard.*" The shipmaster immediately commands his boatswain to "speak to th' mariners" and do it quickly. The boatswain adds his bellowing voice to the cacophony of the storm. Antonio, a passenger on the ship, appears from below, asking for the whereabouts of the master. The boatswain replies: "Do you not hear him? You mar our labour. Keep your cabins. You do assist the storm." He adds: "Silence; trouble us not." Already, the sound of the storm and of human speech are intermingled and juxtaposed. The connection is made explicit in the boatswain's complaint about a human cry he hears from within: "A plague upon this howling! They are louder than the weather, or our office." Sebastian, another passenger, continues the theme with his rebuke to the boatswain: "A pox o'your throat, you bawling, blasphemous, uncharitable dog!" Antonio then refers to the man as "you whoreson insolent noise-maker." When informed that they are about to sink, the boatswain responds: "What, must our mouths be cold?"—by which he means that speech is soon to be curtailed by the water. In this scene, speech and storm are analogized, and there is a war of silence taking place—everyone wants everyone else (including the storm) to be quiet. The fear of death by drowning is the fear of eternal silence, but speech is seen as a form of aggression—as one act of speech attempts to suppress another. There is a tempest of words and weather, with the question raised as to which will exercise the greater power.

In the next scene we discover that Prospero caused the storm by means of his "art" (he enters with magic cloak and staff). He quickly assures his daughter Miranda that no harm was done—in effect, the storm was a fake, a fiction, having no concrete effect, though exciting much emotion. He proceeds to inform her of her background and of how they came to the island, removing his magic cloak for the purpose. He wants her to listen carefully to his speech, to absorb his meaning fully: "The hour's now come. The very minute bids thee ope thine ear, Obey, and be attentive." In reporting his story of betrayal by his brother Antonio, he shows a notable anxiety of attention, repeatedly accusing his daughter of not listening. Linguistic communication requires not just someone speaking but the intended audience listening: Prospero is contending for his daughter's ear, as much as the mariners and nobles were contending for linguistic dominance. "Dost thou attend me?" he truculently asks. "Sir, most heedfully," she dutifully replies. Then again: "Thou attend'st not!" and the reply, "O, good sir, I do." "I pray thee mark me," he persists, ending his oration, "Dost thou hear?" Miranda replies, evidently impatiently, "Your tale, sir, would cure deafness." So great is his anxiety of attention that—now devoid of his magical accessories—he cannot be confident his daughter is listening even when she is maximally attentive. He has an extreme case of the anxiety of all storytellers—indeed, all speakers—namely, that his intended audience will not be interested in what he has to say (an anxiety that must surely have crossed Shakespeare's own mind as a playwright and poet). Prospero is as much addressing the audience of the play, as Shakespeare's surrogate, as he is his own daughter. Without willing ears speakers are stymied, no matter how spellbinding their speech may be.

We next learn that Prospero is a man of the word in a very deep sense. He sacrificed the dukedom of Milan to his "secret studies": "my library/Was dukedom large enough," he avers. Prospero loved his books more than his position and his powers, to the point of neglecting his administrative duties, and allowed Antonio to usurp him. Yet these very books, the source of his loss of political power in Milan, furnish him with magical power on the island. In the end, he will drown his own book, ending his magical powers, but for now he is a supreme sorcerer of the word.

Language again comes to the fore when Caliban makes his clammy entrance. Prospero addresses him thus: "Thou earth, thou, speak!"— as if mere earth could use language. Caliban, resentful of his enslavement, reminds Prospero of the early days when he was taught "how to name the bigger light, and how the less" (the words "sun" and "moon" seem not to have stuck with him). Miranda, recalling the time before Caliban's attempt to violate her, asserts: "I pitied thee, Took pains to make thee speak, taught thee each hour/One thing or another. When thou didst not, savage, Know thine own meaning, but wouldst gabble like/A thing most brutish, I endowed thy purposes/With words that made them known." Caliban tartly replies: "You taught me language, and my profit on't/Is I know how to curse. The red plague rid you/For learning me your language!" Prospero and Miranda construe their linguistic education of Caliban as a civilizing mission, a molding of the brutish into the rational and sensitive; they change his nature for the better (they suppose). But Caliban sees it differently: language took away his innocent unselfconsciousness—it made him able to articulate his misery. Perhaps it even took away his sexual innocence (his attempt on Miranda's honor seems to have followed his induction into the ways of language). He agrees, though, that he was profoundly altered. By learning language he has become susceptible to language, with all its magic and power; and this is a blessing he regards as—at best—mixed. After all, by mastering language (or it mastering him) he can now be commanded to do things, which was not possible before.

When Ferdinand meets Miranda, and learns that she is a "maid," his reply is: "My language! Heavens! I am the best of them that speak this speech, Were I but where 'tis spoken." He is stunned and delighted that they speak the same language, and can thus enter into intimate communication. Prospero's very first words to Ferdinand are: "A word, good sir. I fear you have done yourself some wrong. A word." And he keeps talking about these words, while Miranda assures Ferdinand: "My father's of a better nature, sir, than he appears by speech." Ariel tells Prospero that he shall obey his commands "To th' syllable." Here is language referring to language (what logicians call a "metalanguage"), keeping itself constantly in view.

The first scene of the second act sustains the commentary on matters linguistic. Antonio says of Gonzalo: "Fie, what a spendthrift is he of his tongue!" and "If but one of his pockets could speak, would it not say he lies?" and "His word is more than the miraculous harp." Alonso complains testily about Gonzalo's fluency: "You cram these words into mine ears against/The stomach of my sense." And so the scene continues, with references to "sleepy language" and a "hollow burst of bellowing." Stefano comments upon the combined linguistic skills of Caliban and Trinculo, as the creature beneath the gaberdine: "His forward voice now is to speak well of his friend; his backward voice is to utter foul speeches and to detract." He later remarks: "My man-monster hath drowned his tongue in sack."

When Caliban plots to murder Prospero, he locates his master's power in words: "Remember/First to possess his books, for without them/He's but a sot as I am, nor hath not/One spirit to command—they all do hate him/As rootedly as I. Burn but his books." He also comments on the mingling of sounds the island affords: "Be not afeard. The isle is full of noises, Sounds, and sweet airs, that give delight and hurt not. Sometimes a thousand twangling instruments/Will hum about mine ears, and sometimes voices/That if I then had waked after long sleep/Will make me sleep again." In the same vein, Alonso describes the spirits that surround them in these words: "Such shapes, such gesture, and such sound, expressing—Although they want the use of tongue—a kind/Of excellent dumb discourse." Later he comments: "Methought the billows spoke and told me of it, The winds did sing it to me, and the thunder, That deep and dreadful organ-pipe, pronounced/The name of Prosper." Here we have the comparison of natural and human sounds, with the former also said to convey meaning. Because we humans are such profoundly linguistic creatures, we are apt to find language everywhere—as if nature herself speaks to us (comfortingly or threateningly).

Amid all this barrage of sound, Prospero seeks the end of language, at least momentarily. "No tongue, all eyes! Be silent," he commands the lovers, Ferdinand and Miranda. Later he says: "Sweet now, silence. Juno and Ceres whisper seriously. There's something else to do. Hush, and be mute, Or else our spell is marred." When he vows to drown his book, he is silencing it far more thoroughly than if he had burned it, where it might emit a faint final crackle. He wants an end to words, to the linguistic storm. Yet he cannot abjure language entirely, and he is obliged to tell his tale to Alonso, who comments at the end of the play: "I long/To hear the story of your life, which must/Take the ear strangely." We are trapped in language, formed by it, slaves to it; we feel a desire to break its bounds and distance ourselves from it. It is both marvelous and corrupting, sublime and base (and at its most ostensibly sublime it can be basest). There is a whole complex of attitudes toward language expressed here, but the desire for silence is certainly strongly accented. After all, what we mainly desire of a tempest is that it should cease and return the world to peace and quiet.

I don't think Shakespeare is offering us any very definite thesis about language in this play—that would be alien to his method in general; what I think he is giving us is a multifaceted treatment of the phenomenon of language, noticing the complexity of our relationship to it. He is exploring human language as a naturalist might, simply describing meticulously how it fits into human life: its role in love, in aggression, in politics, in the father/child relationship, and in the way it structures the individual mind. And he is expressing a deep ambivalence about language—its power to illuminate and deceive, to inspire and subdue, to civilize and corrupt. Having made a career from language, Shakespeare is reflecting, late in that career, on the medium through which he wove his own spells, and wondering if now might be the time for silence. Like Prospero, Shakespeare is an artist in words, steeped in them, bound to his "book"—and it is irresistibly tempting to discern a shadow of the playwright in the character of Prospero (as many commentators have). In any case, self-consciousness about language would certainly characterize such a linguistically accomplished author as Shakespeare.

*   *   *

This brings us to the question of the symbolic status of the main figures of the play. Shakespeare is not in general an allegorical writer; his characters are fully rounded human beings, and the action concerns them directly. But in *Tempest* the impression of allegory is strong: the characters "stand" for something. As I just noted, Prospero is readily interpreted as Shakespeare's representative, and there is no doubt that he is intended to stand for the idea of the artist. He refers constantly to "mine art," as in: "The direful spectacle of the wreck, which touched/The very virtue of compassion in thee, I have with such provision in mine art/So safely ordered that there is no soul—No, not so much perdition as an hair/Betid to any creature in the vessel, Which thou heard'st cry, which thou saw'st sink." In other words, it was just a *performance*, giving only the impression of catastrophe, from which all the actors emerged unscathed. Prospero devised this performance and arranged to have it enacted: it was a piece of dramatic art (occurring within a piece of dramatic art). As he says to Ariel, his agent in the matter: "Hast thou, spirit, Performed to point the tempest that I bade thee?" The characters didn't know the storm was essentially fictitious, and so performed their roles with authenticity, but all along it was just a piece of make-believe. Similarly, Prospero orchestrates the romance between Ferdinand and Miranda, though they too don't know that they are players in his creation. He also arranges the disposition of the marooned nobles on the island, manipulating them as he deems fit. He creates and directs the entire drama, employing his "so potent art." He is like an artist with the power to determine the fate of his fictional creations. Accordingly, he has the aspect of a tyrant, as all artists inherently must. He is also described as a storyteller, initially to Miranda, but later by Alonso. In the epilogue, addressing the audience, he tells us: "Gentle breath of yours my sails/Must fill, or else my project fails, Which was to please. Now I want/Spirits to enforce, art to enchant." Here he is acknowledging his role as an artist engaged on an aesthetic project. He wanted to please his daughter by his "art" and he also wants to please the audience (the name Miranda means "onlooker," and certainly Prospero makes her his audience repeatedly). Once again, Shakespeare is introducing theatricality into the lives of his characters. This is exactly why Prospero displays that anxiety of attention I mentioned earlier: he is an artist unsure of the interest of his audience. He wants Miranda (the onlooker) to listen, but he knows he needs to tell a good tale if he is to keep her attention—just as Shakespeare himself needs to. For all his magical powers, he cannot *compel* attention; he must earn it. He is also reclusive, spending all his time in his library in Milan and his "cell" on the island; and Shakespeare must have been somewhat reclusive too, despite his forays to the Globe (Prospero mentions the "great globe" in a speech I shall come back to). And there is a kind of harshness to him that suggests intoxication with power—the power to make things happen as he imagines them. This is not an idealized portrait of the artist, as a softhearted sensitive, but as someone who dabbles in what Prospero calls his "rough magic"—an apt enough description of Shakespeare's own tough and penetrating style. There is something lacking in Prospero in the kindness department (despite his late forgiveness of his enemies), and I think this is part of Shakespeare's picture of an artist. Prospero can be touchy and insecure, as well as proud of his own prowess—the very essence of an artist, one might say.

Then who is Ariel, Prospero's agent in creation? He is, evidently, the creative spirit in the artist. Prospero refers to him often as "my spirit," as well as "my diligence," "my tricksy spirit," and "my brave spirit." These could as well be descriptions of a part of himself, of a faculty within himself. When he wants a project executed, performed, he calls upon this spirit to do the work; Ariel is an excellent agency for that purpose—he performed the opening storm, for example, with marvelous drama and verisimilitude. Yet Ariel has an interesting and complex relationship to his master: he was freed by Prospero from twelve years' imprisonment in a pine (by the wicked witch Sycorax), but he is also Prospero's resentful slave, repeatedly pleading for his freedom. He refers to his master's tasks as "work" and "toil" and clearly would rather be off doing what he wants. But Prospero needs him; he can't function as a magician without Ariel's help. The two are scarcely on good terms, and only threats convince Ariel to do as Prospero commands him. If this is intended allegorically, then it presents an interesting picture of the relationship between an artist and his talent. First, the two are somewhat alienated from each other; in particular, the faculty that does the actual creative work feels like a slave to an imperious master. Secondly, the artist is dependent on the disposition of his talent and must do what he can to induce it to work with him. Ariel seems to enjoy his work up to a point, but he longs for his freedom—he wants to relax. And isn't the creative spirit in the artist in a comparable position? Art is hard work, and the creative spirit sometimes flags: it needs rest and silence. Prospero is always instructing Ariel to perform one more task for him before he can be released; but that could well be a description of the artist's relationship to his own talent. Prospero is fond of Ariel ("Why, that's my dainty Ariel! I shall miss thee"), but there is always an element of domination or exploitation in their relationship—as the light and fiery spirit is forced to carry out his master's strenuous bidding. It is easy to see this relationship as a parable of Shakespeare's own relationship to his talent at this late stage of his career: he has flogged it mercilessly for years, but now it is time to give it a rest—to let it retire from its creative exertions. It has served him well, no doubt, but there has always been an element of resentment, a longing for freedom (it couldn't have been easy to write all those plays and put them on the stage). Shakespeare's retirement to Stratford, to spend time with his eldest daughter, Susanna, after a strenuous theatrical career in London, is certainly analogous to Prospero's abjuring of his magic art and his return to Milan with his adored daughter. To do these things, the artists must bid farewell to their artistic spirits—to the agency within them that performs the creative magic.

How does Caliban find his place in this picture? He is the animal aspect of the human being, the squelchy, sticky part; the part that forages to survive; that is crude, concupiscent, vicious, gullible, and rather pitiful. It is hard to have much affection for Caliban—rape and murder fall within his repertoire—but he has a kind of pathos, a downtrodden and despised wretchedness. He is governed by fear as well as by ill-informed adoration, by resentment as well as sub-servience. His animal nature sits uneasily with the civilized veneer he has picked up from Prospero and Miranda. He is, as it were, the beastlike underbelly of even the most refined of human beings. When Prospero says of him, "This thing of darkness I/Acknowledge mine," he is putting the point perfectly: this dark and despicable thing must be acknowledged as part of the baggage of being human. Caliban is the human as animal, and this too has its place in defining humanity. " 'Tis a villain, sir, I do not love to look on," observes Miranda. Prospero replies: "But as 'tis, We cannot miss him. He does make our fire, Fetch in our wood, and serves in offices/That profit us." We may not like to "look on" our animal nature, but without it we would be bereft of material support—it is essential to our ability to transcend it. Prospero calls Caliban his "tortoise," describes him as "filth," and as "hag-seed"—stressing his subhuman nature—but without him he would be at a loss to survive. Caliban is the agent of his bodily needs.

That is not to say that Caliban has no other meaning in the play: he is clearly also a representative of an enslaved population, a "sav-age" who has been trained in the ways of civilization (with only par-tial success). But I think Shakespeare wants us to appreciate that we each carry our own personal Caliban around with us, as part of our very identity: we too are of the earth, with our own filth, the seed of some "hag" or other. Caliban gets drunk at one point and falls for the loutish Stefano, but the effects of drunkenness on the typical male of the species (which Shakespeare often refers to) are not so different: give a man a few glasses of "sack" and you will see his inner Caliban emerge intact—lecherous, gullible, messy, violent. And even a great artist cannot manage without his own Caliban to negotiate the natural world in which he is condemned to live. Is not the human body itself a kind of rebellious slave that we force to do things against its natural inclinations, and which occasionally over-whelms our better judgment? The split between our animal nature and our "higher" nature, uneasily conjoined as these are, resembles the fraught relationship between the superior Prospero (duke and artist) and his inferior companion (slave and sop). Caliban is an earthy organism, while Ariel is an airy sprite—and Prospero, as a human being, is a kind of compound of the two, equally dependent on both of them.

If Ariel and Caliban can be seen as aspects of a single self, what is Miranda—surely she is a separate person? She is Prospero's daughter, of course, and also his audience, as well as a player in a drama of his creation: but can she in any way be regarded as yet another facet of Prospero's identity? I think she can—as the artist's *internal* audience. Any artist, particularly a playwright, must envisage an audience as he or she composes: the aim is to "please" this audience, to command its attention. But the actual audience is not generally in on the act of creation, so the audience must be merely notional, that is, imagined. Thus the artist has an imaginary audience at his elbow as he composes. This audience can be as hard—or harder—to please than any actual audience, depending on the psychology and standards of the artist. That anxiety of attention I have mentioned has its inner counterpart: can the artist capture his *own* interest? Thus, Miranda can be seen as yet another aspect of the artist's consciousness (this is not, of course, incompatible with her also being an external audience of her father's overt speech acts). If so, we can now detect three separate components to Prospero's identity: his creative spirit, his animal self, and his internal audience—his critical self-consciousness. Each pulls in its own direction and has its own priorities, but each must be placated, or at least controlled. The play, then, is an allegory of the solitary artist's mind and its inner architecture

And now there is one more important point to be made: the tempest named in the play's title might be viewed as a very specific kind of linguistic phenomenon—the act or product of creation itself. Thus the play refers to itself in its title: *it* is a tempest. Creation is a tempest of the mind, and it results in an aesthetic tempest.

I have cited Montaigne many times in the course of this book, noting possible influences on Shakespeare, or at least commonalities. The most well-known passage from Montaigne that has shaped Shakespeare's text is from his essay "On the Cannibals." It runs:

I would tell Plato that those people [the so-called savages] have no trade of any kind, no acquaintance with writing, no knowledge of numbers, no terms for governor or political superior, no practice of subordination or of riches or poverty, no contracts, no inheritances, no divided estates, no occupation but leisure, no concern for kinship—except such as is common to them all—no clothing, no agriculture, no metals, no use of wine or corn. Among them you hear no words for treachery, lying, cheating, avarice, envy, backbiting or forgiveness.[4]

The relevant passage from *Tempest* is put into the garrulous mouth of Gonzalo: "I'th' commonwealth I would by contraries/Execute all things. For no kind of traffic/Would I admit, no name of magistrate; Letters should not be known; riches, poverty, And use of service, none; contract, succession, Bourn, bound of land, tilth, vineyard, none; No use of metal, corn, wine, or oil; No occupation, all men idle, all; And women too—but innocent and pure; No sovereignty—." I quote these passages at length because they illustrate how ready Shakespeare could be to draw directly from Montaigne. It is not that in this particular play the overlap with Montaigne has any great significance—indeed, the context of Gonzalo's speech suggests some skepticism, on Shakespeare's part, toward Montaigne's rosy picture of his primitive society. But it is clear that Shakespeare had read Montaigne carefully, even to the point of paraphrasing him. Less direct, but deeper, sources of influence—such as I have indicated in earlier chapters—then become easier to detect and acknowledge. Shakespeare was clearly taken with the idea of a primitive people, exemplified by Caliban, and the effects that an invading power could have on them, and he chose to set a play about the power of language and art in such a context, where it could provide a counterpoint to those "higher" achievements. What I find interesting here, though, is the fact that Montaigne's footprints should be most evident in a context in which Shakespeare seems least deeply influenced, since his portrait of Caliban does not bear out the positive picture sketched by Montaigne. Was he perhaps quoting a favorite author precisely to show his disagreement with him on a particular point? Was he indicating a chink in Montaigne's otherwise impeccably skeptical and pessimistic armor? Whatever the reason, Montaigne's work is clearly stamped on Shakespeare's text in this play.

Since this is primarily a book about philosophical ideas in Shakespeare, I must mention a passage that has little significance for the play as a whole but that raises a question of philosophy much discussed in subsequent centuries—namely, the relative contributions of nature and nurture to human character and knowledge. Prospero, raging against Caliban's drunken plot to murder him, declares: "A devil, a born devil, on whose nature/Nurture can never stick; on whom my pains, Humanely taken, all, all lost, quite lost, And, as with age, his body uglier grows, So his mind cankers." This may well be the first occurrence in the English language of the words "nature" and "nurture" in this combination, thus setting up, with attractive alliteration, an issue still hotly debated. In later centuries, the empiricists, notably John Locke, maintained that all knowledge and character came from nurture—from the effects of experience and training on an essentially blank slate. The rationalists, on the other hand, such as Leibniz and Descartes, claimed that some knowledge at least was implanted by nature and could not be derived from experience. Shakespeare is not contributing to this debate, obviously, but he is framing the issue in an interesting and suggestive way: he speaks of whether nurture can "stick" on nature. He takes there to be an original nature, an innate constitution, and the task of education is to try to make improvements *adhere* to this original material—and the underlying nature of the organism may be such that these improvements cannot "take." It is not that the mind is just a blank tablet, or an empty box, that can receive anything that comes its way; rather, there has to be a *harmony* between nature and nurture for nurture to make any headway. In the case of Caliban, his original nature simply resists what Prospero has done to ameliorate it: it is *selective* in what it allows to "stick." There is a kind of pessimism about education here that the advocates of the blank slate would never accept—since, for them, the mind is indefinitely open and plastic, able to absorb whatever comes along. In fact, the conception suggested in this brief passage is closer to the orthodox position in contemporary philosophy and psychology, namely that innate constitution *constrains* what can be achieved by way of nurture.[5] You cannot throw just anything at a growing child and expect it to stick; it depends on what the innate constitution prepares the child to receive. In the case of Caliban, it is his moral nature that poses the problem: he is a "born devil," and no amount of moral nurturing can change that, despite superficial appearances. The passage echoes an earlier remark by Miranda on birth and its fatefulness: "Good wombs have borne bad sons." The thought here is that a person may be born bad, so that nothing can be done to mend matters; nurture will not stick. Such seems to be Shakespeare's view of many of his villains: Iago, Regan and Goneril, Edmund. In a word, Shakespeare comes across as a bit of a biological determinist.

Toward the end of the play, Prospero speaks these famous words: "Our revels now are ended. These our actors, As I foretold you, were all spirits, and/Are melted into air, into thin air; And like the baseless fabric of this vision, The cloud-capped towers, the gorgeous palaces, The solemn temples, the great globe itself, Yea, all which it inherit, shall dissolve; And, like this insubstantial pageant faded, Leave not a rack behind. We are such stuff/As dreams are made on, and our little life/Is rounded with a sleep." This could almost have come from *A Midsummer Night's Dream*, with its assimilation of waking and sleeping. The thought appears to be that reality differs not so greatly from fiction in its ultimate destiny, that it too will fade into nothing. Just as a play disappears when the curtain comes down—the world it creates is a temporary one—so everything real will eventually dissolve. Everything has a finite life, especially everything human. Prospero might even have made the point that fiction has *greater* longevity than material things, since Shakespeare's plays, say, will last longer than any building erected in his time; immortality belongs, if anywhere, to the characters of fiction, not those of real life.

The final, resonant sentence bears some scrutiny. What does "we" refer to? It is generally taken to refer to human beings—you, me, William Shakespeare. But perhaps it refers back to "our actors," those melting spirits—that is, its reference is to the characters *of fiction*. Then the point of the line is that fictional characters are made of the same stuff as dreams. That point has the advantage of being a pretty accurate description of what a fictional character is, since dreams themselves are a species of fiction. Prospero is thus reminding the audience that what they have just witnessed is analogous to a dream, so that they have in effect been asleep during the performance—the very point made by Puck in the epilogue to *Dream*. The alternative interpretation—that "we" refers to the human beings of real life—has some poetic power, but construed as a statement of literal fact suffers from the defect of being false. It is just not true that flesh-and-blood people are made of the stuff of dreams: *they are not fictional entities*. I, say, am not a fictional entity, as Hamlet is one, and my reality is not dependent on my being dreamed by someone. I am not merely a character in someone's dream, in someone's imagination. True, we are dreamers; and true, dreaming and waking bleed into each other: but false, that we are, ontologically, dream characters. It *might* be, as Descartes suggested, that all this is just a dream I am having; but again, that is not to say that my reality is constituted by someone's dream. Even if I am always dreaming, I am not thereby myself a fictional character—a person *from* a dream. I am, in a word, real. "I dream, therefore I exist (nonfictionally)" is a perfectly logical inference.

A third possible interpretation is that "we" refers to regular humans but that the word "on" must be construed differently. We are not made *of* the stuff of dreams, but dreams are made *from* us: the dream machinery uses us, real people, as the basis for its fictions. I dream about someone I know, but this person exists outside my dream and is the raw material from which my dream constructs its fantasy. Then the line says that people are the kinds of things that dreams are *about*. This, again, is obviously true, but seems a little banal, and somewhat contrived as an interpretation of Shakespeare's line. Maybe we could read the line as saying that we real people will eventually fade away, just as the characters of our dreams fade rapidly from our consciousness—even though there is no ontological parity between the two. All these are possible interpretations, but none seems to me wholly satisfactory. This, the most famous line of the play, very often quoted as expressing a deep truth, thus strikes me as difficult to interpret, and appears to belong elsewhere. On balance, I favor the first interpretation—but then nothing interesting about real humans follows.

However, the concluding part of the line—"our little life/Is rounded with a sleep"—poses no difficulties of interpretation. Life is short, and on either side of it is the equivalent of sleep, that is, unconsciousness. Death is the nothingness that follows life, and before birth we are likewise nothing. The line does, though, interestingly suggest symmetry between the times preceding and following life: the Big Sleep surrounds life at *both* ends. What is curious is that we are apt to think of the second sleep (death) as infinitely tragic, while the first we don't find tragic at all. But why is it worse not to exist for an eternity *after* one's life than not to *have* existed for an eternity *before* one's life? After all, both periods involve a very large stretch of time in which one is not alive![6] I am not saying that Shakespeare was intending to raise this conundrum, but his line naturally leads to it. We were just as dead before life as we will be after it.

EIGHT

Shakespeare and Gender

It is well known (the film *Shakespeare in Love* makes much of the fact) that in Shakespeare's time the roles of women were played by young men or boys. This is sufficiently alien to us that it is difficult to imagine what it would involve, both for the actors and for the audience. Male actors would have to present themselves as psychologically female; they would have to fully embody or realize a female character. They would have to convey a convincing impression of femaleness to the audience—not just in voice and bearing but also in the depths of personality. They would be required to project a female self (as Erving Goffman would put it). Nor was this just a matter of playing small parts with limited range; Shakespeare's women are as various and detailed as any in literature, and often occupy large tracts of the action. Just imagine what it would take for an Elizabethan lad to play the role of, say, Cleopatra! Evidently, the actors managed it with some success, or else the plays would have fallen flat. They were able to produce an *illusion* of womanhood. They could absorb a female character into their psyche and project it to an audience. And we should bear in mind that Shakespeare's women never appear as anything other than entirely female: we don't ever have the sense that they are boys pretending to be women! Desdemona, for example, does not enter the imagination as some sort of hybrid of male and female elements, as the male actor who played her must have been. Adopting the role of a Shakespearean heroine must have been no small undertaking, but evidently it was possible. The relationship between biology and psychology is sufficiently flexible to allow it. It is not that a biological male *cannot*, as a matter of natural law, play the part of a woman, with her distinctive psychology. The dramaturgical talents of the human species are creative enough to make this feasible.

I remind the reader of this familiar fact of Elizabethan theater in order to discuss its converse: that in Shakespeare we sometimes find female characters playing the part of a male. A particular character, introduced to us as female, often markedly so, is required by the action to adopt the role of a man, and she does so with aplomb and complete cogency. She can absorb and project a male self. Her natural biology is bracketed in enacting a male psychology—or so we are inclined to put it. (In fact, I think this device is designed to call into question the whole idea of a clearly defined male or female psychology—but we will get to that later.) Let us be very clear about what such an impersonation (the word is accurate) would have involved on Shakespeare's stage: a male playing a female who is playing a male. The male actor has to project a male psychology (so called) through the psychology of a female: he must embed the acted male in the acted female. Given the principle that, if X is acting Y and Y is acting Z, then X is acting Z (the transitivity of the acting relation), we can say that in such a case a male is *acting being a male*. If a boy is acting a female character that is acting being a male, then that boy is acting being a male—so he is acting being of the gender he actually is (as well as acting being the other gender). This is not, of course, generally true of acting: if a male is playing the part of a male character, he is not *acting* being a male, that is, pretending to be something he is not. But a female character that is acting the part of a male *is* pretending to be a male, and it is a male actor that is playing that female part. This is a pretty complex nexus of genders—of coincident psychologies. It suggests an enormous plasticity in gender identity, psychologically speaking.

The philosophical question at issue here is this: What kind of fact is it to possess a specific psychological gender? What makes persons the sex they are, from a psychological point of view? We know what makes persons the sex they are biologically—namely, *biology*, a certain natural fact about the world (described by the sciences of genetics and physiology). But what gives persons their sexual identity at the level of character? In particular, how fixed is this? How conventional is it? Where does it originate? The suggestion I want to make is that, for Shakespeare, there is something irreducibly *theatrical* about gender identity. Just as he adopts a theatrical model of the constitution of the self (as I discussed particularly in relation to *Hamlet*), so he regards possessing a male or female self as, at least partly, theatrical. In being psychologically male we *play the role* of a male, according to our imaginative and other resources. The boy actor on the stage plays the role of a female, but he also, in real life, plays the role of a male: he creates himself *as* male, by a process analogous to acting. It is the fact that a female character from Shakespeare can play the part of a man so well that shows that we are always acting—that the adoption of a psychological gender is essentially theatrical. In other words, the process of assuming a gender identity is intentional, creative, and optional. We are all, so to speak, self-made men (or women). Just as a character in Shakespeare can play the role of a king, or a fool, or a false friend, thereby deploying his or her natural theatrical talents, so, more radically, a character plays a particular gender role—generally, the role conventionally allotted by society. The role-playing involved in a female acting the part of a male actually spreads to all aspects of our social existence, according to the theatrical model of the self.

Let us consider a specific and instructive case: Portia playing the role of the male Doctor of Law, Balthasar, in *The Merchant of Venice*. Portia, when we first encounter her, is a beautiful princess, subservient to her dead father's wishes, and engaged upon a bizarre lottery (itself theatrical in character) for her hand in marriage—the lottery of the three caskets. She is witty and sparkling enough, but no astute logician and dialectician. When Bassanio wins her hand, she is all becoming modesty:

You see me, Lord Bassanio, where I stand,
Such as I am. Though for myself alone
I would not be ambitious in my wish
To wish myself much better, yet for you
I would be trebled twenty times myself,
A thousand times more fair, ten thousand times more rich,
That only to stand high in your account
I might in virtues, beauties, livings, friends,
Exceed account. But the full sum of me
Is sum of nothing; which, to term in gross,
Is an unlessoned girl, unschooled, unpractised;
Happy in this, she is not yet so old
But she may learn.

That last statement will be spectacularly refuted by her perfor-
mance at the play's end in the role of Balthasar the lawyer, but at pre-
sent she is playing her role as marriageable princess to perfection.
When later she conceives the idea of intervening in the trial of
Antonio (the merchant of the title) she expresses her confidence in
her acting talents. Asked by her servant Nerissa whether their hus-
bands will see them in Venice, she replies:

They shall, Nerissa, but in such a habit
That they shall think we are accomplished
With that we lack. I'll hold thee any wager,
When we are both accoutered like young men
I'll prove the prettier fellow of the two,
And wear my dagger with the braver grace,
And speak between the change of man and boy
With a reed voice, and turn two mincing steps
Into a manly stride, and speak of frays
Like a fine bragging youth, and tell quaint lies
How honorable ladies sought my love,
Which I denying, they fell sick and died.
I could not do withal.
Then I'll repent,

And wish for all that that I had not killed them;
And twenty of these puny lies I'll tell,
That men shall swear I have discontinued school
Above a twelvemonth. I have within my mind
A thousand raw tricks of these bragging Jacks
Which I will practise.

Nerissa's astonished reply is: "What, shall we turn to men?" Here Portia speaks like an actor who has done her research: she has observed her subject, noted his idiosyncrasies, catalogued his traits, and now she is ready to put on a fine performance. She knows that she can play the part of a man with cogency and credibility (certainly, she plays the part of princess wonderfully). This brave and manly front, which the male of the species so proudly affects, she finds all too easy to imitate: she will have no trouble acting the part that they themselves (somewhat woodenly) act.

When it comes to it, however, the part she must play is far more exigent. Within the court, itself a stagelike arena, she must put on a performance that is beyond anyone else there to perform. She immediately commands the court with her eloquence and probity, her concision and firmness ("I am informed throughly of the cause. Which is the merchant here, and which the Jew?"). She delivers the superb speech that begins, "The quality of mercy is not strained," exhibiting both her command of the law and its limitations as a guide to morality. First she plays the part of advocate on Shylock's behalf, acknowledging the legal correctness of his claim, with no "womanly" shrinking from the brutality to be enacted—"The court awards it, and the law doth give it," she declares. But then comes the marvelously dramatic, and clearly calculated, "Tarry a little," as she begins her logical dissection of Shylock's "bond." He can take his pound of flesh, but must shed no blood, on penalty of law, and he must cut precisely a pound, neither more nor less, under like penalty. Shylock backs down, but Portia seizes the dramatic moment, obviously relishing her performance: "Tarry, Jew," she says, to a hushed audience, and proceeds to unleash the full weight of the law on Shylock's head. She has them all in the palm of her hand, masterfully constructing her legal demonstration.

So convincing is she in the role that even her future husband does not recognize her ("Were you the doctor and I knew you not?"). She has completely transformed herself from the super-feminine, somewhat giddy princess into a sharp-minded, cool-headed legal genius. She has adopted this conventionally male role and played it far more adeptly than anyone else in the court. There is thus nothing essentially male about this role, if that means that it is tied to biological identity; it is more a matter of theatrical talent than biological destiny. And the reason she can play the role of a man so well is that this is a *role*, no matter who plays it. If a male had turned in the same performance, we would have supposed it natural to his sex; but really he would have been acting in just as theatrical a manner as Portia. It is as if Shakespeare is giving us a proof that gender is theatrical, by pointing out that a woman could precisely duplicate the performance of a man.

If we ask ourselves whether Portia retained her usual female self during her performance as a male lawyer, the answer is not clear. Certainly, there is no sign in her behavior, as thus disguised, to indicate that she is anything but what she purports to be; we do not perceive her "true" feminine nature peeping through the chinks in her acting skills. *We* are convinced that she possesses "male" characteristics, of mind and language, manner and deportment. Does she *feel* herself to be feminine beneath her disguise, as if her female self is breathing just beneath the surface? That also seems doubtful: she fully absorbs the role, taking it into her inner constitution. For the duration, she *is* a man—psychologically, intellectually. Or rather, this whole way of thinking about character falls apart. By playing the part of a man so well, she shows that there is nothing essentially *male* about it. It is not that she is pretending to be what she is not; she really becomes what she acts—mentally. She is no more inwardly female during the performance than she is inwardly male the rest of the time. All along she had the latent capacity to play the role of a crack attorney, while also being able to act the part of a princess—just as she has the latent capacity to act being a princess while playing the part of a male attorney. The question, "Which of these is her real self?" has no definitive answer. Selves are theatrical constructs, created for suitable circumstances and audiences, not essences implanted from above. She is just as "authentic" in the court scene as she is in her own court. So, at least, Shakespeare seems to be suggesting (plausibly, I think).

A similar transformation occurs in Rosalind's disguise as Ganymede in *As You Like It.* The disguise is adopted for a utilitarian end (as with Portia), namely self-protection, but one has the feeling that she enjoys the disguise for its own sake (as Portia clearly does), since she keeps it up for much longer than is strictly necessary. In the case of Rosalind, the success of the disguise is in a way greater than Portia's, at least as a theatrical feat, because she succeeds in having Phoebe fall in love with her as Ganymede. This is the ultimate in gender reversal: she can even play the role of male lover. She can project male allure, male sexuality, thus canceling her own hidden femininity. In the end, Rosalind is like nothing so much as a male/female hybrid—an "inter-sexual." And we must remember that she was played by a male actor—a male who spends most of the time acting the male that Rosalind pretends to be. The question of where personal reality ends and acting begins becomes moot.

Perhaps it is not surprising that this play contains arguably the most famous of Shakespeare's invocations of the theatrical model of life, spoken by Jaques:

All the world's a stage,
And all the men and women merely players.
They have their exits and their entrances,
And one man in his time plays many parts,
His acts being seven ages. At first the infant,
Mewling and puking in the nurse's arms.
Then the whining schoolboy with his satchel
And shining morning face, creeping like snail
Unwillingly to school. And the lover,
Sighing like furnace, with a woeful ballad
Made to his mistress' eyebrow. Then, a soldier,
Full of strange oaths, and bearded like the pard,
Jealous in honor, sudden, and quick in quarrel,

Seeking the bubble reputation
Even in the cannon's mouth. And then the justice,
In fair round belly with good capon lined,
With eyes severe and beard of formal cut,
Full of wise saws and modern instances;
And so he plays his part. The sixth age shifts
Into the lean and slippered pantaloon,
With spectacles on nose and pouch on side,
His youthful hose, well saved, a world too wide
For his shrunk shank, and his big, manly voice,
Turning again toward childish treble, pipes
And whistles in his sound. Last scene of all,
That ends this strange, eventful history,
Is second childishness and mere oblivion,
Sans teeth, sans eyes, sans taste, sans everything.

We may note three things about this emblematic passage. The first is that life is said to consist of a *succession* of distinct roles, not a single role, and not a passage from nonacting to acting—just as a professional actor plays a succession of roles. In Rosalind's case, she for a time played the part of a man in a wood, in which she acquitted herself splendidly, while playing other roles at other times. The second point is that each age is characterized by the type of *voice* deployed by the aging individual; and voice is surely the main instrument of any stage actor—as well as being vital to the successful performance of many a real-life role. The actor must have a good and adaptable voice, suiting it to the character being played; and, according to Jaques, the voice of a man is the key to his personality (Rosalind would have to deepen her voice, as would Portia). Third, the passage begins by explicitly separating male from female—not "people," it says, but "men and women." This fits the idea that that distinction is itself theatrically grounded, construed as a matter of psychology or character. Men play at being men and women play at being women, but sometimes men play women and women play men, with no real loss of authenticity. I don't think the point here has to do with homosexuality, still less transvestites and the like; I think it pertains to the theatricality of the self, as an ontological thesis. Gender boundaries may be crossed, and sexual distinctions blurred, but at the root of all this is a deep fact about human psychology: that we are all, to some degree or other, actors on a stage—we employ the techniques of actors in relation to a specific audience. The point is not that a biological male can have a "woman's personality," or vice versa; it is that the very constitution of personality has theatrical roots. As Goffman would insist, any piece of social behavior is inevitably a presentation of the self, guided and controlled by the agent, calculated to create a particular impression on the audience; and acting precisely is the intentional control of behavior so as to produce the impression of a specific self. The stage metaphor, of which Shakespeare was so fond, suggests that this theatricality is pervasive and fundamental in the human psyche. And it applies as much to acting male or female as to anything else.

These reflections on gender connect with three other Shakespearean themes we have encountered. The first is the place of free action in constituting personal identity or self. In a word: you are what you freely act. As we saw particularly in the case of *Macbeth*, Shakespeare depicts human action as shaping character, not merely flowing from it. A decision to act in a certain way—to perform a certain role—has implications for the self that ensues. There is not a fixed psychological nature from which actions derive, as water may be drawn from a well; there is more of a dynamic interplay between character and conduct. You cannot keep your soul unspotted from your deeds, in other words. The outward seeps inward, carving a path to the personality. This general thesis has application in the case of gender, because here too action plays a formative role: if someone acts in a "male" way, she will acquire "male" characteristics—she will absorb a "male" personality. Persona becomes personality. That was Macbeth's problem, but it is also, less harrowingly, true of gender-specific behavior. Or, more positively: rejoice in what you do, because it will stick. By acting *as if* she is an expert lawyer, confident and competent, Portia *becomes* these things—she absorbs them into her being. And such actions are performed *freely*, as an exercise of pure will: so personality can be an upshot of free action. Portia makes the unforced decision to play a certain role, and as a result of this exercise in volition she comes to instantiate a particular personality. Personality is not something *given* to us, out of our hands, a matter of brute biology (or astrology); it is something over which we have voluntary control. The genesis of personality is rooted in free choice for Shakespeare (though only up to a point: see the next chapter); and this applies equally to male and female personality.

Secondly, there is a connection between this conception of the self and the problem of other minds. Put crudely: we cannot straightforwardly infer a "male" mind from a male body or a "female" mind from a female body. There can be mismatches between biological gender and psychological gender. Portia gives the impression of being male in both these dimensions during the court scene, but that is contingent: the male self she brings to bear then is available to her even in her outwardly female manifestation. She harbors her "inner male" even as she is outwardly the beautiful feminine princess. Since gender is theatrical, and therefore chosen, a person may adopt a psychological gender that does not "fit" his or her biological gender; the two are not necessarily correlated. And this means that you can't infer one from the other: you can't assume that because someone has a female body she has a "female mind," and similarly for males. Regan and Goneril might well be accused of harboring male selves (in serpent form) beneath their womanly exteriors; certainly they have the hardness, harshness, and ruthlessness usually supposed the precinct of the male. The mind is something different from the body and is not infallibly revealed in it, and this impenetrability applies equally to matters of psychological gender. Let me put it this way: the people around Portia were blind to an aspect of her mind—its strongly "male" quality (in both senses of the word "quality"). We have a natural weakness for going by outward appearances (Shakespeare's target in so many of his works), but in the matter of gender, as in all other matters of psychology, that weakness can lead us into serious error. Thus the true nature of Portia's mind comes as a surprise even to her closest intimates. This, then, is another exam-

ple of the epistemological slippage between body and mind we have
noted repeatedly.

Lastly, I return to Hamlet, prince not just of Denmark, but also of
personal indeterminacy. It has sometimes been suggested that
Hamlet is an intrinsically female character, a woman dressed in
man's clothing; accordingly, he should be played by a female actor
(Sarah Bernhardt in fact played him, apparently successfully). Now I
would agree that his maleness is not strongly marked (except per-
haps in his more ribald and misogynistic moments), but the reason
is not that he is "really" female in his nature. It is that his character is
sufficiently amorphous and variable that almost any interpretation
fits it. He is, in effect, indeterminate between man and woman, psy-
chologically speaking—rather as he vacillates between poet and war-
rior, lover and hater. He is gender-neutral, perhaps, or at least not
gender-committed. "To be, or not to be"—a stoic or a fighter, he
wonders: but perhaps also male or female (in the psychological
sense). He is not strongly marked for maleness as a character
because he is not strongly marked for anything much (except a wit, a
mocker, and a wordsmith). He escapes traditional characterological
categories, including gender categories. So he makes sense as a
woman, as he also makes sense as a man: but his very indeterminacy
makes him transcend either simple category. He has the universality
of the unmade—the not yet determined. If he sometimes seems to
act in a conventionally female way—in his fussiness, his excess of
scruple, his balking at the brutish—that is because he hasn't yet
made up his mind about what character he wants his life to instanti-
ate. He will achieve a recognizable gender only when, if ever, he finds
a suitable role.

NINE

Shakespeare
and Psychology

Shakespeare was clearly fascinated by the workings of the human mind. His dramas are *inward* dramas—"psychodramas"—with much of the significant action occurring within the souls of the characters. And he looks at the human mind in the round: not merely ordinary rational waking consciousness, but also dreaming, madness, delusion, seizures, and extremes of emotion. He is interested in abnormal psychology (so-called) as much as the normal kind, and he sees how one can flow or mutate into the other. His emphasis on the theatrical aspects of personality is part of this more general interest in the mind's operations. It is often said that Shakespeare was a brilliant psychologist, meaning that he had a deep understanding of human nature; in particular, his grasp of psychological types is unparalleled. That is no doubt true, but he also approached the mind in the spirit of a scientist—he is interested in how it *works*, what the components are, and how they interact. This is part of what I have been calling Shakespeare's naturalism: he approaches the human mind as an impartial observer and recorder, noting similarities and distinctions, trying to provide an accurate account of a natural phenomenon. Odd out-of-the-way mental phenomena catch his attention. Oversimplifications are exposed. Variety is respected. Areas of ignorance are admitted to be such. In this, Shakespeare is very much like Montaigne, whose *Essays* are explicitly designed as forays into naturalistic psychology—with Montaigne himself as the primary (but not the sole) subject. Both authors aim to give us a clear portrait of human psychological nature, open to the phenomena in all their richness and complexity, and not preconditioned by some antecedent dogma or ideology, religious or scientific. Thus both authors are, above all, *candid*—unflinching, unsparing, forthright. All forms of human aggression, weakness, dishonesty, and folly are ruthlessly laid bare. Yet both acknowledge, and are sensitive to, the existence of human virtue; they do not fall for the romance of total darkness. Shakespeare gives us a panoramic perspective on the human mind, an all-inclusive accounting (as Montaigne also aims to do), as if he were aiming for a kind of completeness. No one could accuse Shakespeare of blink-eredness, of narrowness of vision. All human life appears to be there.

It might be thought that Shakespeare was laboring under a disadvantage as a naturalistic psychologist, namely that he was writing at a time when science in general, and psychology in particular, was in its infancy (had hardly even been conceived). Where could he go to discover the latest research findings on the human mind? Where were the laboratories and institutes? Which psychological experts might he consult? Surely, his knowledge of psychology must have been crude and incomplete, just a hash of folk wisdom with no scientific credentials. His knowledge of physics, chemistry, astronomy, and biology was extremely limited, given the state of these fields at the time, so must not his knowledge of psychology have been correspondingly limited? Sigmund Freud, say, was four hundred years in the future, and hardly conceivable in Shakespeare's day. How then could Shakespeare hope to say anything useful about psychology?

All that is true enough, but I think that actually the primitive state of science and psychology acted as an *aid* to Shakespeare in understanding the mind. He could be a *naturalist* without being a *scientist*. That is to say, he could observe the human mind in all its glory and oddity without feeling the need to slot his findings into some preconceived theoretical framework (this is allied to the "negative capability" Keats found in Shakespeare, which I mentioned in chapter 1). In fact, Shakespeare was in a uniquely advantageous position at the end of the sixteenth century: the old religious dogmas and lack of curiosity about nature were crumbling, and yet theoretical science had not yet imprinted itself on the intellectual outlook of mankind. No longer was it compulsory to look at man as the Bible portrayed him (or, more accurately, as the established church did)—as the embodiment of some supernatural entity called "spirit" and defined by the ethical precepts of Christianity; but neither had science schooled people in notions of law and mechanism, forces and equations, determinism and causality. In short, Shakespeare wasn't caught between the Bible and Newton's *Principia*, as if one of these had to be the ultimate model for understanding the human mind. He didn't have to view the mind through the lens of scientific mechanism *or* the lens of religious supernaturalism—as if the mind had to behave like either a billiard ball or a mystical infusion from God. Shakespeare could look at the mind without theoretical or metaphysical preconceptions, and he had a remarkably beady eye. What he offers us is the human mind *as we recognize it*—as we experience it in the marketplace and the home. He is not informing us of facts about human nature of which we have no prior knowledge (as if he were a geographer returning from distant lands); he provides instead the shock of recognition—dramatically presenting human psychology as we humans experience it. He enables us to develop the understanding we already have of our own nature. For this he has no need of recondite findings, statistical results, or clinical experience; he can proceed from common observation, adjoined to imaginative thought and supreme intelligence.

What, then, were Shakespeare's particular psychological insights or themes? Aside from the theatrical model of self, which I have already discussed at length, I think it was the recognition of hidden inexplicable forces operating on what we usually regard as the rational mind. Ordinary rationality is vulnerable, Shakespeare teaches us, to influences whose source is unclear but whose effects are palpable. We are not fully autonomous beings, in the sense that we are in control of the determinants of our thoughts, feelings, and actions.

Reason is readily usurped and warped. Insanity can be just a breath away, prowling the perimeters of ordinary rationality. The rational self is *fragile*—susceptible to all manner of forces that assail it. Thus we often don't know why we do what we do; we can give no good *reason* for our actions. We mystify ourselves, as well as others. Hamlet cannot understand why he delays the moment of revenge. Othello's calm and control crack under Iago's farfetched suggestions, till he falls frothing into a fit. Macbeth is wholly unprepared for the psychological effects of his crimes, and his imagination becomes his worst enemy. Lear has no idea what his banishment of Cordelia will do to his psyche, and his madness is the last thing he would have expected from his exalted position as king. In *A Midsummer Night's Dream* love comes from a magical potion, not reason, with human desire seen as the result of forces unknown to the conscious self (in *The Tempest*, too, love comes clothed in the irrational). All these characters think they are far more in control of themselves than they really are. They are undermined by forces operating within their own minds, as much as by external circumstances.

This point of view is formulated with notable directness in a striking speech of Shylock's in *The Merchant of Venice*. He is pressed by the court to explain why he will not accept the repayment of his debt in full and forgo the pound of flesh he is insisting upon. He replies:

> You'll ask me why I rather choose to have
> a weight of carrion flesh than to receive
> Three thousand ducats. I'll not answer that,
> But say it is my humour. Is it answered?
> What if my house is troubled with a rat,
> And I be pleased to give ten thousand ducats
> To have it baned? What, are you answered yet?
> Some men there are love not a gaping pig,
> Some that are mad if they behold a cat,
> And others when the bagpipe sings i'th' nose
> Cannot contain their urine; for affection,
> Mistress of passion, sways it to the mood

Of what it likes or loathes. Now for your answer:
As there is no firm reason to be rendered
Why he cannot abide a gaping pig
Why he a harmless necessary cat,
Why he a woollen bagpipe, but of force
Must yield to such inevitable shame
As to offend himself being offended,
So can I give no reason, nor I will not,
More than a lodged hate and a certain loathing
I bear Antonio, that I follow thus
A losing suit against him. Are you answered?

The court wishes Shylock to provide a *reason* for his insistence—a proposition that anyone can see would justify seeking the pound of flesh. Shylock answers by stressing psychological individuality and the power of what today we would call phobia. He cannot provide a reason that *anyone* can share, because his hatred results from his own peculiarities—he just happens to loathe Antonio. This is simply the way he feels. He compares his attitude to those odd, unaccountable phobias that afflict people—revulsion at gaping pigs, or cats, or bagpipes (I once saw a man on television who could not abide to be near *celery*—though other vegetables were fine). Shylock's point is that these people could not supply a *reason* for their revulsion either; it is just the way they are made, whatever the cause. It may be mysterious, but it *is so*. If Macbeth were asked why he lets his imagination get the better of him, he will not be able to justify his response; it is simply the way his mind works—and he can't do much about it. Such psychological syndromes defy rationality, and yet they are powerful shapers of conduct and emotion. Urinating at the sound of bagpipes has no conceivable justification, but that doesn't prevent some people suffering from the problem (at least according to friend Shylock). There simply are these mysterious forces that impinge on the human mind, interfering with the desires of the conscious will.

Dreams illustrate the point clearly. Dreaming is not a rational activity; it is not like trying to solve a mathematical problem or finding your way home. The sources of our dreams are obscure—and dreams are rife with phobias, enigmas, and bizarre behavior. Shakespeare clearly had a strong interest in dreams and was fully aware of their peculiarities (recall Bottom's baffled description of his "bottomless" dream in *Dream*). Dreaming and insanity are close cousins, and neither can be subsumed under canons of rationality. The forces that control dreaming and insanity are obscure and unruly. Macbeth acts like a waking dreamer, hallucinating daggers and ghosts, and Lady Macbeth relives in her sleep the villainous acts of her waking life. Shakespeare sees that we cannot separate and contrast the rational conscious mind, on the one hand, and the irrational sleeping mind of the dreamer, on the other; the unruliness of the latter seeps into the former. The conscious mind can be as subject to hidden irrational forces as the mind of the unconscious dreamer. Eruptions from elsewhere can occur in both states.

It is impossible at this point not to be reminded of Freud. Freud, like Shakespeare, was interested in the irrational, in dreaming, in fantasy, in the mental quirks that can overwhelm conscious reason, in phobias, and in neurosis. Freud certainly believed that the rational mind is subject to hidden forces that can rise up and usurp conscious reason. Shylock's list of psychic peculiarities would have been grist to the psychoanalytic mill. Both authors oppose the model of the mind that views us as rational deliberators, fully aware of, and master over, the factors that shape our actions (roughly, the *res cogitans* of Descartes). The psyche is more like a seething pit of warring factions than an orderly and unified progression of logically consequential thoughts. There is much more (and also much less) to the mind than rational calculations and transparent reasons, according to both Freud and Shakespeare. Is it correct, then, to regard Shakespeare as a kind of proto-Freud? Did he anticipate Freud's distinctive doctrines? Is Freud the up-to-date scientific version of Shakespeare? Certainly, Freud drew sustenance from Shakespeare, writing a famous essay on the Oedipal complex he thought he discerned in *Hamlet*. But how deep does the similarity go?

I think that, despite superficial appearances, it would be a serious mistake to read Freud's distinctive doctrines into Shakespeare's text. The two central Freudian concepts at issue are the unconscious and the Oedipus complex. Freud believed that the unconscious is formed by active repression, whereby unpalatable emotions and memories are suppressed and form a residue of unconscious material that influences conscious life—these being mostly sexual in nature (though also aggressive). Thus he shares with Shakespeare the idea of hidden forces operating on the conscious mind; but he gives this general idea a specific twist, via the notion of repression. Does Shakespeare believe in an unconscious in that specific sense? No doubt he believes in an unconscious in *some* sense, since he posits forces from outside the conscious mind that affect what goes on within it; but the nature of these forces is left completely unspecified. They might stem from entirely physical causes in the nervous system, having no mental reality at all: something about the physical makeup of Shylock's bagpipes phobic causes him to behave the way he does, but this has no mental characterization. There may be no explanation of this quirk at the level of psychology. It is a far cry from this very thin notion of the unconscious to Freud's theory of repressed psychological material, with its doctrine of two levels of psychological reality, the conscious and the unconscious. And I see nothing in Shakespeare to suggest *this* notion of the unconscious— the notion of material that is psychologically disturbing being buried below conscious ground. In Shylock's speech, there is no hint that his "neurotics" have repressed emotions or memories, or that anything untoward happened during their infancy. Nor does *Macbeth* ever suggest that the repressed unconscious of Macbeth is the cause of his problems. His imagination is not under his control, and its causal background must therefore lie outside his will; but there is no suggestion that repressed material in his unconscious is calling the shots. No doubt his guilt is playing a role, but he is quite conscious of that; what he doesn't know is by what mechanism his guilt is hijacking his imagination. The workings of his mind are not transparent to him—but that is *not* to say that he suffers from Freudian repression. What would he be repressing and why? He knows just how ambitious he is, and how ruthless—he has not intentionally forgotten these aspects of himself. What is the bagpipes man repressing and why? There is no hint of an answer in Shakespeare, or even the hint that there might *be* an explanation of a Freudian type. I think Shakespeare's position here is that we *just don't know* what accounts for these odd phenomena, while Freud's position is that we do know—it is the repressed unconscious doing its disruptive thing. Freud claims understanding, while Shakespeare confesses ignorance. Nature is mysterious in many ways, Shakespeare seems to be saying, and this is just one of them. He is certainly not claiming knowledge of an unconscious formed by repression of disturbing psychological elements. That is an imposition of Freud's, not Shakespeare's. Shakespeare has observed, as a naturalistic psychologist, that there are such phenomena, but he is not going so far as to produce a *theory* of them—he is not trying to be a scientist in this sense. He describes, but he does not explain; he articulates, but he does not reduce.

What about Freud's hypothesis of the Oedipus complex, the supposed love of mother and hatred of father that is supposed to afflict early psychosexual development? The standard psychoanalytic explanation of Hamlet's dilatoriness in killing his uncle is that he is really in love with his mother and wants to destroy his father, which is why he fails to exact vengeance on the uncle who killed his father; unconsciously, he is *glad* his father is dead—and now he just needs to kill his uncle in order to regain his mother. However, this is surely a very farfetched explanation of Hamlet's motivation, and it has no basis whatever in the text. Hamlet gives every impression, by word and deed, of loving his deceased father, and he shows no gratitude whatsoever toward Claudius for killing him. Nor does he seem at all fond of his mother, come to that. He is slow to kill his uncle because of his melancholy and his inability to play the theatrical role of avenger; there is no indication of repressed hatred of his father, or sexual desire for his mother, in anything he says or does. Of course, if you happen to be a theorist who is convinced that *everyone*, as a matter of psychological law, suffers from a repressed Oedipus complex, then you will attempt to subsume Hamlet under that theory. But there is nothing in the play as such to support such an interpretation, and Shakespeare is apparently quite oblivious to any Oedipal suggestions in his story. Hamlet is indeed subject to obscure forces molding his conduct (or absence of it), but these forces are not Oedipal in nature; his case is far more singular than such an account would imply. He is, it is true, disturbed and horrified by the idea of sex between his uncle and his mother; but his reason for this is the perfectly intelligible one that it so soon follows his father's death, and is close to incestuous. There is no sense in the play that he is *jealous* of his uncle—any more than he was of his father. Trying to force *Hamlet* into the Freudian template of the (alleged) Oedipus complex is procrustean in the extreme.

This takes us to a profound difference between Shakespeare's psychological outlook and Freud's. Freud is post-Newtonian and imbued with the ideal of scientific generality: a good theory of the human mind must consist of laws that specify how *any* human mind functions. Thus all (male) humans are subject to the Oedipus complex, with the resulting sexual repression, and the later manifestations of that repression (females get their analogous Electra complex). There is psychological *uniformity* across people. Human personality is fundamentally invariant. But Shakespeare is pre-Newtonian and hence not dazzled by the ideal of universal law. Accordingly, his characters possess a rich and irreducible variety. They all have sensation, passion, reason, will, and imagination (in varying combinations and strengths), but their individuality is very marked. You never feel you are meeting the same person twice, watching identical psychological machinery grind through its routines. Even when characters are in some respects similar—as with, say, Iago in *Othello* and Edmund in *Lear*—clear differences are indicated. There is never any sense that different individuals are just the working out of the same fundamental personality type—whereas this is Freud's basic assumption. Shakespeare is acutely sensitive to the variability of human personality, and also to the difficulty of appreciating that fact. He has no wish to assimilate, to reduce, to level. In this he is the exact opposite of Freud (and many another psychologist), who always claimed to find uniformities lurking behind surface variety. Freud is forever subsuming different phenomena under the same rubric, with sexual repression the driving force of almost everything, like Newton unifying the fall of an apple and the movements of the planets—dreams, say, turning out to share the same deep structure as slips of the tongue. Insight, in this scientific way of thinking, is identified with generalizing, with finding a common cause. But Shakespeare is content to recognize variety, to celebrate it even. Each human being, in Shakespeare's universe, is an original, not a variation on a prototype. Hamlet would not have allowed Iago to bamboozle him, as Othello did; Macbeth would never be as slow to act as Hamlet; Portia would not have permitted herself to get into the mess that Cordelia and Desdemona do. It is not just that Shakespeare is a good enough artist to avoid repetition; it is that he is making a *point* about human psychology—that it is infinitely various. He feels under no pressure to emulate Newton in producing a general theory of human traits, the analogue of Newton's law of gravity, since Newton was a thing of the future. The Freudian idea that *everyone* (male) is sexually in love with his mother and desires his father's death would, I surmise, strike Shakespeare as preposterous. Even within the same family offspring can have widely divergent personalities—as with Regan and Goneril, compared to Cordelia (not much love of father from the first two). The grounds of these differences remain a mystery, for Shakespeare, but he is quite clear that such differences exist. And even today the basis of personality differences remains obscure (the usual talk of genes and environment is pretty much hand-waving without much more detailed causal hypotheses). We still really have only the sketchiest of ideas about why we are the way we are. In sum: Freud is *looking* for psychological generalities about human character (and thinks he has found them), whereas Shakespeare is not even in that line of business—he is the faithful student of natural variety and irreducible singularity.

If I were asked what most distinguishes Shakespeare's psychology from that of his predecessors and contemporaries (as well as descendants), I would say it is his emphasis on imagination. The traditional psychology of disparate mental faculties posited sensation, reason, passion, and will, with imagination tacked on as a by-product of sensation; imagination, in the form of mental images, was regarded as just a degenerate remnant of sensation. The imagination was not accorded a significant originative role, but was taken to be merely a faded residue of perception.[1] In Shakespeare, however, the imagination becomes active, even dominant, and it is held to run all through mental life. Imagination is what unites the lover, the poet, and the lunatic (according to A Midsummer Night's Dream); it is what unhinges Macbeth; it works to inflame Othello's jealousy; and Hamlet is highly imaginative in speech and thought process. Dreaming and madness, frequent Shakespearean themes, are the imagination uncoupled from reason, left to its own peculiar devices. Imagination is not just an idle aftereffect of perception; it is a potent source of emotion, and hence action. It is a full-blown mental faculty in its own right, in Shakespeare's handling of it. And it puts the notion of creativity at the heart of the human psyche, since imagination and creativity are interwoven. In a certain sense, then, everyone is an imaginative artist for Shakespeare, because everyone has the power to generate imaginary worlds, for good or ill.

What Shakespeare indisputably excels at is giving us detailed portraits of human vices and failings—as well as, sometimes, of human virtues. He dissects ambition, jealousy, arrogance, evil, irresoluteness, resentment, naivete, credulity, and all the rest, with remarkable acuity and subtlety. He is a moral psychologist, first and foremost. He knows that human psychology and ethical evaluation are never far apart. For the human mind has considerations of morality built into its very structure. We cannot really describe a person's psychology without adverting to moral matters, since virtues and vices make up character. One person is described as kind, generous, open-minded, and judicious; another is said to be cruel, miserly, closed-minded, and rash: these are all aspects of character, and they are all morally evaluative. There is no value-free description of human psychological nature. This takes us to the topic of the next chapter.

TEN

Shakespeare and Ethics

Questions of right and wrong could hardly be more paramount in Shakespeare's works; the plays are essays in moral . . . moral what? What kind of moralist *is* Shakespeare? Hazlitt makes these intriguing remarks about Shakespeare as moralist, in the course of his discussion of *Measure for Measure*:

> Shakespeare was in one sense the least moral of all writers; for morality (commonly so called) is made up of antipathies; and his talent consisted in sympathy with human nature, in all its shapes, degrees, depressions, and elevations. The object of the pedantic moralist is to find out the bad in everything: his was to show that "there is some soul of goodness in things evil" . . . In one sense, Shakespeare was no moralist at all: in another, he was the greatest of all moralists. He was a moralist in the same sense in which nature is one. He taught what he had learnt from her. He showed the greatest knowledge of humanity with the greatest fellow-feeling for it.[1]

I sense an important bushel of truth in these remarks, though as they stand they are hardly pellucid. Hazlitt is opposing two senses of the word "moralist" and suggesting that in one sense Shakespeare is a moralist (a great one), while in the other he is not. The second sense is easier to elucidate: Shakespeare was not in the business of issuing condemnations, or instituting social reforms, or chastising evildoers. His writings are not hortatory, not preachy, and not didactic. His plays are not ethical precepts dressed up in dramatic form. There are, to be sure, places where some moral sentiment is allowed to breathe, where a spirit of advocacy seems evident. I think here of Lear's late and hard-won compassion for the poor: "Poor naked wretches, wheresoe'er you are, That bide the pelting of this pitiless night, How shall your houseless heads and unfed sides, Your looped and windowed raggedness, defend you/From seasons such as these? O, I have ta'en/Too little care of this! Take physic, pomp, Expose thyself to feel what wretches feel, That thou mayst shake the superflux to them/And show the heavens more just." It is hard to read this eloquent plea for social justice as anything other than Shakespeare revealing his own sympathy for the poor and downtrodden, and criticizing those in power who refuse to acknowledge such injustices. But, in the context of the play, the meaning of the passage is primarily to indicate Lear's transformation of character, from arrogantly royal to compassionately human (or animal). We have no awkward sense of the playwright intruding didactically on the action. There is also a moralistic passage from *The Merchant of Venice*, put into the otherwise unsympathetic mouth of Shylock, addressed to the Venetian court: "You have among you many a purchased slave/Which like your asses and your dogs and mules, You use in abject and in slavish parts/Because you bought them. Shall I say to you/'Let them be free, marry them to your heirs. Why sweat they under their burdens? Let their beds/Be made as soft as yours, and let their palates/Be seasoned with such viands'? You will answer 'The slaves are ours.' So do I answer you. The pound of flesh which I demand of him/Is dearly bought. 'Tis mine, and I will have it." Now admittedly Shylock's fervent abolitionism is mainly casuistry, aiming as it does to bolster his claim on Antonio's flesh; but he presents a good case, and again it is hard to deny that Shakespeare must have known this (and perhaps delighted in the incongruity of placing it thus). The injustice of slavery is certainly strongly and persuasively registered in the speech. Shakespeare obviously understood well

enough that brute asymmetries of power account for such differ-
ences in social standing, and that while some prosper others lan-
guish through no fault of their own. What we would now call social
inequality is something of which he was clearly quite aware.
Shakespeare was, in this limited sense, a "liberal." But such passages
are rare and somewhat incidental. No Shakespeare play can be
described as primarily designed to achieve some political or moral
end. Social reform was not the point of his art. Nor does he seem
concerned to express his own antipathy (to use Hazlitt's term)
toward his individual characters; vividly presented as they are,
authorial censure is not much in evidence. Iago is manifestly a despi-
cable swine of a man, but we don't get treated to anything much in
the way of overt condemnation (though Emilia certainly gives him a
mouthful). The audience doesn't feel that it is being cautioned about
becoming Iago-like. Moral knuckle rapping is not Shakespeare's
style. His concern is far more with realistic and dramatic portrayal.

In what sense, then, *is* Shakespeare a moralist? For Hazlitt is cer-
tainly right that there is scarcely a writer in the English language into
whose works moral content is more strongly infused. The texture of
the plays pullulates with questions of right and wrong, of good and
evil. The question is *how* Shakespeare interweaves drama, psychol-
ogy, and morality. I think Hazlitt is wrong to suppose that
Shakespeare was anxious to show that there is always "some soul of
goodness in things evil," as if he wanted to mitigate outright evil in
people. He certainly did not believe, on the evidence of his plays,
that everyone, no matter how overtly nasty, has a heart of gold, or
even that the blackest soul has a sliver of decency in it. Iago is unre-
servedly evil—there is no "soul of goodness" in him. The same is
true of Regan and Goneril, who are quite free of redeeming qualities
(Edmund has a last-minute spasm of decency). Shakespeare's point
is not that conventional morality is too harsh or too black-and-white
or too obsessed with wickedness and sin. On the contrary, he has an
extremely bleak view of human wickedness, as of the cosmos itself
(as I argued in respect of *King Lear*). However, I think Hazlitt is right
to draw attention to Shakespeare's affinity with nature. Indeed, that
fits with the general thesis of this book, namely that Shakespeare was

a kind of naturalist—an artist whose reportorial power was intended to lie as close to nature as possible. If Shakespeare could have merged with nature (while retaining his artistic powers), he would have. He brings morality into the heart of his dramas because *morality is part of nature*. It is part of what constitutes the thing we call human nature—our nature as responsible and autonomous persons.

For Shakespeare's characters are, above all, ethical beings. They are *defined* by their moral qualities, their virtues and vices, their propensities toward good and bad. They make an ethical impression on the audience, from the moment of their introduction. We cannot see them as anything other than morally constituted beings, living embodiments of vice and virtue. Thus they elicit from us the attitudes appropriate to moral evaluation—admiration and disgust, approval and condemnation. In witnessing a Shakespeare play our consciousness is engaged morally in an intense and unavoidable way. The plays are *about* good and evil, and the human relationship to these ethical categories. What makes Shakespeare a great moralist, as Hazlitt intimates, is that he is expert at expressing and dramatizing moral questions—at exposing the *workings* of good and evil, in the individual soul and in social relationships (especially families). This is what I meant in the last chapter by saying that Shakespeare is a great *moral* psychologist. He depicts psychology morally and morality psychologically. Not that he is the only writer to do that—it might be said to be the aim of all serious literature—but he did it supremely and influentially. His depiction of Iago, say, is an essay primarily in the inner psychology of evil—not so much in its outward effects (or even its causes). He wants us to enter fully into the evil mind, properly hushed. Likewise, his depiction of Macbeth is a portrait of the ruthlessly ambitious mind—of what the vice of ruthless ambition is like psychologically. He is describing the ethical *in* the psychological.

When I say that morality is part of nature, I mean that in a quite specific sense. Human character is defined, in large part, by the virtues and vices. If I ask you to describe a friend of yours, you will proceed by listing his or her virtues and vices (as well as other traits): you will say she is generous or kind or considerate or selfless; or

mean or self-centered or short-tempered or vain. You will list traits
that have a moral dimension. Such descriptions imply moral evalua-
tions—attitudes of approval and disapproval. If you were forbidden
from using such concepts, your description of your friend would be
thin and uninformative. So, to describe human nature at all fully and
accurately, we must make use of moral categories—because human
character is *constituted* by virtues and vices. It is constituted by these
moral qualities just as much as it is constituted by nonmoral quali-
ties—height and weight, intelligence, sense of humor, extraversion
and introversion. Virtues and vices are qualities people intrinsically
have—they are part of their nature as persons. Thus nature presents
these qualities to our observation, and if we are out to record what
nature contains we must include them. They are not constituents of
some supernatural transcendent realm, removed from the hum-
drum realities of human nature. They are, in one sense, entirely nat-
ural properties—they are part of what human beings naturally *are*.
They are *in* nature, not *above* it.

Accordingly, Shakespeare, as a dramatic naturalist, must give us a
rendering of this part of nature. The sense in which he is a great
moralist is that he is an expert recorder of nature in its moral aspect.
And not merely a disinterested recorder: for Shakespeare is a moral
being, like the rest of us. As he records, he also evaluates; or better,
he provides us with the materials with which to evaluate. All he
needs to do is accurately describe; it is left to the audience's moral
sense to supply the moral assessment. Thus we find ourselves
engaged morally, though the author has not proffered any moral
opinions of his own: *he doesn't need to*. All he needs to provide is
insight, understanding, and descriptive accuracy (as well as poetic
expressiveness and so on); our own capacity for moral judgment will
take care of the rest. His task is essentially *cognitive*: he must share his
knowledge of moral psychology with the audience, leaving the eval-
uative part to them. It is what Shakespeare *knows* of humanity that
distinguishes him as a moralist—not the rightness of his ethical pro-
nouncements. What he does is make himself, as author, morally
transparent—so that we don't see his moral opinions, but see instead
the reality he is depicting, in all its moral glory (and ignominy). He

shows us moral reality, without commentary. His aim as author is to disappear morally.

And yet there is something more to it than that (which is more or less the orthodox view of what a dramatic artist must do). Shakespeare's treatment of moral matters is not *clinical*: he is not the scientist peering disinterestedly into the microscope and monotonously recording his findings. He is not morally detached (if he were, we might also be). There is, one wants to say, *humanity* about his recordings—what Hazlitt calls his "fellow-feeling." This is hard to articulate, but Shakespeare seems to present a moral stance of his own toward humanity in the round—a kind of brotherly compassion. It is not tolerance exactly—it could hardly be said that he tolerates Iago—but it partakes of that quality. It is the feeling we have that he is *with* his characters, that he and they occupy the same world, that nothing is alien to him. Certainly, his esteem for his virtuous characters is palpable (Desdemona, Cordelia, Edgar), and his way with human imperfection is always one of comprehension (all the tragic heroes). It is as if he always wants to forgive; he doesn't enjoy condemnation. He is pained by humanity, also amused by it, but he wishes it well. I don't sense misanthropy in Shakespeare, though disillusionment seems evident; there is no harshness in his portraits, nothing icy or vindictive. Perhaps he is most to be compared to a disappointed lover—one who had great hopes for humanity, but found his hopes crushed. And this too is a kind of moral stance: don't turn away from human nature; don't refuse to engage with it. Although Shakespeare himself is conspicuously absent from his plays, an attitude of authorial engagement is pervasive. Every character must be given his due, artistically, no matter how loathsome or low or lightweight he may be. Everyone deserves attentive description.

Can we construct any ranking of the virtues and vices, as Shakespeare's plays present them? Which virtue is primary, and what is the principal vice? I don't mean to ask which virtues and vices did Shakespeare himself think to be the primary ones—that is not a question to which we are ever going to be able to provide a firm answer; I mean, what do the plays themselves tell us about the primacy of the virtues and vices? The question does not permit of a rigorously fortified answer, but some impressions may be recorded. In line with everything I have said so far, I would nominate *deception* as the number one vice and *honesty* as the number one virtue, so far as Shakespeare's text is concerned. The chief weapon of the villainous Shakespearean characters is always deception, and not, say, outright brutality: Claudius's deception in the murder of his brother; Iago's deception of Othello; Macbeth's deception of the assassinated Duncan; Edmund's deception of his father and brother; Regan's and Goneril's deception of their father. Some of these characters find deception easier to pull off than others, but all fall into it with remarkable alacrity, as if it were a way of life for them, a matter of course. Some are veritable artists of deception, raising it to a high level of expertise, with many a bell and whistle. Iago doesn't seem all that keen on acts of violence themselves, but he certainly relishes his deceptive scheming. Deception is not just a necessary means to nefarious ends, but an evil end in its own right. It is a basic form of power over other people, an assertion of individual will. To deceive someone is to destroy his relationship to the truth, to alienate him from the real world. And lying is a kind of insult to the other person's intelligence, as well as an abrogation of trust. It undermines community and cooperation. It attempts to make a fool out of the other person. It compromises language as a means for the transmission of knowledge.[2] Iago's kind of massive, persistent, elaborate lie is an attempt to create an entire false world for the victim to believe in—a delusion of dreamlike proportions. It is painful to observe a person who has been deluded by lies, who lives in an unreal world built on misrepresentation. And the exposure of the lie occasions extremes of anger and a sense of betrayal. Shakespeare is right to give it the ethical prominence he does. Evil intentions almost always need a shield, a cover, and deception is what gives such intentions traction.

Honesty is correspondingly the primary virtue in Shakespeare. His morally exemplary characters are first and foremost purveyors of the truth—candid to a fault. One thinks of Desdemona's guileless endorsement of Cassio's suit, and her inability to understand Emilia's tolerance of infidelity and the deception that accompanies it. She is always plainspoken, forthright, and accurate in her statements. Cordelia too seems incapable of lying, even when morally that might be the better course (as in her refusal to exaggerate her love for her father). Horatio is also notably straightforward. And there are many minor characters, from fools to madmen, gravediggers to servants, who speak the truth plainly and without circumspection. Dishonesty is the mark of the schemer, while honesty is the mark of someone with nothing to hide. This is why there is no greater villain in Shakespeare than someone who has a reputation for honesty but is actually anything but—as with the constantly commended "honest Iago." That is an inversion of the greatest vice for the greatest virtue, and it shows that the detection of moral qualities is by no means easy.

Deception is also, at a more philosophical level, a misuse of our very nature as embodied minds. Because the mind is essentially hidden, relative to the body, and can only be inferred from what the body publicly provides, deception arises from disjoining the two. The honest person knows he is inherently psychologically opaque to others and tries to overcome the epistemological abyss by offering reliable signs of his inner being; he tries to compensate for the structural problem of other minds. But the dishonest person exploits his essential invisibility, making his body misrepresent his mind. He capitalizes on the weakness inherent in the other's position, trading on that weakness for his own ends. He knows that the other cannot see inside his soul, and he seizes on that fact to present a false appearance. He exploits the other's epistemological limitations, instead of helping to overcome them. The deceiver is therefore like someone who uses another person's innate handicap against him. Knowing that the other is in effect deaf and blind with respect to what is going on inside his mind, he decides to exploit that deficiency for his own ends. But the honest person makes a sincere effort to guide and assist the handicapped other, providing just the right clues to reveal her inner reality. Honesty is helping the afflicted, while dishonesty is exploiting the affliction. Truthfulness and sincerity are ways to mend the divide between mind and body, while their opposites revel in, and abuse, that divide.

Ambition comes in second, for Shakespeare—or rather, ruthless ambition does. Macbeth is ambitious to be king and might have become so if he had waited, but (egged on by his wife) he pushes scruple aside to realize his ambitions. Iago was ambitious for promotion and furious when Cassio was preferred over him (his ambition then turned deadly). Claudius killed his own brother to be king and possess the woman he desired (his sister-in-law). Regan and Goneril are ambitious to be powerful queens, even if it means trampling over their father and sister. Ambition, in this sense, is yearning for what you do not deserve, and resenting not having it. It entails the use of immoral means to achieve the end in question. Ordinary ambition—the desire for one's own betterment—is not in itself a vice, but it can easily slide into one. Ambition becomes a vice when it is married to impatience or unscrupulousness or simple insensitivity. Shakespeare must have been ambitious, but, to judge from his work, he earned his success; there will have been others of his time with like ambitions and less success—and who might have resented his. He would likely have had some acquaintance with ambition of the ruthless and resentful kind. The trouble with ambition is that it is invariably competitive: what one person gains, the other loses. One person always gains success at someone else's expense, as the real world is constructed—even when the ambition is fairly implemented. In Shakespeare, this element of competitiveness is strongly marked: one person goes up as another comes down. Hence ambition is inherently destructive of others, which is why it often involves the death of the rival. Shakespeare sees that ambition is always, at bottom, interpersonal conflict, with the standing temptation toward immoral means of advancement.

Hard-heartedness is, I would say, third on Shakespeare's list. Regan and Goneril have it in the extreme—toward their father, notably, but also toward the blinded Gloucester. It is deadening of feeling, a willed rejection of compassion. (Iago is not exactly hard-hearted: he never had a heart to deaden, and compassion is simply outside his sphere of comprehension.) But hard-heartedness, in less extreme forms, is quite common in Shakespeare. It comes out, disturbingly, in the attitudes of fathers toward their daughters, particularly when it comes to marriage. Fathers are forever ignoring the pleas of their daughters to marry the man they love, turning a stony indifference toward their daughters' wishes (Egeus's attitude toward Hermia's desire to marry Lysander in *A Midsummer Night's Dream* is a good example, and *Romeo and Juliet* is built around the same theme). Hamlet, to his discredit, displays considerable hard-heartedness toward Ophelia, occasioning her death by probable suicide. Edmund is simply a callous bastard. Lady Macbeth schools herself in hardness of heart (she is a willing pupil), memorably telling her hesitant husband: "I have given suck, and know/How tender 'tis to love the babe that milks me. I would, while it was smiling in my face, Have plucked my nipple from his boneless gums/and dashed the brains out, had I so sworn/as you have done to this." Macbeth himself has a heart of purest flint by play's end (he orders his rival's children butchered). There is no shortage of emotional calcification in Shakespeare, and with it brutality and murder (the blinding of Gloucester being perhaps the most searing). It is the most terrifying of vices (if that is not too weak a word), because it can permit the cruelest of acts; and it is impervious to moral appeal. I think Shakespeare finds it commonplace, in varying degrees; true sensitivity of heart is more rarely encountered in his universe. The numbing of the soul he finds more routine than its continuing receptivity. Shakespeare's characters inhabit a harsh world, and tenderheartedness is unlikely to survive its rigors.

Let me finally mention humor in this catalogue of sins and graces. Is a sense of humor something that connotes goodness of character in Shakespeare? There is a conventional idea that the evil man is dour and humorless, while the pure of heart are always ready with a winning laugh. Nothing like this, however, is to be found in Shakespeare's world. Fools and jesters are apt to be full of humor, professionally so, but they tend not to be full-blooded characters; they are certainly not supposed to be particularly virtuous. The wittiest of Shakespeare's characters, I would say, is Hamlet, but his humor is apt to be mocking, off-color, and downright tasteless; it comes not in the service of light and munificence, but as a reflection of his own torment and turmoil. He makes you laugh, but uncomfortably (as when he mockingly replies to Ophelia's desperately sincere "I think nothing, my lord," with the flippant "That's a fair thought to lie between a maid's legs"). Humor, in Hamlet's mouth, is a means of diversion, of distancing; he is not some jolly bundle of laughs. Falstaff in the *Henry* plays is amusing and likable in a roguish way, though not conventionally moral. And of course there are many other characters, of varying virtue, in Shakespeare with something funny to say. But Iago, of all people, is depicted as quite a comedian: he brims with witticisms, with humorous paradoxes, with gibes and one-liners. He is always sniggering about something. He finds the nastily funny phrase ("Your daughter and the Moor are now making the beast with two backs," he remarks to Brabanzio). He derives tremendous amusement from his wicked plot, and regards his victims as risible clowns. His gruffly jocose manner is no doubt helpful in concealing his inner evil, but it is not just an act to cover his designs; he really does have a developed sense of humor. Indeed, it is integral to his wickedness, since it is cynical and ironic, dismissive and unfeeling. Nor can we report that Shakespeare's unqualifiedly virtuous characters have much in the way of wit: Desdemona and Cordelia, say, are far too serious to go in for humorous sallies. Portia can be witty and satirical, but here too this seems incidental to her virtues (she is all seriousness when she gets to the trial of Antonio). All in all, humor in Shakespeare bears little direct relation to virtue. It is morally neutral, if not skewed toward the bad end of the moral spectrum.

I should consider one other question: to what extent is Shakespeare's morality religiously inspired or biblically based? Of course, he lived at a time in which morality was, at least officially, derived from the teachings of the church, and was supposed to enjoy divine backing. To be good was to be approved by God; to be bad was to be disapproved by Him. God's justice was supposed to reveal itself in the world, and in the afterlife. Sainthood was conceived as a dispensation from God, while wickedness was an effusion of the Devil. Did Shakespeare absorb this traditional way of thinking about morality? It is quite clear to me that he did not; his moral thinking is entirely secular. That is not to say that he had no belief in the Christian God—this is not a matter on which we can hope to have any decisive information—but it is to say that, as morality is presented in his plays, it bears no stamp of religion. The virtues and vices of the characters are presented as natural facts about them, sometimes as a matter of birth, not results of communication with God or Satan. Iago, indeed, is far too egotistical to suppose that his evil might come from beyond himself. Characters very rarely pray, an exception being Claudius when Hamlet has the opportunity to kill him—and he is a villain. The Bible is not quoted as a source of moral authority. The impression given (and it is particularly strong in *Lear*) is that right and wrong are human matters—not reflections of a supernatural netherworld. There is never so much as a hint that Edmund might be the plaything of Satan, or that Cordelia is God's emissary.

This is of a piece with Shakespeare's entrenched naturalism: he represents the human world as self-contained, and as continuous with nature, not as beholden to a divine (or satanic) reality. The moral dimension of man is as much a natural fact about him as eating, drinking, and talking. I am not saying that Shakespeare has no truck at all with the supernatural: he does make use of assorted witches, ghosts, soothsayers, sorcerers, sprites, and spirits. But these play no part in constituting the moral being of his characters; they are auxiliaries to the action, not elements of the human moral drama. We are never encouraged to believe that to be virtuous or vicious is to have a soul that either God or the Devil has left a deposit in. Neither is there any sense that God is supervising the proceedings, doling out punishments and rewards according to the moral standing of the agents. The universe seems to operate with sublime indifference to the moral status of human beings, visiting suffering on the virtuous and prosperity on the wicked in equal measure. When the wicked perish it is typically through their own actions and the efforts of the relatively virtuous. No act of God ever steps in to vanquish the wicked before they have done their evil work. From an ethical point of view, the supernatural has been expunged from Shakespeare's worldview. Nor is the figure of Christ ever offered as a paradigm of virtue. Shakespeare's ethics seem to come from somewhere else entirely.

ELEVEN

Shakespeare and Tragedy

What is the general shape of a Shakespearean tragedy? What do Shakespeare's tragic plays have in common? What is the essence of tragedy, as Shakespeare conceives it? If we look at *Hamlet, Othello, Macbeth,* and *King Lear* (the canonical Shakespearean tragedies), what pattern emerges? These plays form, it seems, a natural aesthetic kind (as do his comedies), and we ought to be able to say something general about the class. Of course, it may be that nothing general can be said—that there is no common essence here. Wittgenstein accustomed us to the notion of an indefinable but unified concept, a concept that does not work by having an analysis in terms of necessary and sufficient conditions.[1] His famous example was the concept *game*: if we think of all the things we call games, we will not find a common thread running through them, since they vary so enormously (compare football and chess, say, or solitaire and hopscotch). Instead, Wittgenstein insisted, there is a whole network of similarities—what he called a "family resemblance"—that holds instances of the concept together, with no shared essence. Following this conception, the concept *tragedy* might be claimed to be a family resemblance concept, so that the plays we bring under that concept are united by nothing more than rough overlaps and vague resemblances; there is, accordingly, nothing useful we can say by way of general definition or analysis. That is a theoretical possibility, but I think we should explore the concept first before throwing up our hands; we should make an effort to find out whether we can provide a useful analysis of the concept before declaring that there is no such analysis. And I believe we shall see that we can provide an illuminating account of the essence of Shakespearean tragedy (I will not inquire as to whether this account can be applied to everything we call tragedy). There are, I believe, common elements to each of Shakespeare's great tragic plays that explain why we so naturally group them together. What, then, are these elements?

The first and most obvious element is *death*. In each of the tragedies the protagonist dies: the person named in the title of the play meets his end. He is not the only one, of course; typically, members of his family (wife, parent, children) also die—those emotionally close to him. The villains of the piece die too: Claudius, Iago (though not during the action of the play—but we are assured of his execution), Macbeth and his wife, Lear's wicked daughters, the bastard Edmund, and the traitor Cornwall. And various others, innocent or tainted, likewise meet violent ends. A Shakespearean tragedy is drenched in death; its color is death. We are also made *witness* to the death of the protagonists: powerful images of death and dying are presented to us. The reality of death is brought fully home to the audience. And surely, we call these plays tragic precisely because they eventuate in death: it is the death of the protagonist that is tragic—this is a "tragic death" (as opposed to the other kind). The plays also involve great suffering, the onset of insanity, drastic diminishment, loss of reputation, even maiming; but it is the death of the central figures that qualifies the events as genuinely tragic.

It is worth pondering why this is so. Could there be a tragedy that did not involve death, but only something short of it? Perhaps; but it would not be a *Shakespearean* tragedy. There is undoubtedly something terrible about Gloucester's blinding, but it is not itself a tragic event (unless we see blindness as the analogue of death—the death of a sense). Othello's suffering is frightful to behold, but by itself does not amount to tragedy. Lear's insanity is infinitely sad, but does not rise to the level of the tragic (unless, again, we think of madness as the end of the self). Macbeth's torments are searing, but they do not by themselves evoke the sense of a tragic end. Only death—with its irrevocable finality, its sense of utter annihilation—can give us the authentic feel of the tragic. Why? Is it because it reminds us of the basic tragedy of life—that we must all die? Is this the central tragic fact? No, because the fact of death is not itself tragic: that is, Shakespeare's plays are not tragedies simply because they contain this bare fact. They contain it in a particular *way* (the nature of which it is our purpose to examine). Mere accidental death or death from disease and old age are not tragic facts in Shakespeare's tragedies, and seldom (if ever) occur. Such deaths may be sad, but they are not the stuff of *tragedy*. The critical question is what *effect* the death of Shakespeare's protagonists has on the audience. And how does this effect differ from the effects of other sorts of calamity suffered by the characters?

One possible suggestion is that tragic death makes us recognize the futility of life, since it can be snuffed out for so little reason. If the lives of these great figures can be extinguished so easily, so point-lessly, what point can there be in our own petty lives? If great souls cannot be immortal, what significance can there be in the lives of lesser beings? Thus, on this suggestion, we come away from a Shakespearean tragedy resigned to the meaninglessness of our lives. Death is central to tragedy, then, because of the shadow it casts over life: it makes us value life less, and hence we become more resigned to losing it. However, I think this suggestion is the exact opposite of the truth. Death in a Shakespearean tragedy does not have the effect of lessening our attachment to life, or making life seem cheap and dispensable—as if what can end so abruptly and gratuitously could not have had much value all along. On the contrary, in Shakespeare's tragedies the deaths of the protagonists remind us of how *valuable* life is—of how *much* is lost when death supervenes. The plays achieve this aim by presenting individuals in whom the force of life is exceptionally strong. Shakespeare's protagonists are always excep-tional beings, and along two dimensions. First, they are socially exceptional: they are kings or princes or (in the case of Othello) prominent generals—so that in their individual lives the lives of many others are bound up. But second, and more significant, they are *inwardly* exceptional: they have spiritual intensity, magnitude of soul. The flame of life burns strong in them. Hamlet is a kind of wayward genius, a fizzing ball of verbal pyrotechnics and trenchant reflection; he is loved and admired by all. Othello is noble, dignified, commanding, and passionate; he is greatly valued by the state (despite his alien hue); Desdemona loves his inner spirit. Macbeth is a brave and effective soldier, but also a passionate and imaginative soul, devoted to his wife; his mind is a cauldron of contradictory impulses, bubbling and spewing forth. Lear, for all his folly, is a man of towering emotion, of searing eloquence, of enormous wounds; he is a lightning storm of intense feeling. Each of these characters is a dense concentration of life forces—not "larger than life," but life in its condensed essence. They are not conventionally "good" people, but there is no denying their exceptionality. They take life at full throttle.

And their death accordingly produces a very specific effect—namely, an impression of what A. C. Bradley called *waste*.[2] We feel, in watching a Shakespearean tragedy, that these exceptional lives have been wasted, thrown away. When such a life is ended something very significant—something very *large*—has been lost. Thus the death of a character like this brings home to us how vital and significant life is. We are presented with a character whose life is magnified, beyond the normal, and when it ends we sense the end of something magnificent—not in the moral sense, but in the sense of sheer natural force. We see that something truly great has ended. That great thing has been wasted, since the death was not in the service of some larger good. It need not have happened. It was mandated neither by nature nor duty. And this sense of enormous waste only arises because of the magnitude of what has been extinguished.

Thus, the reason that death is a critical component in Shakespeare's tragedies is that only death can make us recognize the importance of life. Other types of calamity leave the person alive, and hence still manifesting the life force. Only death puts a definitive end to life, and by representing the absence of life we appreciate its presence. Death is, as it were, the great backdrop to life—its frame, the dark expanse around the spotlight. In a sense, then, a

Shakespearean tragedy is *about life*, by contrasting it with death. The real tragedy is not the inevitability of death or its eternality or the poverty of life; it is the very richness and power of life, and the fact that it can be brought pointlessly to an end. It is the fact that *such a thing* ends that is tragic. The play is really about *this* thing, not the death that throws it into relief. The death of the hero is just a means to the end of exhibiting his life. All dramatic works exhibit life in one way or another, but only tragedy exhibits it against the background of death. Death is crucial to its effect precisely because life can best be appreciated against the reality of its absence. This is why suffering and loss, though they are ingredients of Shakespearean tragedy, are not of its essence.

But we have not yet said what it is about death in Shakespeare's plays that confers tragedy upon them. After all, the protagonists could have died in any number of ways and the same blazing life would have ended. If Macbeth had fallen off his horse, or Othello eaten bad fish, or Hamlet knocked his head on the door, or Lear had a heart attack, then the same people would have met their end—the same vitality would have been terminated. But this would not a tragedy make. The death has to occur in a specific way for the effect to be tragic; and the hard question is what exactly this way is. We now know that death is a *necessary* condition for tragedy, but it is clearly not *sufficient*—the death has to come about in a specific fashion. The death has to be *caused* in a particular way, and our next question is what this causation must comprise.

The usual answer to that question is that the tragic death must result from the *character* of the person who dies: the person must have a hand in his or her own death. This is clearly true of Shakespeare's tragic protagonists (though it is less clearly true of subsidiary characters in the plays); but it is very vague as it stands—and it runs into the problem that simple suicide, which is a case of a person causing his own death if anything is, does not itself count as tragic, as opposed to sad or regrettable or pathetic. The person's character must lead to his death in a particular way, which we have still not yet identified. The classic Aristotelian answer to the question is that a tragedy is a story in which an otherwise noble person has an isolated flaw of character that leads to his death—the "tragic flaw theory"[3] We need the nobility if we are to sympathize with the character and regard his death as a waste, and we also need the idea of a flaw to see justice, or at least appropriateness, in the final death. It is the flaw that leads to the tragic outcome, and the outcome is tragic because the flaw occurs in someone otherwise admirable. Something bad leads to something bad, in other words, but the badness does not belong to an outright villain (there is nothing tragic about Iago's death). In the case of Hamlet, then, we have his irresoluteness; Othello has the weaknesses of credulity and a jealous nature; Macbeth has a lust for power and position; Lear is vain and imperious. These flaws are what power the tragedy, according to the Aristotelian view, producing the sense of tragedy in the audience. The protagonists are, to some degree, responsible for their own deaths, because they let their fatal flaw dominate their otherwise fine nature.

I think this view is itself fatally flawed. First, the nobility part: Is it really true that each of these Shakespearean characters has an intrinsically noble nature qualified by a single weakness? Are these all morally admirable men who suffer from a local shortcoming? That might be true of Othello, but I doubt it captures the other three. Hamlet can be cruel and unkind, as well as irresolute; his callous treatment of Polonius, as well as his cruelty toward Ophelia, shows that he is not always morally sensitive. He is extremely intelligent, but he is not terribly ethical. Macbeth seems to me hardly moral at all: he is violent, murderous, and acquisitive, as well as superstitious and deceptive—it isn't that he is basically a fine fellow except for the small matter of his ambitiousness. Nor is Lear a noble man: his petulance, pettiness, and vindictiveness are apparent from the start—he is a tyrant and a bully. None of these men could be called evil, exactly, but to describe them as noble strikes me as an exaggeration at best. They have "greatness of spirit," in the sense of inward vitality, but moral distinction is not what they impress us with. Certainly, they are always surrounded by people who are their clear moral superiors: Horatio is a more moral man than Hamlet; Macbeth is morally outshone by Macduff and Malcolm (and indeed by almost everyone in the play); Lear cannot hold an ethical candle to Edgar, Kent, and Gloucester, not to mention Cordelia. Morally, these men are at best mediocrities; so the sense of tragedy we feel cannot stem from seeing men of exceptional *moral* quality brought low and destroyed.

Secondly, the tragic flaw part: is this really the right way to conceive of the cause of the tragedy? I would not say that these characters have some isolated and localized weakness, at odds with the rest of what they are; the problem of character they have is pervasive and systematic. It defines them. It comes from their entire being. Hamlet is (initially) indecisive through and through, overly thoughtful, and shy of rough revenge; this is not just one small speck on his personality. Othello is credulous and jealous, but also lacking in sophistication, and susceptible to racial insecurity; Iago taps into his very core, not merely trading upon some peripheral foible. Macbeth is eaten up with ambition, and easily swayed by his wife's taunts; these attributes define him—they are not just incongruous minor failings. Lear is not an excellent king and father who slipped up one day because of some outlying flaw: his foolish test of his daughters' love is entirely characteristic of him, his essence. The failings here are nothing like an ugly little chip on an otherwise sturdy frame. But, even putting that point aside, the tragic flaw theory runs into an insuperable problem: if these are characters with a fatal flaw, *why hasn't it manifested itself before?* That is: if these are standing traits of character, which themselves cause the tragic outcome, why haven't they operated in like manner earlier? The traits have long been in place, but only now do they generate the kind of catastrophe they do. Why? Shouldn't there have been lots of tragedies along the road, as the fatal flaw worked its tragic way into the world?

I take it the answer to this question is obvious, but it is important: *because the right circumstances for tragedy had not yet arisen.* It is these men with these characters, placed in these circumstances, which leads to tragedy, not the characters of the men considered in isolation. Character and situation *combine* to set the tragic wheels in motion. It is the situation in which the irresolute Hamlet finds himself that leads to the tragic outcome: the need to avenge his father's murder and assert his right to the throne. His indecisiveness might not have led to any real problems if he hadn't faced a situation for which he is so constitutionally unsuited. Likewise, Othello had been doing just fine before he encountered the scheming and insidious Iago—at the precise moment that he, a soldierly black man, won the heart of a beautiful and sophisticated white girl. It is this situation, so alien to his experience and expertise, which throws him into a tragic downward spiral. Macbeth had been a worthy and admired soldier, a favorite of King Duncan, until he met the witches, was browbeaten by his wife, and had the opportunity to murder Duncan as he slept. The situation is what unleashes the ambition he nurtures but has hitherto kept under control. And Lear, accustomed to power and privilege, finds himself in the novel predicament of wanting to retire and being hopelessly wrong about his daughters; the situation of dependence on others is one he has never encountered before. In all these cases, the protagonist is placed in circumstances for which he is unprepared and unsuited. His character by itself might never have led to tragic consequences, but for the situation in which it must function. The circumstances alone would not lead to tragedy, if a different character were placed in them (Othello in Hamlet's position, say, or vice versa); and the character alone would likewise not lead to tragedy, if those circumstances had not arisen: it is the combination that sparks the tragic outcome. And this combination has a special quality: the character is unsuited to the situation, out of his element.

I shall accordingly say that the cause of the tragedy is best described as the *mismatch* of character and situation. There is no intrinsically fatal flaw of character, which would lead to tragedy even in normal circumstances; there is only a type of personality that, *in that situation*, generates tragic consequences—and such a situation might never have arisen. Thus there is always an element of *bad luck* in Shakespearean tragedy: it is just unfortunate that these particular characters find themselves in those very situations—situations to which they are temperamentally unsuited. Their weaknesses (which are general, not local) are transformed by the circumstances into potentially dangerous forces, so that their failings become magnified and volatile. The underlying tragedy is that character and circumstances have collided in this way, with catastrophic results (essentially, death). Once we see the hero placed in this situation, knowing his personal limitations, we sense the looming presence of tragedy; we know that he won't be able to cope with it—that he will act wrongly, badly, foolishly. We have a presentiment of tragedy when we register the mismatch between character and circumstances; this is when the tragic note is struck, and the rest is just working out the consequences of the mismatch. Tragedy is set in motion when the character is inadequate to the situation in which he finds himself. This is why we feel that the entire setup is tragic—the unlucky convergence of a particular personality and a recalcitrant situation (relative to that personality). It is not that the individual is in himself tragic (a "tragic hero"); it is the way he and his world *mesh* (or fail to) that is tragic. Abstractly put, the essential tragic fact is that the world does not always conform itself to our contingent strengths and weaknesses.

The essence of Shakespeare's tragedies, then, is that the death of the protagonist results from the mismatch between his character and the situation he finds himself occupying (where this character is of an exceptionally vivid and forceful sort). But there is another element that I believe is crucial to the tragic effect of these plays, namely that someone conspicuously virtuous or innocent should also die as a result of the protagonist's actions. While it would be hard to maintain that Hamlet or Othello or Lear *deserved* to die (Macbeth is another case), they do bear some burden of responsibility for their own deaths: it was their actions, culpable as they were, that set the tragic mechanism in motion. So our sympathy for them, though real, is somewhat qualified; the tragic effect is muted. But when an innocent dies the full horror of the events is evident and undeniable; now the heart is more unequivocally wrenched. The death of Desdemona is the most powerful example of this, and certainly adds infinitely to the tragic effect of the play. Ophelia's death, the indirect result of Hamlet's killing of her father, and perhaps his rejection of her, also contributes strongly to the tragedy of the play. In *Macbeth*, the execution of Macduff's wife and children fulfills this dramatic role: these are completely innocent bystanders to the main action. In *Lear*, it is Cordelia's death that pulls most powerfully at the heartstrings; indeed, without it, the tragedy would not have an ingredient I am saying is essential to the full Shakespearean effect. The causation runs from the character-in-situation to that character's death, but it also spills over, from its own awful energy, into the lives of others, who are swept up in it toward their own doom. And the fact that they are virtuous and innocent prevents us from supposing that there is some kind of rough justice in the universe, illustrated by the demise of the protagonist; for not *all* the deaths in the play can be regarded as instantiating such justice. In these latter cases, the sense of waste is at its most poignant, and the value of what is snuffed out most salient. A Shakespearean tragedy always contains this kind of wholly unjust death.

It is worth distinguishing between two kinds of mismatch between character and situation: affective and cognitive. The two are connected, because emotions affect judgment, and vice versa; but in different cases one or the other characterization seems more apt. In the case of Hamlet, the mismatch belongs on the affective side: he is not ignorant of the truth about his father's death, nor does he substantially misjudge the situation he is in; it is, rather, that he is temperamentally unsuited to carrying out the revenge he knows is required. He makes no *cognitive* blunder. But in the case of Othello, Macbeth, and Lear the mismatch takes the form of misjudgment (no doubt aided by affective factors). Othello makes a huge error of judgment and has totally false beliefs about the situation he is in: he is ignorant, and to some extent culpably so. His beliefs fail to match the truth of his circumstances. If he had true beliefs, we don't doubt that—unlike Hamlet—he would be able to do what is necessary (cut Iago down where he stands). His emotional makeup permits his cognitive flaw, but it is the cognitive mismatch that drives the tragedy. Macbeth also makes a mistake of judgment, this time about himself:

he fails to realize how his conscience will affect him, and what the consequences of his actions will be. Part of his situation is his own psychological nature, particularly his emotion-driven imagination; and he is wrong about this—he is cognitively deficient with respect to self-knowledge. (He is also far too credulous when it comes to witches.) Lear is massively deluded about the characters and intentions of those around him—cognitively utterly at sea. He completely misjudges Regan, Goneril, and Cordelia, and is likewise ignorant of Kent and others. His rashness of judgment and his complacency in error lie at the heart of the tragic mechanism of the play—though, again, they are conditioned by temperamental or affective factors. So cognitive mismatch is critical in each of these plays except *Hamlet*, and falsity of belief is the clearest way that a person can become detached from his environment—and hence be confounded by it. Even in *Hamlet* the lack of adequacy to the situation is partly cognitive, because Hamlet is slow to see that his position is untenable unless he deals decisively with his uncle; it is only a matter of time before Claudius will seek to have him removed too. So these are all dramas in which the protagonist's cognitive faculties let him down: the situation he is in is not one he can quite get his mind around. In the last analysis, then, these tragedies stem from a certain kind of cognitive defect—which is precisely a type of mismatch between person and situation. We might say that in each of these cases the protagonist is temperamentally unable to form true beliefs about the situation in which he finds himself. The tragedy, in other words, has an epistemological dimension: the story is tragic *because* of epistemological inadequacy (*inter alia*, of course).

It is sometimes supposed that the tragic outcome of a Shakespearean tragedy is inevitable—that there is really no other way that things could have turned out. Once we see the characters and the situation they are in, we can predict with certainty that things will end badly. I think this is wrong, at least with respect to Shakespeare's tragedies. In the first place, the tragic outcome is always a result of human decision—of free action. It is what the protagonist freely decides to do or not do that determines the end result: Hamlet declining to kill his uncle when he has the opportunity; Othello undertaking to smother Desdemona; Macbeth deciding to murder Duncan in his bed; Lear inviting his daughters to declare their love for him and banishing Cordelia. No one forced these characters to do any of these things; they were free agents. At any point the character could have done otherwise. In the second place, Shakespeare often introduces elements of chance into his dramas, and these are critical to the tragic result: it is chance that makes Hamlet come across Claudius alone at his prayers; it is chance that enables Iago to secure Desdemona's handkerchief and deploy it to deceive Othello; it is chance that brings Duncan unsuspectingly into the Macbeth household; it is chance that allows Cordelia to be hanged because Edgar is too late to save her. The objective world colludes in tragedy, in the sense that accidents can further the tragic action. But this produces in us the sense that the tragic outcome is not predestined; it might at any time be halted and reversed. Bad luck plays its indispensable part. Things *might* have turned out better; but chance intervenes and things proceed along the tragic track. And it is the fact that the tragedy does not strike us as inevitable that makes us feel its force more powerfully: it heightens our sense of the gratuitous in it—the contingent, the avoidable. These are deaths that are poignant in proportion as they are preventable. A Shakespearean tragic death is not one that results from some sort of structural or teleological fact about the universe, a death wish at the root of things. There is no necessity about Shakespearean tragedy.

TWELVE

Shakespeare's Genius

It is difficult to write about Shakespeare without wanting to articulate what his peculiar genius consists in. He strikes one as a unique phenomenon, as existing in a class of his own, and one would like to be able to say what raises him to that level. But the task is a demanding one, partly because it is in general hard to capture the nature of genius, and partly because Shakespeare presents so many aspects. There is a danger of windy rhapsodizing, of palpitating "Bardolatry," when what is required is some kind of illuminating analysis. To be sure, we can report that his gifts and achievement are at an exceptionally high level, and there is nothing to prevent us noting his poetic talent, his dramatic sense, his metaphorical power, his depth of characterization: but what we really seek is something that singles him out—that conveys the particular quality and feel of his work. He has the usual talents of a man of his calling to a high degree, yes, but can we say anything to capture what it is that marks him out as an artist? Is his distinction merely quantitative or is it qualitative? Is he just more omnivorous, versatile, and capacious than other writers, or is there a particular quality to his work? Is there a characteristically *Shakespearean* genius?

One reply to this question is suggested by everything I have said in this book so far: Shakespeare combines the philosophical and the dramatic in a uniquely powerful and compelling way. He takes an abstract theme—the nature of the self, the problem of other minds—

and succeeds in embedding it in concrete living characters, in such a way that the theme is vitalized and the characters are rendered emblematic. He dramatizes (and makes poetic) deep structural facts about the human condition. Something profound is always at stake in his plays. Hazlitt tells us that Shakespeare was at least as good a philosopher as he was a poet; right, but we can also say that he is a philosophical poet and a poetic philosopher. He brings the two together; he welds them into one. All this is perfectly reasonable—but I don't think it suffices. Other writers have combined the abstract and the dramatic, if not quite as forcefully (the list is long: Dante, Pope, Milton, Voltaire, et al); but Shakespeare does it in a particular *way*— his entire method seems unique (or at least very rare). He is a different *kind* of artist, one feels. Can we narrow this down further?

It might be thought definitive of the genius that he alters our vision of reality by imposing his own new vision. We see the world in a certain way, and then the genius comes along and imposes his own stamp on things; henceforth we see the world through *his* eyes. This description particularly fits the genius of science: Newton made us see the world as unified by universal natural laws, a kind of vast mechanism subject to a handful of mathematical principles; Einstein taught us to see that space, time, and motion do not have the absoluteness we supposed; Darwin made us look at nature as the outcome of blind natural forces, not as the creation of a divine architect. But the same can also be said of the artist: the artist gives us a new way of looking at things (cubism, impressionism, literary modernism). The emphasis here is on novelty, creation, invention, altered perception. The genius changes our sensibility, making us see things differently. He does not passively reflect the status quo (where is the genius in that?); he upsets the apple cart, he shakes us up. The genius is a visionary, who persuades us to relinquish our old worldview for the fresh one he has constructed. The force of his creativity is evident to us; his identity as genius is imprinted on our minds.

I would say that this is *not* what is characteristic of Shakespeare's genius. Borges remarked that Shakespeare is "everyone and no one,"[1] and Hazlitt has the following to say about Shakespeare's talent:

> It was only by representing others, that he became himself. He could go out of himself, and express the soul of Cleopatra; but in his own person [in his poems and sonnets], he appeared to be always waiting for the prompter's cue. In expressing the thoughts of others, he seemed inspired; in expressing his own, he was a mechanic. The license of an assumed character was necessary to restore his genius to the privileges of nature, and to give him courage to break through the tyranny of fashion, the trammels of custom . . . Shakespeare's imagination, by identifying itself with the strongest characters in the most trying circumstances, grappled at once with nature, and trampled the littleness of art under his feet.[2]

Borges and Hazlitt are onto the same point: Shakespeare's magnificence lies not in his presence in everything he wrote, but in his *absence*. Hazlitt opposes art and nature, suggesting that Shakespeare was free to represent nature precisely when he was not laboring under the demands of art. This fits nicely with my theme that Shakespeare is best seen as a kind of naturalist—a patient and disinterested observer and recorder. A naturalist has no wish to impose his vision of reality upon nature; he wishes, more modestly, simply to record nature as he experiences it. His aim is not to construct, but to reflect. The point Borges and Hazlitt are making is that this aim is best achieved by Shakespeare when he is occupying the position of someone else; then he can give himself up to nature, be its faithful servant. His own identity is bracketed, and the identity of his subject shines through. Of course, it shines through a mind with great gifts of intelligence and language, but the stance is still one of resolute naturalism. Shakespeare's aim is to disappear as an artist, so that we feel that he is giving us nature in the raw. This is why it is so difficult to single out any character in a Shakespeare play as representative of the author's perspective; he seems to be everywhere and nowhere. There is no authorial perspective, no skewing and prompting (Iago is as lovingly portrayed as Desdemona). We accordingly have the impression of living conscious beings—not as the artist wishes us to see or interpret them, according to his personal vision of reality, but the beings themselves. We *meet* these characters, in all their rough authenticity.

We can sum this up by saying that Shakespeare's art is *imitative* or *mimetic*. He is giving us what is already there, not imposing a new vision. Shakespeare was himself an actor, of course, and I would not be surprised if he was an excellent mimic. He can take on the role of another person with consummate ease and skill (I think here of the related talent possessed by the actor Peter Sellers), speaking, thinking, and feeling like that other person. His characters are not mediated and filtered through his own personality; rather, they mediate *him*. He inhabits the character, bringing it to uncanny life in his own self. I imagine Shakespeare composing his plays by speaking out loud the parts he has written, using different voices, stances, and so on—so that he can be sure he has expunged himself from the product (anything that sounds a bit too much like William S. he crosses out). Possibly in real life he was fluid of character, not locked into one type of personality; or maybe he had the ability to shed his identity once he began to create another character. In either case, he had the capacity to fully realize the character he was portraying. Thus his characters, in all their variety, are never just versions of himself—as the characters of many writers are: they are individuals in their own right. His genius lies in flawless imitations of imaginary characters, not in bringing his own identity into the picture. He is, as Borges says, everyone and no one: every character contains the spirit of the author, and yet the author himself is nowhere to be seen. In this way he was able to depict humanity with an unprecedented accuracy and depth.

In *Shakespeare: The Invention of the Human*, Harold Bloom contends that Shakespeare invented human nature, as we now understand it.[3] This is a striking claim, since one would have thought that he merely reflected what was there already. He certainly didn't invent the human in the way that James Watt invented the steam engine. Rather, Shakespeare depicted human nature as he found it around him in the world, as it existed independently of his efforts. He discovered, clarified, and exhibited human nature; he didn't (literally) *invent* it, in the sense of bringing it into being. He *discovered* it in the sense that writers and dramatists had not theretofore achieved the degree of realistic naturalism that he achieved, and perhaps saw no particular reason to aim at such naturalism. He also discovered that human nature as it exists is itself a fit subject for literature, as opposed to merely gesturing at it in the service of some religious or mythological or moral precept. He *clarified* the human by engaging in careful investigation of the inward and outward life of human beings, articulating what previously had been at best implicit. He analyzed and dissected, striving for complete perspicuity. And he *exhibited* the human by exploiting all the resources of poetry, dramatic form, and theatrical presentation at his considerable disposal. But he didn't really *invent* humanity, if that is taken to mean that he constructed it and imposed it on the world. It was there anyway, waiting to be discovered, clarified, and exhibited.

However, Bloom may not be making any such literal claim of invention. He might be saying, less dramatically, that Shakespeare invented a new way of *representing* the human—and that, I think, is true. He represents humanity with an unprecedented depth and complexity, inwardly and outwardly; and he does so by meticulous attention to reality. But Bloom might also be making the point that Shakespeare's representations of the human have themselves causally influenced what we are today. By clarifying and exhibiting the human, he presented audiences with a picture of themselves that they could not help but absorb. Since we are reflective, self-conscious creatures, we respond to representations of ourselves—they modify us. Shakespeare's representational power was so enormous, so grippingly memorable, that subsequent generations were changed by his productions. In other words, humanity may have imitated Shakespeare's imitations of humanity. Thus, in this sense, Shakespeare created human nature, as it now exists, at least in some measure. So pervasive has his influence on the culture been—so ingrained are his words and his characters—that we cannot help but be shaped by his work. We are all, to some indefinite degree, Shakespeare's progeny. And, if he is right that we are naturally theatrical creatures, it is entirely possible that his theatrical constructions should become the basis of the theatrical selves we project in daily life. You might, to put it crudely, become like Hamlet simply by seeing Hamlet on stage. This, too, seems to me plausible. Shakespeare's very fidelity to human nature, as he observed it, has come to modify human nature. But this is not to rescind the point that Shakespeare's genius is of the mimetic kind— that he represented what he found to be already there. Bloom's formulation threatens to obscure this truth, though (as I have said) it can be interpreted in less contentious ways.

To my original question, then, I return the following answer: Shakespeare's peculiar genius should be seen in his submission to nature. He didn't impose his own vision on reality; he let reality impose itself on his vision. He told us how the world looks from the perspective of itself. And the world never looked the same again.

NOTES

Chapter One: General Themes

1. William Hazlitt, *Characters of Shakespeare's Plays* (Whitefish, Mt.: Kessinger Publishing. www.kessinger.net, 2005), 50.

2. Ibid., 60.

3. Two notable exceptions are Stanley Cavell in *Disowning Knowledge* (Cambridge: Cambridge University Press, 2003) and Millicent Bell in *Shakespeare's Tragic Skepticism* (New Haven, Conn.: Yale University Press, 2002)—though both books largely confine themselves to questions of epistemology in Shakespeare.

4. Plato, *The Republic* (London: Penguin Books, 1998), esp. part 7, book 7.

5. See Richard Popkin, *The History of Scepticism* (Oxford: Oxford University Press, 2003), for an account of Greek skepticism and its influence.

6. The essay is in *Michel de Montaigne: The Complete Essays*, trans. M. A. Screech (London: Penguin Books, 1991).

7. The most thorough discussion I know of Montaigne's influence on Shakespeare is Bell's *Shakespeare's Tragic Skepticism*. However, there are many passages from Montaigne I cite that Bell does not, and I suggest many more areas of specific overlap. Still, we are generally of like mind.

8. David Hume, *A Treatise of Human Nature* (London: Penguin Books, 1985), part 3, section 14.

9. This celebrated line is from a letter Keats wrote to his brothers in 1817, speaking of a conversation he had had with a friend.

Chapter Two: A Midsummer Night's Dream

1. René Descartes, *Meditations* (London: Penguin Books, 1998), First Meditation.

2. Michel de Montaigne, *Michel de Montaigne: The Complete Essays*, trans. M. A. Screech (London: Penguin Books, 1991), 674.

3. Ibid., 67.

4. Ludwig Wittgenstein, *Philosophical Investigations* (Oxford: Basil Blackwell, 1974), part 2; see also Colin McGinn, *Mindsight: Image, Dream, Meaning* (Cambridge, Mass.: Harvard University Press, 2004), chapter 3.

Chapter Three: Hamlet

1. David Hume, *A Treatise of Human Nature* (London: Penguin Books, 1985), part 4, section 6.

2. Michel de Montaigne, *Michel de Montaigne: The Complete Essays*, trans. M. A. Screech (London: Penguin Books, 1991), 640.

3. Ibid., 680.

4. Ibid., 380.

5. Ibid., 1222.

6. Quoted in *The Presentation of Self in Everyday Life* (New York: Doubleday, 1959), 75–76.

7. Quoted in Harold Bloom, *Shakespeare: The Invention of the Human* (New York: Riverhead Books, 1998), 417.

8. See Donald Davidson, "How Is Weakness of the Will Possible?" in *Essays on Actions and Events* (Oxford: Oxford University Press, 1980).

9. Montaigne, 8.

10. Ibid., 548.

11. Ibid., 373.

12. For a defense of mysterianism, see Colin McGinn, *The Mysterious Flame* (New York: Basic Books, 1999).

13. Montaigne, 52.

14. Ibid.

Chapter Four: Othello

1. David Hume, *A Treatise of Human Nature* (London: Penguin Books, 1985), part 3, especially section 14.

2. Michel de Montaigne, *Michel de Montaigne: The Complete Essays*, trans. M. A. Screech (London: Penguin Books, 1991), 711.

3. Ibid.

4. As reported in the glossary to the Oxford edition of *William Shakespeare: The Complete Works*, ed. Stanley Wells and Gary Taylor (Oxford: Oxford University Press, 1988).

5. See Colin McGinn, *Ethics, Evil, and Fiction* (Oxford: Oxford University Press, 1997), chapter 4, for a discussion of the explanatory puzzles generated by the purely evil agent.

6. Montaigne, 484.

7. William Hazlitt, *Characters of Shakespeare's Plays* (Whitefish, Mt.: Kessinger Publishing. www.kessinger.net, 2005), 50–51.

8. W. H. Auden, *Lectures on Shakespeare*, ed. Arthur Kirsch (Princeton, N.J.: Princeton University Press, 2000), 205.

9. Quoted in ibid., 199.

Chapter Five: Macbeth

1. See Colin McGinn, *Mindsight: Image, Dream, Meaning* (Cambridge, Mass.: Harvard University Press, 2004), on imagination and the mind's eye.

2. David Hume, *A Treatise of Human Nature* (London: Penguin Books, 1985), part 1, section 1.

3. Michel de Montaigne, *Michel de Montaigne: The Complete Essays*, trans. M. A. Screech (London: Penguin Books, 1991), 109.

4. Ibid., 1234.

5. A. C. Bradley, *Shakespearean Tragedy* (London: Penguin Books, 1991; originally published 1904), 354.

6. For a discussion of Shakespeare and Catholicism, see Stephen Greenblatt, *Will in the World* (New York: W. W. Norton, 2004), and Clare Asquith, *Shadowplay: The Hidden Beliefs and Coded Politics of William Shakespeare* (New York: Public Affairs, 2005).

Chapter Six: King Lear

1. David Hume, *A Treatise of Human Nature* (London: Penguin Books, 1985), part 3, section 14.

2. Jean-Paul Sartre entitled his metaphysical masterwork *Being and Nothingness* (London: Methuen and Co., 1969).

3. Michel de Montaigne, *Michel de Montaigne: The Complete Essays*, trans. M. A. Screech (London: Penguin Books, 1991), 500.

4. Ibid., 509.

5. Ibid., 1224.

6. See Colin McGinn, *Ethics, Evil, and Fiction* (Oxford: Oxford University Press, 1997), chapter 4.

Chapter Seven: The Tempest

1. Ludwig Wittgenstein, *Philosophical Investigations* (Oxford: Basil Blackwell, 1974), section 109.

2. The arch proponent of this type of view is Gottlob Frege, the mathematician and main founder of analytical philosophy: see *The Frege Reader*, ed. Michael Beaney (Oxford: Basil Blackwell, 1997), for a selection of his works.

3. In addition to Frege, Karl Popper adopted such a position: see *Objective Knowledge* (Oxford: Oxford University Press, 1972).

4. Michel de Montaigne, *Michel de Montaigne: The Complete Essays*, trans. M. A. Screech (London: Penguin Books, 1991), 233.

5. See, for example, Steven Pinker, *The Language Instinct* (New York: HarperCollins Publishers, 1994).

6. For a discussion of this conundrum, see Thomas Nagel, *The View from Nowhere* (Oxford: Oxford University Press, 1986), chapter 11, section 3.

Chapter Nine: Shakespeare and Psychology

1. For a discussion see Colin McGinn, *Mindsight: Image, Dream, Meaning* (Cambridge, Mass.: Harvard University Press, 2004), chapter 1.

Chapter Ten: Shakespeare and Ethics

1. William Hazlitt, *Characters of Shakespeare's Plays* (Whitefish, Mt.: Kessinger Publishing. www.kessinger.net, 2005), 217.

2. For a discussion of the virtues of truthfulness see Bernard Williams, *Truth and Truthfulness* (Princeton, N.J.: Princeton University Press, 2002).

Chapter Eleven: Shakespeare and Tragedy

1. Ludwig Wittgenstein, *Philosophical Investigations* (Oxford: Basil Blackwell, 1974), section 66.

2. A. C. Bradley, *Shakespearean Tragedy* (London: Penguin Books, 1991; originally published 1904), lecture 1.

3. For a discussion see Walter Kaufman, *Tragedy and Philosophy* (Princeton, N.J.: Princeton University Press, 1968).

Chapter Twelve: Shakespeare's Genius

1. Quoted in Harold Bloom, *Shakespeare: The Invention of the Human* (New York: Riverhead Books, 1998), xxi.

2. William Hazlitt, *Characters of Shakespeare's Plays* (Whitefish, Mt.: Kessinger Publishing. www.kessinger.net, 2005), 231.

3. Thus Bloom: "Shakespeare essentially invented human personality as we continue to know and value it," 290.

# BIBLIOGRAPHY

This list contains both books I refer to in the text and books I consulted while preparing mine. It is by no means intended as a complete bibliography on Shakespeare, even from a philosophical perspective. I used the Oxford edition *William Shakespeare: The Complete Works*, edited by Stanley Wells and Gary Taylor (Oxford: Oxford University Press, 1988), and all quotations are from this work.

Asquith, Clare. *Shadowplay: The Hidden Beliefs and Coded Politics of William Shakespeare*. New York: Public Affairs, 2005.

Auden, W. H. *Lectures on Shakespeare*, ed. Arthur Kirsch. Princeton, N.J.: Princeton University Press, 2000.

Bell, Millicent. *Shakespeare's Tragic Skepticism*. New Haven, Conn.: Yale University Press, 2002.

Bloom, Harold. *Shakespeare: The Invention of the Human*. New York: Riverhead Books, 1998.

Bradley, A. C. *Shakespearean Tragedy*. London: Penguin Books, 1991; originally published 1904.

Cavell, Stanley. *Disowning Knowledge: In Seven Plays of Shakespeare*. Cambridge: Cambridge University Press, 2003.

Davidson, Donald. "How Is Weakness of the Will Possible?" in *Essays on Actions and Events*. Oxford: Oxford University Press, 1980.

Descartes, René. *Meditations*. London: Penguin Books, 1998.

Frege, Gottlob. *The Frege Reader*, ed. Michael Beaney. Oxford: Basil Blackwell, 1997.

Frye, Northrop. *Northrop Frye on Shakespeare*. New Haven, Conn.: Yale University Press, 1986.

Garber, Marjorie. *Shakespeare After All*. New York: Pantheon Books, 2004.

Goffman, Erving. *The Presentation of Self in Everyday Life*. New York: Doubleday, 1959.

Greenblatt, Stephen. *Will in the World: How Shakespeare Became Shakespeare*. New York: W. W. Norton, 2004.

Hazlitt, William. *Characters of Shakespeare's Plays*. Whitefish, Mt.: Kessinger Publishing, www.kessinger.net, 2005.

Hume, David. *A Treatise of Human Nature*. London: Penguin Books, 1985; originally published 1739.

Kaufman, Walter. *Tragedy and Philosophy*. Princeton, N.J.: Princeton University Press, 1968.

McGinn, Colin. *Ethics, Evil, and Fiction*. Oxford: Oxford University Press, 1997.

―――. *The Mysterious Flame*. New York: Basic Books, 1999.

―――. *Mindsight: Image, Dream, Meaning*. Cambridge, Mass.: Harvard University Press, 2004.

Montaigne, Michel de. *Michel de Montaigne: The Complete Essays*, trans. and ed. M. A. Screech. London: Penguin Books, 1991.

Nagel, Thomas, *The View from Nowhere*. Oxford: Oxford University Press, 1986.

O'Toole, Fintan. *Shakespeare Is Hard, but So Is Life*. London: Granta Books, 2002.

Pinker, Steven. *The Language Instinct*. New York: HarperCollins Publishers, 1994.

Plato. *The Republic*. London: Penguin Books, 1987.

Popkin, Richard. *The History of Scepticism: From Savonarola to Bayle*. Oxford: Oxford University Press, 2003.

Popper, Karl. *Objective Knowledge*. Oxford: Oxford University Press, 1972.

Sartre, Jean-Paul. *Being and Nothingness*. London: Methuen and Co Ltd., 1969.

Shapiro, James. *A Year in the Life of William Shakespeare*: 1599. New York: HarperCollins Publishers, 2005.

Williams, Bernard. *Truth and Truthfulness*. Princeton, N.J.: Princeton University Press, 2002.

Wittgenstein, Ludwig. *Philosophical Investigations*. Oxford: Basil Blackwell, 1974.

INDEX

215